"Patience Hope? Still a virgin?

At her age? Hold the front page. How can this be? Why has this girl never bagged herself a bit of the other? Is she scared? Or worse — is she frigid?"

Penny stared at the girl, not quite sure what to make of the rather odd speech. "To be quite honest, I was shocked to hear your little revelation. I assumed you'd lost your virginity years ago."

"Why? Do I come across as some kind of a slut?"

"No, of course not. It's just that most girls of our generation don't hold onto it for so long."

"I decided to wait."

"What for?"

Patience shrugged, not too sure of her motives. "The right man, I suppose."

"I assume he never turned up."

"What do you think?"

They shared a knowing girlie moment.

"I guess I wanted my first time to be special."

"The first time is never special. It's awkward. And painful. And a total disaster."

"It doesn't have to be, surely."

A stern look from Penny. "Believe me, it always is."

"Well, if it's that bad, I'd better get it over and done with. I'm determined to find myself a shag. Preferably today."

Also recommended...

You may also like these other ForbiddenFiction works:

Blindsided by **Ann Ruby**

It begins as a case of mistaken identity. Brenda is escaping into the mountains of Montana for a week of relaxation. Instead, she finds herself naked and pressed against a hard, aroused man, intent on a weekend of sexual domination. When the real submissive walks in on them, he realizes the mistake made at the front desk and is horrified, willing to do whatever he can to make things right. Brenda is intrigued. When she asks him to take her on as a substitute, he is blindsided! Can a weekend that satisfies their deepest desires, both sexually and emotionally, turn into more?

http://forbiddenfiction.com/library/story/AR1-1.000009

Heart of Brass by **KJ Kabza**

Dr. Jameson H. Dashiell, inventor of over 20 unique sex Machines designed to "safely treat and tame lascivious desire," must find a way to treat the beautiful and insatiable Lady Gallantine without losing his professional self-control–or losing his life at the hands of her father, the suspicious and overbearing Duke.

http://forbiddenfiction.com/library/story/KJK-1.000025

Patience is a Virgin

Mikey Jackson

ForbiddenFiction
www.forbiddenfiction.com

an imprint of

Fantastic Fiction Publishing
www.fantasticfictionpublishing.com

PATIENCE IS A VIRGIN

A Forbidden Fiction book

Fantastic Fiction Publishing
Hayward, California

CREDITS
Editor: Lon Sarver
Cover Design: D.M. Atkins
Cover photo: Otto Kalman at Dreamstime
Production Editor: Erika L Firanc
Proofreading: Kailin Morgan

SKU: MJ1-000039-02 FFP
ISBN: 978-1-62234-088-0

Published in the United States of America

DISCLAIMER

This book is a work of fiction which contains explicit erotic content; it is intended for mature readers. Do not read this if it's not legal for you.

All the characters, locations and events herein are fictional. While elements of existing locations or historical characters or events may be used fictitiously, any resemblance to actual people, places or events is coincidental.

This story is not intended to be used as an instruction manual. It may contain descriptions of erotic acts that are immoral, illegal, or unsafe. Do not take the events in this story as proof of the plausibility or safety of any particular practice.

Contents

Chapter 1
Secrets and Lies

"How many men have you had in your life?"

Uh oh. Awkward question alert.

Patience Hope wished she hadn't suggested the game now. But she was drunk. Very drunk. Not hopelessly bladdered. Just lingering at the point where proposals of the insane variety always seemed like good ideas at the time.

Such as, "Hey, how about we play the Truth Game?"

It was her birthday. Twenty-five years of age. And how was she celebrating such a milestone occasion? Partying hard amidst the bright lights and big city of London perchance? Doing England proud by flying the flag of drink, debauchery and a bloody good knees-up? Nope. Far from it. Patience was at home, sharing a bottle of supermarket vodka with her flatmate Penny Baker, a trainee nurse who had only chosen her career path because she thought it would be just like her favourite TV medical dramas; handsome surgeons, steamy affairs and perfect hair that never fell out of place.

Penny sat beside her boyfriend of three months, two days, twenty-two hours and four minutes. Yes, the lass kept note of the exact time since first kiss — or fuck, whichever came first — of boyfriends with obsessive accuracy. Dave was his name. Just Dave. Nobody seemed to know his surname, especially Penny whose strategy was to fuck first, then if the man was any good, move on to stage two, i.e. conversation. Like, with big words and everything. But judging by the incessant roar of uninhibited passion that shook the flat whenever Dave stayed over, stage one was stuck in a permanent loop.

"Answer the question, Patience," ordered a grinning Penny.

1

"What question?"

Good idea. Maybe Penny had forgotten what she'd asked her.

The flatmate playfully rolled her eyes. "How many men have you had in your life?"

Bugger. She hadn't forgotten.

Patience was a virgin. This very fact made it difficult to offer a suitable response to Penny's query. It was rare these days for females of the species to notch up an innings of a quarter of a century without dipping their toes into some kind of sexual undertaking. But Patience had somehow managed it, untainted and pure.

Her mother had always told her it didn't matter. "Don't rush into it, Patience, my dear," the parent had advised her young daughter all those years ago. "Sex is highly overrated. Don't dish it out to all and sundry. Instead, wait for the right man to come along. Remember. Your virginity is your most precious possession."

Ah, but times had changed. Drastically. Nowadays, a modern girl's most precious possession was her mobile phone.

Yet even in an age where sex could be found everywhere — on TV, over the internet, in glossy gossip magazines, not to mention in almost all pop music videos, especially those involving rappers spitting constant drivel about their oh-so-amazing hedonistic lifestyles — Patience had rigidly adhered to her mother's wishes, refusing to dive into the sordid lake of lust, open legs first. The water was far too cold for her liking. And it was bound to leave a bad taste in her mouth.

A rogue thought made a guest appearance in her head. Was she actually following her mother's wishes, or was she simply too afraid to part her thigh-gates for the somewhat scary opposite sex, using her mother's advice as an excuse? Hmm. Probably a bit of both.

Sexual intercourse was something Patience had never been particularly bothered about. Contrary to popular opinion, the act of fornication was not the be all and end all of everything. There were far more important things in life than a mere fifteen minutes of sweaty panting. Or twenty minutes if extra time was required to peel off skinny jeans. This girl was determined not to allow sex to govern her life.

She'd always been proud of this achievement.

Until now.

Right at this very moment, it was a major league embarrassment.

Why? Simple. This very predicament was hitting home to Patience that being a virgin aged twenty-five was, for want of better words, weird, irregular, unheard of, and, oh, my God, dare she think it? Abnormal. In fact, her V status was downright peculiar of the highest, uppermost, mountainous order, especially in this day and age. If her dark and dismal secret got out, she'd be a social outcast. Debates would be held. Questions would be asked. Why does this girl remain unprodded by manly fingers at her age? Don't members of the opposite sex find her attractive? Does she like her own sex perhaps, as in her own gender? Or, perish the thought, was this poor and unfortunate freak of nature born without a vagina?

Think, girl, think. Get yourself out of this tight spot. Preferably with the majority of your dignity intact.

Aha. Then, an idea.

"Do you mean, how many boyfriends have I had?"

Good thinking. Sure to work.

Penny screwed up her face, just as she would if all heads in the room had suddenly turned bright green with yellow spots. "Like, no. How many men have you had? As in, fucked. Shagged. Laid. Bonked. Screwed. Slept with."

Bugger.

Had Patience ever enjoyed the company of a proper boyfriend? No. Not unless she counted holding hands way back in her first year of little-tiny-youngster school with — um — that boy with the black hair whose name had long since fled her memory. Mind you, from what she could recall, the relationship only lasted five minutes. On the sixth minute, she found herself dumped in favour of that pig-tailed girl with the freckles and bad teeth. Little wotsername, the lass whose father owned a confectionery shop.

And oh, God, thinking about it, she couldn't remember ever having to turn anybody down. Which meant nobody had ever asked to take her to bed. Argh! Never once propositioned was more blush-inducing than being a virgin. What was wrong with her? She was hardly unattractive, but at the same time not exactly stunning either. Somewhere safely in between. Not fat. Not thin. A hectic disorder of mousy hair of differing natural shades that couldn't decide whether it was light brown or fair. And hey. Somebody had once told her she had a relatively cute face. This was a plus. But she supposed her mother didn't really count.

Yet even the most ugly girls received regular helpings of Saturday Night Salami, and that was a fact. She'd listened in on many a bar convo between peroxide floozies, all encrusted in thick slaps of make-up stained with fake tan, comparing notes about their illicit conquests, to be fully up to speed with that particular statistic.

How tragic. Stuck indoors when she should be out socialising. London was calling, but Patience wasn't answering the phone. She should be out drinking her own bodyweight of happy juice in a trendy bar. Or whining badly at a karaoke night to that song where an afraid and petrified woman, whose ex has turned up on her doorstep, suddenly becomes strong and vows to survive. Or whatever it was that quarter-century women did for kicks these days. Instead, here she was, teetering dangerously on the wrong side of tipsy, being practically forced to admit that her private parts had — wait for it — never been touched by human hands. Except her own.

How would she get out of this one? Simple. Be a little economical with the truth.

"I've had loads of men. So many, I've lost count."

Oh, dear. Economical was not one of her strong points.

Penny frowned, sceptical. "Oh? I've never seen you bring any-body back."

Double bugger.

The recovery came in the form of, "When I have a one-night stand, I always make a rule of going back to their place. You really think I want drag-backs knowing where I live? God, that would be, like, ask-ing for trouble."

Penny nodded in agreement. "Good point."

Patience smiled. Things were looking up. The revelation of the big V was set to remain classified.

"Strange," piped up Dave, scratching his head. "Nobody's ever mentioned shagging you before."

Fuck's sake! She'd forgotten about the Male Conquest Grapevine, the legendary virtual swap shop where all men traded their dirty deeds. It was a well-known fact that if a girl parted her legs for one guy, then a hundred more men would know all about it by close of business the next day. Intimacy was no longer sacred. Dirty laundry was a free-for-all, with the ins and outs of each sexual encounter dutifully cast into the public domain for the whole world to see. Females and all they stood for, considered not as equals but as trophies. Mere badges to be collected. Was it really a wonder why Patience had avoided genital-to-genital contact for so long?

"That's because I only choose nice guys who keep their gobs shut," Patience responded.

"I didn't realise men like that existed," commented Penny.

"Nor did I," said Dave, showing a blatant disregard for his own gender.

"Oh, they do," replied Patience. "But they're very rare. Almost extinct these days."

Penny was not prepared to let up on such a gaping plot hole. "If they're so hard to come by, how come you've had loads of them?"

Triple bugger.

"Either you've been bloody fortunate in your sex life," the flatmate continued, "or you're lying through your teeth."

Patience sucked in a sharp pocket of air, gobsmacked by her friend's treachery. "How could you even think that?"

"Because I don't believe a word you're saying."

"But I have had sex. I'm not a virgin," stressed Patience, applying just a tad too much emphasis on the V word for her own good.

Penny's brow creased with suspicion. "This debate is about the number of men you reckon you've had. I never mentioned virginity."

"What virginity? I told you, I'm not a virgin."

"There you go again. Protesting too much. Patience, have you actually bedded anybody in your life?"

Patience's mouth flopped open at such an accusation. Or rather, an anti-accusation, seeing as Penny had charged her with the crime of not doing something.

"Of course I have!" Proverbial spade in hand, using it to full effect. "I've had more men than hot dinners." Proverbial hole dug deeper and deeper.

Penny and Dave didn't look at all converted.

"In fact, I'm quite the expert," Patience added to enhance her point.

Then she winced. Argh! Why had she spat out such a dweebish line? The proverbial hole was noticeably increasing in size with every ticking second.

Penny scoffed, amused by such overt insistence. "Something tells me you've never laid eyes on a willy-winky, let alone had one between your legs."

This was in fact true, but top secret, information known only to Patience. The girl had never witnessed a bona fide example of real-life, up close and personal male genitalia. Such opportunities hadn't really come her way. Being an only child, she was hardly able to satisfy early adolescent curiosity with sneaky peeks at male siblings through a part-open bathroom door. Nor had a flasher ever displayed his wares to her in the park. Sure, she'd seen the odd photograph or two of a penis on the internet. And rather worse for wear examples in Penny's medical textbooks. But not properly. And never once in the flesh.

Patience now had two choices. Either admit to her total inexperience of the opposite sex. Or dig that hole even deeper.

"Get real. I've seen hundreds."

Uh oh. The proverbial hole was now a proverbial canyon.

"If that's the case," bit back Dave, "what do they look like?"

"Um. Hairy."

Penny laughed. "Willies aren't hairy."

Patience stumbled awkwardly with, "Surrounded by hair, covered by hair, same difference."

Dave joined Penny's giggle club.

Annoyed by such scathing ridicule, Patience continued with, "This is stupid. Everybody knows what they look like. Walk through any subway and they're scrawled all over the walls."

"Graffiti cocks are nothing like the real thing," said Dave.

"Yeah? So why do blokes draw them like that?"

Dave shrugged his shoulders, clueless. "We just do. It's the law."

"I remember a guy once," recalled Penny, "who was admitted to the Emergency Department after slicing a big slit right the way across his bell-end with a bread knife. The idiot took the design of cartoon cocks as gospel and thought something was wrong with his own. What a dick. Him, I mean, not his thingy." A giggle. "Mind you, cartoon vaginas are even worse. Have you seen them? They look like dirty great open scalpel wounds with false beards."

"Best not to let Patience near any sharp instruments then," quipped Dave.

Penny and Dave erupted with laughter. Patience failed to see the funny side.

"Yeah, har frigging har. Look, Penny, this isn't fair. You see cocks all the time. You're a nurse."

Penny responded with, "Ah, but you claim to have seen hundreds."

"Yes, but I prefer to have sex in the dark," Patience retaliated. "And besides. If a guy's on top of me, my eyes are up here." She pointed to her eyes. "And his cock's down there." She indicated to her groin. "So it's not as if I get much of a chance to study the dangly bits."

Penny and Dave smirked, totally unconvinced.

"Oh, Patience," Penny said. "Why don't you just tell us the truth?"

"I am telling you the frigging truth."

"Are you sure about that?" asked Dave.

"Yes."

Okay, so it was another lie. But only a little white one. Not the kind of deceit that could break up lovers or tear friendships to shreds. It didn't affect or hurt anybody else, so it was perfectly justified. Nothing but an insignificant fib with one sole purpose. To protect a hugely embarrassing secret.

Penny said, "You are amongst friends, Patience."

Yeah, right. "Am I?"

"Yes. You are."

Yeah, right again. With bells on. "It certainly doesn't feel like it." She eyed their amused faces and added, "Oh, look, can we please drop this subject?"

Penny and Dave in harmony. "No."

"Why the fuck not?"

"Because you haven't answered the question yet?" said Penny.

"What bloody question?"

Yeah, yeah, so it was a long shot. But temporary amnesia during stressful episodes was certainly not uncommon. And this was without a doubt an episode of the stressful variety.

Penny reminded the girl—yet again—with, "How many men have you had in your life?"

Bugger. Fake temporary amnesia, not quite so convincing after all. Funnily enough, a few years back, she'd been offered some cut-price acting lessons. She wished she'd taken up the offer now.

Ah, well. There was just one more option available.

Patience exercised her lawful right to remain silent.

Dave said, "If it's any consolation, Patience, I've never had a man either."

Yeah, very frigging funny. "That's because you're a hetero male."

Penny rubbed Patience's arm as some form of solace, even though the trainee nurse was the one dishing out the very reason why she required said solace in the first place. "There's no shame in being a virgin."

Patience rolled her eyes. How many more bloody times? "I told you. I am not one of—" A brief wrestle to complete her reply. "—those kind of people."

Oo-er. Now she was treating virgins like some kind of ethnic minority.

Dave smirked in a haughty fashion. "Well, we think you are."

"I am not a virgin."

Penny and Dave: "You are a virgin."

"I'm not!"

"You are!"

"I'm bloody not!"

"You bloody are!"

Patience could hold back the rage no longer. She stood bolt upright and exploded, big-time. "All right, all right, I fucking admit it! I'm a virgin! A girl of the V variety. Not featured as a notch on anybody's bedpost! I've never had sex in my entire life! Not once! Not ever! Happy now?"

Cue the post-outburst awkward silence from her two friends.

Bugger.

It was an age-old, well-known fact that secrets and lies always harboured the bad habit of coming out in the end. But Patience had hoped the hush-hush snippet of private information she'd kept under wraps for the past few years would remain forever undiscovered. Ah, but no. Fat chance of that. News of such a startling revelation was bound to spread like wildfire. By this time tomorrow, the whole town would know all about her un-dirty little secret.

Argh!

Her credibility as a modern civilian now stood cold and naked on the pedestal of scrutiny, awaiting an unfair trial of laughter and mockery. She'd never live this down. Ever.

"And now I'm off to bed," Patience growled, heading for the nearest available exit. "In the same way I retire every frigging night. Alone!"

In the history of the flat, no door had ever been slammed so hard.

Dave threw Penny an unsure glance. "Was it something we said?"

Chapter 2
Through the Keyhole

Virginity.

It had been Patience's most closely guarded secret.

And now it was out.

Oh, the shame. A virgin at twenty-five. Twenty bloody five, for God's sake. Such a daunting prospect made her feel nauseous. The worry was almost too much to bear. Which was why, just over an hour after making her door-slamming exit, sleep had failed to take a foothold. Instead, the poor girl lay wide awake in bed, staring up at a badly painted ceiling.

Up until now, it had been easy to conceal her virginity. During her formative secondary school years, she often heard playground tales of a handful of the older girls doing it before the age of consent. Such infamous stardom was strictly reserved for cool girls only. The absolute elite. Pretty things with model looks. Or failing that, the owners of the biggest breasts. At the time, their peers had thought of such a glittery, regal select few as popular and sensational—

"Wow, she did it last night with him! He's got a car and everything! And he's eighteen!"

—but in retrospect were remembered not so fondly as nothing more than dirty, easy sluts.

Patience failed to reach the dizzy heights of the school's in-crowd. Way too plain. And definitely not fashionable enough. Not that she'd ever wanted to be part of what she saw as a cut-throat circus of social acceptance. Fake bitches, the lot of them. As a result, she blended seamlessly into the fuzzy grey background shared by all the other ordinary kids, and as such, was never questioned about the status of her virginity. No point in asking. Fuzzy grey people weren't big news. Not interesting enough. This was most fortunate.

The post-school-first-job-mid-to-late-teenage phase of her life then came knocking on her door. It was a period that noticeably lacked the blatant schoolchild immaturity that had come before it. A far more reserved time where nobody asked juvenile questions such as, "Are you still a virgin?" because everybody assumed that everybody else was doing it. So therefore, her secret remained safe. In fact, watertight.

So why the fuck was it that women crashing into their twenties suddenly reverted back to the infantile behaviour of yesteryear, as if embroiled in some kind of regressive exodus towards being twelve and three quarters all over again? Furthermore, twenty-somethings were inherently louder these days. Far more brash. And were getting two, three, four, even five times more drunk than the supposed wild and reckless teenage community. What the hell was going on? A mass quarter life crisis perhaps?

Actually, thinking about it, why was she pinning the blame on the twenty-something crowd as a whole? Her angst was mainly directed at Penny. In fact, totally directed. The same Penny who claimed to be her friend. The very same Penny who had totally ripped the piss out of her for being a virgin.

Bitch.

Did she class Penny as a proper friend? Probably not. A mate perhaps. Somebody with whom to get drunk. But not a true companion who would be there in her hour of need.

She'd only known the girl for six months. Patience had placed an advert in the local rag for a new flatmate after the previous lass eloped with a Greek waiter. Penny turned out to be the only prospective tenant who hadn't scared her. And so she got the gig. But now, half a year down the line, Patience figured she might have been better off offering the flatshare to Sidney, the one-eyed taxidermist with a penchant for rubber and bondage.

Hold on a minute. So what if she was a virgin at twenty-five? Did it really matter? No. It didn't. Did it make her a freak? No. It didn't. Actually, yes, it did matter. And if Patience herself ever happened to stumble across another girl of the same age who was a virgin, then she too would think something along the lines of, "That girl must be some kind of freak."

As the good old English age of consent was sixteen, Patience had been sexually legal for nine years, yet had done absolutely nothing about it. What a waste of nigh on a decade. Argh! Of course, the question in her somewhat racing mind was simple. What the hell was she going to do about it?

Well?

Her lone debate found itself disturbed by the sound of playful pre-sex giggles coming from Penny's room. Uh oh. The lovers had hit the sack. But of course, sleep was not on their immediate agenda.

A rhapsody of erotic audio filled the air every time Dave stayed over. The first movement would consist of giggles, stop-its and shushes. A suite of oohs and ahhs would then play over a bed-squeak accompaniment, culminating in a crescendo of opera-like shrieks as their love — or rather, lust — was finally realised. At first, Patience had blocked out the racket with a strategically placed pillow over her head, praying to God, Allah or anybody else willing to listen that the sex-obsessed idiots would bloody get it over and done with as soon as possible. But recently, and rather alarmingly, she'd found the couple's cries of passion strangely alluring.

Patience threw open her duvet and crept gingerly across the room. She opened the door and peered out. Penny's bedroom was situated directly opposite, door shut tight. The hallway was in near-darkness; the only illumination, a slender finger of light striking out like a white hot sword from Penny's keyhole. The flatmate always did it with the light on. She was a girl who preferred to see everything as it happened.

There had been one or two occasions lately where Patience had wondered what it would be like to spy through that keyhole. What would she see? And how would she feel when she saw it? But no. She couldn't possibly do that. No way. What they were doing behind that closed door was private. She had to respect that. No, no, no. The Forbidden Keyhole would remain forever out of bounds.

Patience kept her own door wide open and returned to the safety of her bed. And there she lay. As quiet as she could. Listening out for any sounds. Attempting to guess which stage the lovers had reached. They couldn't have got far. They'd only just started a minute ago. Oh, hold on. A giggle. Then an ohh from Penny. And a muffled mmm from Dave. It could be anything. Dave kissing her neck perhaps. Or fondling her breasts. Maybe Penny cupping his balls? Difficult to ascertain.

She slipped her right hand beneath her pyjama bottoms, where it rested upon her pubic mound for a moment before sliding down a little further. Her index and middle fingers joined as one and found her clitoris. She closed her eyes and began to stimulate herself with soft, circular motions, applying more pressure upon hearing every fresh moan and murmur from Penny's bedroom.

"Oooh!" It was Penny's voice. More prominent than before. "Ooohhh, God!" And there it was again. Even louder. Dave was certainly doing something right. Exactly what was anybody's guess.

Patience's left hand decided to join in, her clammy digits exploring the soft flesh between her legs. She parted herself wider and allowed eager fingers to burrow between her lips. She was rather surprised by how wet she had become in such a short time.

"Oooooh! Fuck!"

It was Penny again. The girl was without a doubt enjoying herself in that room. What was Dave's secret?

Patience paused, her breath bated, keenly awaiting the next cry. She opened her eyes and peered through the open door into the corridor. That's when she found herself drawn to the light. The Forbidden Keyhole.

No. She couldn't possibly do that.

She stroked her moist crevice with her left hand whilst polishing her clitoris with her right. Wisps of air escaped from her part-open mouth as she pushed her middle finger against the entrance to her love tunnel, not quite entering, loitering nearby. Just enough stimulation to make her want so much more.

It was no good. The temptation was too great. The Forbidden Keyhole was beckoning. Calling out to her. Drawing her closer. She climbed out of bed and inched carefully towards her goal. She knew she shouldn't. It was wrong. Immoral. An invasion of privacy. But she couldn't help herself. It was too late. She was already sold.

Second thoughts. What if she was caught? What would she do or say? How would she survive the protests, the arguments, the fallout?

Could she take the shame?

Well?

Ah, sod it. What did she care? It was the risk that made it all the more exciting.

Patience stepped into the gloom of the hallway. She prepared to position her eye, but found herself halted by the sudden arrival of third thoughts. She stood up straight and mulled things over, reconsidering all pros and cons. She'd fully made up her mind in the bedroom, but upon reaching her destination, found herself debating once more whether or not to take the plunge. The voice in her head seemed to be well up for it. Go on, girl. Take a peek. Penny and Dave would be none the wiser. They were simply doing what came naturally to them. Fucking like rabbits. And would they actually mind being watched? Hmm. Not sure. Penny was pretty open-minded in her attitudes towards sex and its many varied forms. And Dave looked like the kind of bloke who would be game for anything. But voyeurism without consent? It was a whole new ball game. Totally uncharted territory.

Oh, God, it was so wrong. And bloody nerve-racking. She could feel her heart working overtime, pounding against her ribs, winding her, choking her, labouring her breath. Her insides were being twisted, wrenched, tied in knots. Her whole body was shaking violently. Was it the fear of being caught? Or the fear of the unknown?

Her right hand returned to the warmth of her pyjama bottoms. She ran a finger under her pussy. Fuck, she was soaked down there. Totally flooded. A new ocean had been formed within minutes. The rest of her trembling body was unsure of where to go from here, but her vagina knew exactly what it wanted.

Behind that door, the murmurs continued. Penny and Dave were getting down to some seriously heavy petting for sure. And here stood Patience. Outside their bedroom door. Listening in.

She knew things were moving fast sex-wise between the amorous couple. After all, she'd overheard this same series of events unfold so many times over the past three months, two days, and however many hours, (she didn't keep count like Penny did) she could write the bloody script. Patience had satisfied herself to the music of their fucking on several occasions, striving to come when they came, which was not as easy as it sounded.

And now she was blessed with the added opportunity to enjoy it all visually too. Live. Unedited. In glorious 3D, i.e. with her own eyes.

Oh, God, she couldn't. It was so wrong.

Yes, she could. Right. Here goes nothing.

Patience squatted low and peeked through the keyhole. Straight away, she recoiled, covering her mouth with the palm of her free hand. She looked in all directions, eyes blinking, brow furrowed, swallowing hard, recovering from what she'd just seen. Naked flesh. Dave's back. And Penny's bosoms. She'd never noticed before, but her flatmate owned a rather fulsome pair.

She spied again, this time not chickening out after the first flash of unclothed skin. Her lower jaw fell open and her eyes widened. Wow, it was most certainly hotting up. Was she prepared to miss a single second of it? No way.

Penny could be seen lying on the bed, legs outstretched. Dave had his back to the keyhole, but it was obvious what was going on. Pussy tasting, of course. Gorging on its delights. Upon every lap of his ever-hungry tongue, Penny's head tilted back and her spine arched upwards, eyes shut tight, mouth wide open. Dave pushed his tongue deeper into her crack with every moan of approval.

In the hallway, Patience was a ball of excitement. Her heart fluttered madly. Butterflies danced — no, scrub that — butterflies rioted in her stomach. She couldn't believe how turned on she was. With a gentle finger, she stroked her sodden lips up and down, round and round, side to side, emulating where she imagined Dave's tongue to be travelling across Penny's pussy. Simulation as well as stimulation was the name of the game here.

Dave and Penny changed angles. Patience's eyes widened. Ooh, look, a flash of his penis. Well, part of it. The groin area at least, where the base of the stalk met a mass of pubic hair. Just for a split second. A blink and she would have missed it. But this was not enough. Patience wanted to see more. Not just a quick teaser. The whole caboodle. His cock in all its glory.

Patience could now see Dave's tongue working its magic across Penny's vagina. The body parts of another woman hadn't been too high on her want-to-look-at list, but the view was surprisingly compelling. Dave licked her crevice in tender upward and downward motions. Patience did the same to herself, but with her fingers. He then flicked his tongue rapidly across Penny's clitoris. Patience tapped her own magic bean with her fingertips. As Dave continued to tongue Penny like a madman, two of his fingers found their way up her entrance, thrusting in and out like pistons.

"Ooooh, fucking yes!" barked Penny, eyes rolling back, whites showing.

Patience's thumb took over drumming duties on her clitoris as she pushed two fingers into her own hole. The digits motioned in and out, in and out, just like Dave was doing to Penny. Fuck, fuck, fucking yeah, this was good stuff. She began to wish it was herself on the bed and not Penny. She yearned to be the lucky lady being pleasured by Dave's fingery-licky party trick. But, hmm. Should she be thinking such a thing? No, not really. But she couldn't help it. The pushing and tapping she was applying to herself was mashing her mind and whipping her body into a frenzy.

Penny's hands fell onto her own breasts and went to work immediately. Kneading them. Pushing them together. Fingers and thumbs on nipples. Rubbing them. Squeezing them. Pinching them hard. On the other side of the keyhole, Patience moved her free hand up to her bosoms and tweaked each nipple in turn as she continued to push two fingers deeper and deeper inside her. Oh God, fucking hell, pressure was building up fast. Her quivering legs began to tingle. Heart in overdrive, boom, boom, boom, her breathing heavy and laboured, huff, huff, huff. Uh oh. She was on the verge of coming. Would she last the distance? She fucking well hoped so.

Patience needed to calm herself down. No, no, no. Don't come yet. Save yourself, girl. Fingers out. Nipples unpinched. Just watch. For now. A few soothing breaths were taken. Then a smile of relief. It was working. The intensity of it all was subsiding. She was all waterfalls down below, and as such, felt a dribble running down her inner thigh. But at least her orgasm would be saved for better things.

It was Dave's turn to lie on the bed. Patience smiled. At last. A good view of his cock. And what a cock it was, loyally standing to attention for his woman like a rocket ready to launch. She couldn't take her eyes off it. Wow. What a monster. Penny was so fortunate. Lucky bitch.

Yeah, yeah, many a time, Patience had heard the tired old adage that size didn't matter, but Penny always stressed that only guys with small willy-winkies quoted that particular line. And she was probably right.

Dave smiled at Penny as she knelt astride him. She wrapped her fingers around his penis and held the stalk in position as she gently lowered herself onto him. And ooh, yes, he was in. Patience exhaled weightily at the sight. Oops. She hastily gagged her mouth with the flat of her palm. Bugger. Did they hear the noise? A quick check. No. Thank fuck for that.

Patience's fingers made a return visit to her clitoris as she watched Penny ride the man. Up and down, up and down, Penny moved, her pussy swallowing his penis whole upon every downward plunge. Dave grabbed her bottom cheeks and squeezed them hard as the couple accelerated their pace; the tempo of each gyration matched perfectly by the rhythm of the watching girl's fingertips on the other side of the door.

Penny leaned forward and placed her hands flat on the bed, positioning herself on all fours over him. Dave thrust his penis upwards, taking charge of the riding. She squealed with delight as his cock pounded into her, harder and harder, faster and faster. In the hallway, Patience slipped a finger back into her hole, powering it rapidly, in and out, in and out, in and out. Fuck, fuck, fuck, she thought, this was total fucking heaven.

It was all building up again inside the watcher. That fizzy, fuzzy sensation. It wouldn't be long now. The final furlong was in sight. Once more, she clasped her mouth with a tight-fitting palm to thwart rogue wails as she worked her pussy harder and harder. Through the keyhole, Penny and Dave gyrated for dear life, hard and fast, hard and fast; her hole being pummelled to oblivion by his rigid weapon. The couple squealed, shouted, swore and spat as they fucked like they'd never fucked before.

"Oh, my fucking God!" shrieked Dave, eyes popping wide open as he smashed his cock relentlessly into her pussy. "I'm going to come!"

"Oh, fuck, I'm coming too!" yelped Penny, continually slamming herself down on Dave's penis, as if her life depended on it.

"Fucking hell, so am I," whispered Patience to herself, trembling, perspiring, working herself faster than ever before.

Penny and Dave's bodies steeled, tensed and quivered in unison as the shared climax made a spectacular entrance. Bang! Ear-piercing screams of sheer ecstasy rang out as the explosive finale completely overwhelmed the couple. Behind the keyhole, Patience slammed her eyes shut, gritted her teeth and growled under her breath as she rode such hectic spasms with glee.

When her orgasm was spent, Patience fell to her knees, sucking in much-needed cool air. In the bedroom, Penny and Dave collapsed flat on the bed, entangled in each other's arms and legs, exhausted but fulfilled.

It had been one hell of an experience.

For all three of them.

Chapter 3

About Last Night

Patience slept well that night. And awoke the next morning with a huge smile on her face. She couldn't erase the previous evening's events from her head. Her heart was all a-flutter. Her pelvis tingled madly, screaming at her to do something about it. And so she did. With her fingers. And some serious rubbing. Playing back in her mind's eye everything she'd witnessed through that keyhole over and over again. Dave's talented tongue upon Penny's welcoming vagina. The sight of Dave's cock in all its glory. And the two of them fucking hard and fast.

Ooh, yes.

It didn't take her long to come. A minute at the most. But it was a bloody good orgasm. A massive explosion. Plenty of excess juice. And as she wiped her sodden fingers with a tissue, she made a mental note in the To Do department of her brain. Change her bed sheets forthwith.

Demented endorphins continued to sprint crazily around her body as she washed and dressed. They made her feel good, on top of the world. But as they wore off, the woes of last night came flooding back. The part of the evening just before Patience's record-breaking door slam. The dark secret that was no longer her own.

Twenty-five-year-old Patience Hope was a virgin. And worse still, Penny and Dave now knew all about it.

Bugger.

Patience walked through the hallway and into the kitchen. Penny stood by the sink, filling the kettle with water. She turned to face the new arrival and smiled sweetly.

"Morning. Coffee?"

"Who else knows?" asked Patience, eyes narrowed, hands on hips.

Penny frowned as she flicked the kettle onto boil. "Sorry?"

"Don't act as if you haven't got a clue what I'm talking about."

Penny shrugged. "I haven't."

Did she really need to spell it out? "Me. Being a virgin. Who have you told?"

"Nobody."

"What about Dave?"

"He already knows. He was here, remember?"

Patience rolled her eyes. "That's not what I meant. Where is he?"

"Where do you think? Work, of course."

"Do you reckon he'll tell his workmates?"

"Why would he?" Penny was clearly growing tired of Patience's needless concern. "It's not as if it's a big deal."

Patience threw her a scowl. "That's not what you thought last night."

Penny plucked two mugs from the cupboard. "Don't you think you're overreacting?"

"No. I don't."

"We were only having a laugh."

"Yes. At my expense." And still not convinced, Patience added, "So you haven't blabbed about it at all?"

"No. How could I have done? I haven't stepped outside the front door yet."

Patience threw her a look. Like, duh. "This is the twenty-first century. You've got umpteen means of communication right here at your disposal. Phone, text, email, instant messaging, social networking, chatrooms, internet forums, shouting out of the window, you must have told somebody, you always do."

Penny stared at her in silence for a moment, disenchanted by the supposition. Then she responded with, "I'm sorry you feel that way, but I haven't said a word about it to anybody. And that's the truth."

Patience couldn't get her head around it. Does not compute, does not compute. "But—it's juicy gossip."

"No, Patience. Juicy gossip is finding out that the doctor I most hate at work is shagging the head consultant's wife. If only, huh? Talk about a blackmail opportunity. Or the wanker bloke I wish my naïve sister would have the sense to dump has got somebody else pregnant. Now that I would love to see happen. Or the shock-horror discovery that Felicity down the road's grandfather is getting married to his eighteen-year-old carer."

Patience's lower jaw flopped loose. "Is that true?"

"Yep."

"But the man's eighty-six years old."

"Eighty-seven actually. He had a birthday last month."

"What does Felicity down the road have to say about it?"

"She reckons it won't last."

Patience scoffed. "If her grandfather's not careful, neither will he." Then an afterthought. "How the hell did it happen in the first place?"

"Felicity down the road reckons it's got something to do with him telling the girl he had money. Can't wait for the tarty little gold-digger to find out it's only a few coins in a piggy bank."

Penny chuckled at the prospect. Patience, unable to share the amusement, began to pace the room, head hung low. Not even the news of Felicity down the road's future teenage step-grandmother could sweep away the current plight from her troubled mind.

"Cheer up, Patience, it might never happen."

"Exactly. I could be a virgin forever."

The kettle reached its boil and clicked off. Penny proceeded to prepare two coffees. Patience dumped herself at the table, elbows upon surface, hands propping up chin. She blew out a sigh of despair.

"They'll all laugh at me."

Penny looked across at her. "No, they won't."

"How can you be so sure?"

"Because me and Dave are the only ones who know. And we won't say anything, I promise."

"Oh, God, I'm a virgin at twenty-five."

Penny brought over the two mugs and joined Patience at the table. "Which is nobody's business but your own."

"People are bound to find out. They always do," said Patience, cupping her coffee in both hands and staring into space. "I mean, it's bound to slip out sooner or later. Just like it did last night."

"Playing the Truth Game was your idea."

"Yeah, and don't I know it? I wish I'd suggested Pin The Tail To The Donkey now." A sip of her coffee, then, "It's no good. I need to resign myself to the fact that secrets are never secrets for very long. Soon, the whole world will know I'm a virgin. I can see the headlines now." And in a faux shocked voice, she continued with, "Patience Hope? Still a virgin? At her age? Hold the front page. How can this be? Why has this girl never bagged herself a bit of the other? Is she scared? Or worse — is she frigid?"

Penny stared at the girl, not quite sure what to make of the rather odd speech. "To be quite honest, I was shocked to hear your little revelation. I assumed you'd lost your virginity years ago."

"Why? Do I come across as some kind of a slut?"

"No, of course not. It's just that most girls of our generation don't hold onto it for so long."

"I decided to wait."

"What for?"

Patience shrugged, not too sure of her motives. "The right man, I suppose."

"I assume he never turned up."

"What do you think?"

They shared a knowing girlie moment.

"I guess I wanted my first time to be special."

"The first time is never special. It's awkward. And painful. And a total disaster."

"It doesn't have to be, surely."

A stern look from Penny. "Believe me, it always is."

"Well, if it's that bad, I'd better get it over and done with. I'm determined to find myself a shag. Preferably today."

"Have patience, Patience. You've saved yourself for this long. Why rush into things now? What if the right man is just around the corner?"

Patience shook her head. "There is no right man. Not for me. He would have shown up by now. I mean, it's not as if I haven't waited long enough."

"Maybe his SatNav is a bit crap."

"It's no good. I need to get rid of this virginity as soon as possible," she stated in no uncertain terms, as if referring to a decrepit pair of shoes or a monster zit on the end of her nose. "It's humiliating."

Patience held her head up high. Steadfast. Unwavering. The girl had reached a major decision and was determined to stick to it. Nobody could talk her out of this one.

Penny conceded and said, "Well, if that's what you want."

"It is."

"In that case, let's get you laid."

"But how?" She gestured to her flatmate, seeking input. "Where do I start?"

"At the beginning, of course. Question one. Who do you fancy?"

The reply came surprisingly fast. "Nobody."

"Okaaaay. Does anybody fancy you?"

"I don't think so."

"There must be somebody out there who likes you."

"Not that I'm aware of."

Penny deflated. "This is going to be a lot more difficult than I thought."

"Tell me about it."

It was true. Nobody fancied her. Or if they did, they certainly knew how to hide it well. She ran through the Patience Hope Good Points checklist in her head. Attractive in a quirky sort of way. Tick. Not exactly overweight. Tick. No acne problem. Tick. Her hair always looked nice. Um. Didn't it? Maybe a smaller tick. And she considered herself relatively fashionable. Or at least above the limits of the social acceptance grey area. Right? Another smaller tick. Oh, and she didn't smell. Big tick. So what was wrong with her? What was it about her appearance that seemed to repel men so much? Did she wear a bloody great sign on her back?

Don't Fancy Me, I'm Horrible.

It was indeed a mystery.

A scary thought then crossed her mind. What if she gave off some kind of pheromone that told—or rather, warned. Yes. Warned—the opposite sex that she was a hopeless virgin? What if it told the male of the species to steer well clear?

"You won't get a decent bonk here, mate. This girl has never been

23

poked."

Oh, God, that could be it. Virgin scent. The downfall of the sexually inexperienced female. A dreaded hormone impossible to mask, no matter how drenched with celebrity-endorsed perfumery.

Maybe she should contact the nearest science lab. Or university. Or wherever, whatever and whoever it was who dealt with such peculiarities. Patience Hope had single-handedly discovered the virgin pheromone. It was a scientific breakthrough. This could make her famous. And rich. They'd name it after her, of course. They'd have to, you see. The Patience hormone. Yes, you heard right. The Patience hormone. Well, come on, get real. They could hardly call it the Hope hormone. That would be a most inappropriate moniker for a chemical that pushed men away.

Curious. In erotic literature, the general consensus was that men liked virgins. Especially the mid life crisis generation, the dirty sods. But it had to be a fallacy. In fact, a total fabrication. Why would any man desire such useless creatures? No experience, for starters, for it had been well documented throughout the ages that guys preferred women who knew exactly what they were doing. And why wouldn't they? Better a satisfying shag than a lifeless sack of potatoes. Then there was the problem of the penis not fitting inside such a tight, never-explored passage. Or upon successful entry, constricted to the point of fainting by the contracting pelvic muscles of an exceptionally tense and panicky beginner. Or was that just a fallacy too? How the hell would she know? She hadn't got that far yet.

Back in the real world, Penny decided to try a different approach. "What about people at work? Any eligible contenders?"

"I don't really know anybody yet. I only started the job last week."

"You mean to say nobody fits in the category of, 'Mmm, not bad. Don't know his name, but I wouldn't mind a bit of a dirty fumble with him?'"

"Most of my colleagues are women."

"Oh. Right."

Patience thought about it some more. "There's a male part-time cleaner. His name's Bob."

Penny smiled. "Now we're getting somewhere."

"But he suffers from chronic body odour."

Penny's smile faded. "Oh. Anybody thought about letting him know?"

"Believe me, they've all thought about it plenty of times. But nobody will risk getting close enough to tell him."

"Fine, I get the hint. Bob's scrubbed off the list. Anybody else?"

Patience nodded. "Yes. Geoff, my manager."

Delight flashed across Penny's face. "Aha. Perfect. Has he tried cracking onto you?"

"He has smiled at me a few times. But that could just be him being friendly." An afterthought. "Or wind." Then more upbeat. "Mind you, I did overhear the other girls saying it will only be a matter of time before he tries to seduce me."

"That's great. It means they know for a fact he likes you."

"No, Penny. It means they know for a fact I'm the only girl in the office he hasn't shagged yet."

"Yes, but don't you see? It's the perfect solution to your problem. Open your legs to Geoffy-boy and say farewell to your virginity."

"But he's my boss."

"So?"

"It would be unprofessional. And unethical."

Penny was having none of it. "Oh, fuck the un words. I thought this was an emergency."

"I'd hardly call it that."

"Wouldn't you? At the beginning of this conversation, losing your virginity was more important to you than oxygen."

Patience took stock of the situation for a moment. Something was not quite right here. At said beginning of conversation, Penny was part of the "virginity is no big deal" crowd. Now the girl was on emergency code red, all systems go, on call and ready to assist in the deflowering of Patience Hope, no matter what, who, how, where, when or why.

"Penny? Are you mocking me?"

A genuine and sincere Penny responded with, "No, of course not. If losing your virginity is that important to you, then as a good mate, I am here to help you in any way I can. Which is why I think it will be a brilliant idea for you to go into work today and open your legs for the boss at the first available opportunity. Preferably during your tea break or lunch hour to avoid any docking of your wages."

Patience felt unsure. "Yes, but banging the boss doesn't feel right."

"Why, what's wrong with him? Is he a total minger?"

"No, he's rather handsome actually."

"And has he got money?"

"He's the boss. Bound to be loaded."

"All the more reason for you to sample his sausage. Who knows? You might bag an exotic holiday out of it. Or a car. Or even a house."

Patience shrank into herself, uneasy. "Maybe this isn't such a good idea after all."

Penny rolled her eyes to the heavens. "Do you want to get shot of your virginity or not?"

"You know I do."

"Then it's settled." Penny was not for turning. "Patience Hope. Today's the day your cherry gets picked."

Patience's mobile phone bleeped for attention. It was a text. She read the message and beamed with glee.

"Who is it?" asked Penny, wanting in.

"Joe. He wants to meet me for a coffee after work. I haven't seen him for months. It will be nice to catch up on things."

"Who's Joe when he's at a coffee shop?"

Patience smiled. "He's my best friend. I've known him ever since primary school. We kind of grew up together."

Things didn't seem to add up for Penny. "So how come you two never got round to exchanging bodily fluids?"

For a moment, a dreamy glint animated Patience's eyes. And then it was gone. "I would if I could, but I can't. Joe's gay."

Penny gave a tut. "What a bummer." Then she realised and checked herself. "The situation, I mean. Not—well, you know."

They laughed. Patience then drained her mug and rose from the table.

"You off to work now?"

Patience nodded. "No rest for the wicked."

Penny offered a wink. "Exactly. Your manager won't know what's hit him."

Patience threw back a smirk as she grabbed her jacket and hand-bag.

"Don't you dare come back here tonight with your virginity in-tact, young lady," warned Penny, parent-like, wry grin. "You'll be in right hot water if you do."

"Yes, Mother," joked Patience, flicking a mock salute.

"Oh, Patience, before you go. You wouldn't happen to know the number of a pest control company, would you? I think we might have mice."

Patience frowned, hovering by the door. "What makes you say that?"

"It's probably just me," replied Penny, "but I'm sure I heard strange noises last night in the hallway."

At that, Patience made her excuses and left.

Quickly.

Chapter 4
Banging the Boss

It was the first time Patience had ever purchased condoms. A sense of daunting tenseness overwhelmed the girl as she plucked a three-pack from the shelf and scurried towards the till. She felt dirty. And guilty. Like she was committing the crime of the century. Her life, her activities, her privacy invaded, for she was sure a million—no, make that a trillion—pairs of eyes were watching her every move.

Once she joined the queue, however, a much-needed dose of head-lifted-high self-assurance kicked in. After all, why be embarrassed by rubbers? Millions of packs were sold every minute of every hour of every day to perfectly normal people from all walks of life who at some point in their upcoming schedule would be having sex. Or planning to. Or rather, hoping to. Just like her. If she played her cards right. This very fact made her feel a part of society. She had something in common with the rest of the world. She now fitted in. No longer an outcast, she was part of the gang.

Bold and proud, she held the colourful little box in plain view of her fellow shoppers. She pretended to read the instructions on the back, but was in actual fact using the method of contraception to mask her virginity. Hey. It's Patience Hope. She's buying condoms. So she must be having sex. Right?

Look at me. I'm a sexually active woman.

Well, almost.

The journey to work was a short bus ride. On this morning's commute, however, there were far more passengers than usual. The weatherman on the local morning news had spoken of the threat of torrential rain. He had to be mistaken, surely, for the sun shone brightly, with plenty of room for the blazing orb to stretch in a cloudless blue sky. But alas, this very fact failed to deter a flurry of astute pedestrians from taking the public transport route. Just this once. Just in case.

The only seating not already taken was the dreaded area everybody strove to avoid. Situated directly above the rear wheels, Old Rumble-Shaky, as the seat was affectionately nicknamed, took the brunt of the vehicle's shakes, shudders and bounces, and would drive even the hardiest stomach to the point of nausea. Many a pavement pizza had found itself delivered by green-faced passengers whose only option was to hastily alight from the bus and lose possession of their stomach contents to the wrath of the seat of doom. Old Rumble-Shaky took no prisoners, period.

It was curious to note that the tremors presently raging underseat seemed to affect Patience in a wholly different and rather bizarre way. Both buttocks were being shaken to the point of submission, and were unlikely to survive the journey in their current shape or form, yet the tingling she felt down below as a result was making her horny again. Of course, the fizzy, fuzzy sensations to which she was currently subscribed were not entirely the fault of mere axle vibrations and unrepaired potholes in the roads.

So what was mainly to blame? Last night, that's what. Or rather, the events of. She'd never witnessed two people fucking before. And how could she have done? The girl had never experienced any type of sexual intercourse live and uncut. Why? Because she was a virgin.

She rolled her mind's eye. Why did she have to keep reminding herself of the fact that she'd never been involved in, and up until last night, never observed any form of naughty action? Oh, apart from randy dogs in parks. But they didn't exactly count. Well, the answer was obvious. She now yearned for a piece of the action. Being left out was horrible. Not fair at all. It seemed like a case of everybody fucking everybody else, then everybody else moving on to anybody else who wanted some more, leaving Patience standing cold, alone and ignored on the sidelines. Or at least that's how it appeared to her.

The fizzing down below showed no signs of fizzling out. Her genital region was on permanent randy alert. The previous evening's clandestine voyeurism had certainly made its mark for sure. However, her non-stop pussy pouting was now becoming rather tiresome, and at the same time, something that couldn't be ignored. Oh, God, if the tingly-binglies failed to subside, she'd have no choice but to sort herself out in the works toilets, blessed with the company of her fellow cubicle dwellers, namely, the work avoiders and secret smokers. Oh, bugger. Why the hell hadn't she taken a cold shower before setting out for the day?

Ten minutes later, she arrived at work. The prospect of yet another mind-numbingly boring day in the office seemed to outweigh the desire to polish her magic bean, and as such, dispelled the fuzzy-wuzzies down below completely. This was most fortunate. Now she could sit tingle free at her desk and devote all her time and effort to wishing she was somewhere else. Somewhere far away. And hot. Near a swimming pool. Where vodka was on permanent tap. And cost nothing to buy. Mmm.

What did Patience do for a living? Simple. Exactly the same as the other women in the office, all hopelessly chained to desks littered with piles of paperwork. Menial administration and secretarial duties. Yay! Whoopee! All hail job satisfaction.

Whatever that was.

Still, at least it paid the bills.

Just about.

It was then when Geoff Denton, the boss, sauntered past. He caught her eye and smiled. Patience returned the gesture. She even added a small wave just for good measure. Oh, look. A wave back. Then the man entered his office. And closed the door behind him.

A couple of the other girls glanced at Patience. They both threw across small smiles. Or were they smirks? Hmm. Not sure. Whatever they were and however they were supposed to be taken was in effect irrelevant. She knew exactly what they meant. Watch out, Patience. Looks like you're next in line for Mr Denton's shaft.

Geoff was dangerously close to being two decades her senior, but looked a lot younger. The dreaded wrinkles hadn't yet taken much of a foothold, and his hair still retained its original factory settings, colour-wise. He was a snappy dresser—ooh, that tailored suit he'd sailed past in a moment ago certainly made his buttocks look shapely—and, yes, no two ways about it, he was pleasing to the eye. But was he the right man to take her virginity? And furthermore, was it really the best of ideas to open her legs for the boss?

He'd have to do. Let's face it. Nobody else seemed to be volunteering their services.

There was one problem. Or rather, several. Namely, all the other women in the office who had sat on his cock and jiggled. Five female colleagues. Yep. Five. She was potentially in the running to be crowned Miss Sloppy Sixth. Not that she relished the prospect of being the latest addition to a long list of boss fuckers. One more notch on his bedpost. Yet another pussy travelling along a never-ending conveyor belt of sexual perks. Yuck. It didn't exactly make her feel special. But alas, it had to be done.

In a way, it was almost laughable. Fellow colleagues, left, right and centre, all falling over themselves to assist in making Geoff's willy wet. Why? To enhance their career prospects, of course—

"Promotion please, Mr Denton."

"Sex first."

"Certainly, Mr Denton, sir. You're the boss." Insert plastic smile here.

—whereas Patience was only considering such a proposal—or rather, Geoff's future request, seeing as he hadn't even attempted to proposition her yet—just to wave goodbye to the thorn in her side that was her bloody virginity.

Maybe it was a good thing that Geoff had been with so many other women. Surely all that practice made him an expert. Right? And by shagging all those girls, Geoff would have picked up squillions of handy sex-enhancing tips and tricks along the way. Right? Which was sure to guarantee Patience absolute paradise in bed.

The. Most. Amazing. Sex. Ever.

Right?

The theory had to be true. Or at least she hoped so. This girl was determined to avoid at all cost the awkward, painful and inevitably disastrous first time that Penny had described as being textbook and unavoidable.

She just hoped Geoff washed his bits thoroughly between conquests.

Patience blinked her way out of the swirling pink mist of her thoughts and landed back inside the four magnolia walls of reality. Geoff stood by the coffee machine at the other side of the room. Aha. This was her chance. Walk over to him. Talk to him. Smile at him. Flutter her eyelashes at him in the way she'd seen it played on TV. You know, as if to say, "Make a play for me, stud. Don't be shy. I'm available right now for a quickie. Mind if we go somewhere a little more private?"

Hmm. Were eyelash flutters really capable of saying so much?

Patience then asked herself a rather more serious question. In her mind, that is. Not aloud. Did planning — or rather, plotting — to throw herself at the first available man make her look a bit cheap? No. Of course it didn't. Far from it.

It made her look totally cheap.

And transparent. And shallow. And easy. And a tart. Oh, and a lady on the embarrassing side of desperate.

Ah, who cares? She'd only look cheap, transparent, shallow, easy, a tart and a lady on the embarrassing side of desperate for one day/night/whatever only. A single meaningless fuck. That's all it would take to free herself from the iron manacles of pure innocence. Goodbye to the virgin. Hello to the blossoming woman of experience. And once she'd got shot of her virginity, she could be far more choosy with any subsequent sexual encounters. It wouldn't even matter if her second shag took several years to find. As long as she got rid of that damned cherry today.

Patience rose from her desk and employed her best bottom wiggle as she sauntered across the room. Hmm. Did she consider a wiggle of the buttocks to be a good idea? Probably not. It lacked a certain grace, making it look like one of her legs was slightly longer than the other. Argh! Stop this madness. Now. She clenched her rear cheeks to disallow further wiggling and joined Geoff at the coffee machine

"This virgin is ridiculous," he growled.

She stepped back a pace, stunned. Could he really tell just by looking at her? The situation was worse than she thought. It was evidentially more than just virgin scent — AKA the Patience hormone — that kept the boys at bay. Virgins were easy to spot by sight too. Bugger.

No wonder no man had ever offered to park his car in her garage.

"Sorry?" she croaked, face contorted.

"This bloody machine. Verging on ridiculous," he said, holding up a plastic cup that contained a strange substance resembling clouded ditchwater. "I tried to order coffee, milk, no sugar. All I got out of it was tea, no milk, five sugars."

Sheer relief from Patience, her face now contortion free.

Note to self: Clean out both ears.

"Oh, I see," she said. "I thought you said —"

Don't say it!

"Thought I said what?" asked a curious Geoff.

Now look what you've done!

It was most fortunate that Geoff then continued his original rant. "For the life of me, I don't understand why they load this machine with tea in the first place. Nobody ever chooses the muck. Looks like dirty washing up water. Tastes like gnat's piss." Then an afterthought and a shrug. "Whatever gnat's piss tastes like." Another quick think, then, "I've always wondered. Do gnats actually urinate?"

"Um. I'm not sure. That Attenborough guy who does those TV nature shows will probably know. He's an expert on animals."

Geoff packed away his irritation and smiled warmly at the girl. "It's Patience, isn't it?"

"That's right, Mr Denton."

"Please. Let's not be so formal. All that Mr Denton nonsense is way too starchy for my liking. You can call me Geoff."

"Okay."

"How are you finding the job?"

Boring. "Fine."

"Happy?"

No. "Yes."

"Oh, Patience." Geoff gave a knowing chuckle. "You must be bored shitless at that desk all day."

Patience grinned. "Just a bit."

"In that case, how would you like a fresh challenge?"

Did a bear shit in the woods? "I'd love it."

Geoff looked pleased. "That's great. Meet me in the car park at three o'clock this afternoon."

"Where will we be heading?" she dared to ask.

"My place."

The drive to Geoff's place only took twenty minutes or so, but the scenery changes were astounding. To a devout London girl like Patience, the sight of the cold and impersonal grey of inner-city concretia surrendering to the far more pleasing earth shades of leafy suburbia proved a somewhat stark contrast. The old adage was true. The grass was categorically greener on the other side.

Geoff climbed out of the vehicle, trotted round to the other side and opened the door for his passenger. Wow, she thought. A gentleman. What a rarity. And a well-deserved tick in her endangered creatures spotter book.

Entering Geoff's home was like walking into another world. The place was huge. And lavishly designed, to boot. Bold, vibrant colours. Fine drapery. Luxurious furnishings that oozed wealth and opulence. For sure, a far cry from her dreary abode. She also noticed something else. There was absolutely no trace of dust to be found anywhere. Not even in any difficult to reach places. His wife's handiwork? Probably not. Mrs Denton was bound to be a lady of leisure who had never held a duster in her life. Cleaning duties? No doubt the sole responsibility of an au pair. Young and female, most definitely, with unlimited access to Geoff's trousersnake.

"Make yourself at home," invited Geoff, gesturing to the sofa.

Patience nodded and parked her posterior. Geoff sat next to her.

"You'll have to excuse the mess."

She looked around and made a face. Eh? What mess?

"My wife, she's out of town for a few days. It's her mother, you see. She's had one of her funny turns." A theatrical roll of the eyes, as if to signify all too frequent bouts from his mother-in-law of the funny turns genus. "So I figured it would be nice for the two of us to take a break from that stuffy old office and work from home."

A small smirk formed on Patience's face. Work from home, eh? She'd never heard it called that before.

Geoff opened his briefcase. From it, he plucked a pile of paperwork. The coffee table became its new home.

"I know it looks a lot, Patience, but I'm sure we'll get through it all in no time."

Patience's face dropped. From a great height. You what? Most blokes lured women to their homes under false pretences. Could this be the first time in Homo sapiens history that a lure was under true unpretences? Hmm. Was true unpretences even a phrase? Who cares? It was official. As a woman, Patience was clearly unlikeable and unappealing, so much so that Geoff, who, let's face it, was famous for his extra-marital conquests, did not wish to place his hands upon her body and squeeze a lot.

It was like she'd been given testicles, only for her boss to kick them. Hard.

Geoff noticed her displeasure at once. "What's the matter?"

"You brought me here to work?"

"Well, yes. What else were you expecting?"

Another kick in her virtual gonads. This time with steel-toed boots. Ouch.

What else was she expecting? Action between the sheets, that's what. How could he even ask such a question? All the other women in the office had no doubt been tempted to his house in exactly the same way. And all the other women in the office had without a doubt felt his cock inside them. Even Sheila, a rather overweight girl who suffered from severe acne and bad breath. So why not Patience Hope? Argh! The very thought of such unjust ostracism—because quite frankly, that's what it was—made her blood boil.

Oh. Hold on a minute. Maybe this was part of the ritual. Maybe he was playing hard to get. Teasing her. Getting her in the mood for what was to follow. Mmm. In that case, it was time for Patience to play along. Roleplay was not exactly her cup of tea. She left dressing up and spouting fictional blurb to the acting profession. But in order to get what she wanted, an episode of give-and-take back scratching was clearly required.

"Okay." She threw him a smile and a wink. "Let's get to work."

Geoff smiled back and tipped a nod. He split the paperwork into two equal piles. One for him. One for her. Patience frowned, unsure of his motives. Um. When was the guy planning on shifting the ceremony forward a notch from just-like-work realism to work-to-sexy fantasy?

"Isn't it best for us to work together?" she queried, laying heavy emphasis on the final two words.

"No."

Ouch.

Geoff elaborated with, "By working separately, we'll be able to shift this load in half the time."

Blimey. This man was not just playing hard to get. He was playing bloody impossible to reach. Still, if that was the way he wanted to play it, then that was the way he'd get it.

Another smile and wink combo from Patience. "Ah, but Geoff," she uttered in her most sexy and seductive voice. Or rather, what she assumed sounded sexy and seductive to men. "Instead of shifting your load, wouldn't you rather —" A pause for dramatic effect. " — blow your load?"

Yeah. That line was good. Clever. Witty. And very provocative. Guaranteed to set the mood, and at the same time kickstart the two of them onto the next level.

But no. It didn't. Insert sigh here.

"I don't think you're getting it," came his reply.

"Yes, I know I'm not bloody getting it!"

Geoff. Taken aback by her sudden bark. "Patience? Is everything all right?"

Huh? What did he mean, is everything all right? Was he being serious? Was this guy really that thick? Was he from this bloody planet? She could feel spasms of rage shimmying inside her trembling body, cranking up unimaginable pressure. It would only take one more stupid line for Patience Hope to explode.

"What is wrong with you?" he asked.

And that was the stupid line.

Boom!

"I'll tell you what's wrong with me, shall I?" she cried out, taking no prisoners as she kicked out a leg and knocked over the coffee table, spilling its paper load onto the carpet. "I thought you'd brought me back to your place because you wanted to fuck me!"

The million decibel outburst was followed by an ice-cold deathly hush. Geoff's lower jaw fell limp. He stared aghast at the girl in stunned silence. Patience winced. Shit. If there was ever a time where she had got everything completely wrong, this was it.

"Oh, God," she squealed. Double face-palm. Crimson-cheeked embarrassment. "I'm sorry. I misread all the signals. Oh, Geoff, I've been so stupid. Please forgive me."

"No, no, no, don't apologise." He placed a gentle hand on her shoulder. "You're right. I do want you."

Eh? Confusion overload. "So why the hell are you getting paperwork out when you should be—" A struggle to complete the question.

"Getting my cock out?" prompted Geoff.

Patience blinked a couple of times. "My version was not quite so graphic. But yes."

"I didn't know if you were interested. The other girls in the office, they all practically threw themselves at me, so I knew exactly where I stood with them. But you—" A shrug.

Patience prompted him with, "But me?" A fishing eyebrow arch. "What about me?"

"You're—"

"I'm what?"

"Different."

"In what way?"

"Not once have you tried to get something out of me—money, a promotion—by opening your legs."

"And that's a bad thing?"

"No. It's great. It made me see you as a challenge. A girl I'd have to work hard at wooing. But then I thought, what if she's a—" His head swayed from side to side whilst attempting to select the correct term. "A—"

Uh oh. V alert! "I'm not a virgin, you know," she blurted out rather too sharply.

Geoff frowned. "I never said you were."

"But that's what you were about to say," she insisted. "I'm right, aren't I?"

Geoff threw her a funny look, prompting the girl to realise she was drawing the wrong kind of attention to herself.

"The phrase I was looking for," he told her, "was good girl."

Oops. "Oh. Right."

"So I set up this little act of luring you to my place just to see what would happen. But once here, I got cold feet. Because I didn't think you were interested."

It took a second or two to sink in. Then came a big smile. "Does this mean — you actually want to fuck me?"

Geoff smiled back. "Yes. Very much so."

For a brief moment, nothing happened. They simply stared at each other in suspended animation, like they were both in a movie where a viewer had hit pause on the DVD player.

It was Geoff who took the plunge. He craned his neck forward and planted a kiss upon her lips. Patience kissed him back. Geoff reached out and wrapped his arms around her body. She did the same. Their mouths pushed together and remained fixed in union. His tongue slipped into her mouth. Mmm. She liked that. Very much.

Patience laid herself on the sofa, allowing Geoff to climb aboard. She pulled the tail of his shirt from the waistband of his trousers. Eager fingers crept under cotton and explored the contoured flesh of his back. She'd never felt the warm skin of a man before. How sad was that? Ah, who cares? It didn't bother her any more. This girl was no longer living in the past. It was here and now, all the way.

Geoff unbuttoned her blouse as he peppered her neck with kisses. He pulled open the garment, revealing ripe breasts cupped in lace. He placed both hands upon them. And squeezed them. Fondled them. Pushed them together. Ooh, yes, she thought. It felt good.

It was only the second time her tits had been touched by male hands. The first time was purely an accident. A packed bus. No free seats. Fellow standing passengers. A dog running out in the road. A sudden stamp on the brakes. And a total stranger stumbling forward, both hands outstretched. The poor guy hadn't meant to cop a feel. So she guessed it didn't count.

And so, correction. This was the first time her tits had (officially) been handled by male extremities.

Geoff's fingers burrowed beneath Patience's bra and found her nipples. They were firm. Erect. Standing to attention for her man. He clasped them between thumb and forefinger and gave them both a gentle squeeze. She let out an involuntary murmur of approval, egging him on to squeeze them harder.

"Ooh, yeah," she growled, smiling. "I like that."

It was true. She did like it. Very much so. She recalled how she'd tweaked her own nipples during the previous evening's voyeurism. But somebody else doing it to her was something else. Wow. Much better. And what's more, she certainly didn't need to run a finger across her crevice to test whether or not she was moist. She could feel the juices flowing freely already.

"What else do you like?" he asked.

This was a tough question for Patience to answer. How the hell did she know what would turn her on? She hadn't experienced anything sexual yet. It was all new to her. A case of trial and error. Like being invited to a posh wedding and tasting those volly-vonty thingies — or whatever they were called — alongside other strange looking and even stranger sounding savouries she'd never heard of before. Some she would cheerily gush about, others she'd turn down with a pained grimace and return half-consumed to the platter and say, "Ooh, no. Never again." Therefore, she assumed going through the motions of sex would be largely similar.

"Well?" he prompted. "What would make you really wet?"

"I don't know," she whispered, grinning at the man on top of her. "Surprise me."

Yes. A perfect reply. And tactical too. The ball was now in his court.

"Okay," he responded, eyes glinting. "I will."

Geoff dismounted and stood up. Patience threw a double take at the size of the bulge in his trousers. Would something of such mass fit inside her? She hoped so. And more worryingly, would it hurt? She hoped not.

"Let's move to the bedroom."

Patience liked the sound of that. "Okay."

"Go upstairs and get undressed," he requested. "The master bedroom is second on the right. I'll join you in a couple of shakes."

A couple of shakes of what? His penis? He'd better not quiver it too much. More than a certain number of shakes constituted a wank. Or at least that's what she'd overheard from immature schoolboys.

Whether there was any truth in the statement remained to be seen. Not that she wanted it proved correct today. And certainly not with Geoff as the test subject. The last thing she needed right now was his lust jelly taking a one-way journey into a tissue in hand, then thrown down the lavatory pan, never to see the light of day again.

Patience climbed the stairs and entered the bedroom. She found it even more ornate and flamboyant than downstairs. A king-size four-poster bed dominated the room, enveloped in lavish, near-transparent drapery. She'd never before laid eyes on such splendour. This was a luxury of which she was not familiar. Had she died and gone to Heaven? It was a feasible explanation.

A smile appeared on her face. Maybe it was a good idea after all to say yes to sex with the boss. Penny would be so jealous when Patience reeled off this particular tale.

She stripped her body of clothing, made herself comfortable on the bed and waited. Ooer. She felt rather exposed and self-conscious in her nakedness. Well, of course she would. It was her first time. Oh, God. Her first time. Nail-biting stuff for sure. She was nervous as hell. It was actually going to happen. Right here. Right now. In this very bed. Wow.

Patience Hope was about to lose her virginity.

Note to self: (Underlined in virtual red ink.) Do not fuck this up.

Chapter 5

Strawberries and Cream

The wait was over. Geoff made his appearance in the bedroom. He was already naked, with both arms tucked behind his back. She couldn't take her eyes off his rigid weapon, aimed upwards, ready to be fired like a missile. Wow. At last. A real cock. In the same room, as opposed to through a keyhole. A stiff member with her name on it.

It was very similar in size to Dave's magnificent specimen. Hmm. Curious. Were they all built to the same specifications? Maybe. Um. Actually, no, they couldn't be. After all, no two vaginas were the same. Not that she'd seen that many in her life, aside from flashes of womanly bits in the school showers after a hockey match. Oh, and Penny's pussy last night which didn't exactly mirror her own genitals. So therefore, the same law of nature had to apply to willies too.

She'd often heard the brash boasts of men about their huge cocks. But saying that, she'd also heard the wives, girlfriends or illicit lovers of said males spout less favourable and undoubtedly more accurate reviews. So yes, they had to be different sizes. Some big, some middling, some bordering on laughable. However, size was all relative. Geoff and Dave both owned what Patience considered as monsters. But, as she didn't have anything else to compare them with, they could in fact be tiny examples, with everybody else's being much bigger.

Oh, why the hell was she even debating the subject? A penis was standing to attention right in front of her eyes. Her job right now was to take advantage of it.

"You look beautiful," Geoff said with a warm smile.

Patience beamed back at him. "Thank you."

And then a thought cropped up in her head. Was he calling her beautiful as an individual person? Or because she was a naked young filly on his bed? There was a difference.

Argh! Stop debating it.

"What are you hiding behind your back?" she asked him.

Geoff's face glimmered with devilish anticipation. He revealed a bowl of strawberries in one hand, a canister of spray cream in the other.

Patience's brow furrowed in question. "Are we eating first?"

"Sort of." He joined her on the bed. "I've always wanted to do this. I keep meaning to suggest it to the wife, but I don't think it's her cup of tea."

This unnerved her slightly. "What exactly are we talking about here?"

"This."

Geoff sprayed a whirl of cream over her left breast. The sudden shock of cold made her recoil. She then smiled at him as he sprayed her right breast and placed one strawberry upon each.

"Well, this is—" She struggled for the right word. "—interesting."

She could feel his hot breath on her chest as he devoured the first strawberry and plunged his lips into the cream. His tongue writhed all over her breast as he lapped up the white stuff. Patience closed her eyes and exhaled. His wet, eager tongue felt good. She couldn't describe the sensation. It was just—different. Like being licked on the neck, but far more potent.

Then onto her right breast. She placed a hand on the back of his head and pushed him closer as he nuzzled on her nipple. His mouth-play was magnificent. It was making her oh so wet down below. The tingly-winglies had returned and were screaming at her once again. In response, her brain yelled, "Get ready, pussy. Company's coming soon in the form of a big, hard dick."

She looked down at the man, checking his progress. Most of the cream had been licked off her tits. He was definitely hungry for her body. Or was it that he simply loved the taste of spray cream? She smiled at the sight of the mess all around his mouth as he relentlessly suckled on her nipples. The term big kid instantly sprang to mind.

Geoff moved further down her body and parted her legs. He took hold of the canister and sprayed cream all over her vagina. Once again, she flinched at the cold. He grinned at the girl and then dived straight in. Oh, fuck, it felt good. Tingles and sensations erupted across her pussy like a succession of active volcanoes as he furiously lapped away like a dog drinking water on a hot day. She was so glad she kept her pubic lawn neat and trim. Geoff choking on a lengthy stray pube would ruin the vibe for sure.

Her boss continued the magic with his insatiable tongue. She'd never experienced anything like it. The licks across her breasts had been pleasing to say the least, but were nowhere near in the same league as this. What she was feeling right now was intense with a capital fucking I. Wow.

Geoff sucked away the cream from around her pussy lips and then ran his tongue along the length of her crack. Her eyes slammed shut and her head tilted back as the man said hello to her clitoris.

"Oh, Geoff," she snarled in ecstasy. "You are fucking amazing."

Spurred on by such animated endorsement, his fervent tongue explored her pussy, up, down, left and right. No part of her vagina was left unlicked. Patience moaned, in fact screeched, with unbridled pleasure as his eager mouth consumed the cocktail of cream and the juice of Patience.

Geoff clambered into a kneeling posture. He wiped away the mess from his face with the back of his hand and reached once again for the canister. This time, however, he pointed it at himself and smothered his penis in its entirety. And then he placed a strawberry upon the tip to complete the decoration.

"Now it's your turn," he said.

Patience froze. Nervous. Apprehensive. Talk about being put on the spot. It was only fair, she supposed. He'd been good enough to eat her. And now it was time to eat him. A reasonable swap. However, there was one problem. She didn't have a clue how it was done. Then again, how difficult could it be? It was sucking a cock, that's all. Rocket science, it was most certainly not. Oh, but hold on. Did she actually have to suck it? Or was the term simply figurative? Why hadn't she done her homework? Had she bitten off more than she could chew? Oh, don't think like that. Talk about tempting fate. Biting anything off would be a grave mistake. For starters, it would spoil the moment.

She sat up on the bed and attempted to pull herself together. She needed to look lively and stop dithering. Did she want to make it easy for Geoff to work out that she was a virgin? No. That would never do. Ah, well. There was only one thing for it. She'd have to play it by ear. Or rather, mouth.

Patience wrapped her fingers around his penis. Through the cool and smooth outer layer of cream, she could feel the glowing warmth of his manhood. So this was what a hard dick felt like in her hands, huh? She could get used to this.

She lowered her head and opened her mouth, plucking the strawberry from his tip with her teeth. She chewed, she swallowed, she peered up at him, she smirked. And then she licked all round his helmet, imagining she was enjoying an ice cream cone on a sunny day.

Question: Was she doing it right?

"Ohh, yessss," murmured Geoff, eyes closed, big smile.

Question answered.

Now more confident, Patience ran her tongue slowly down the length of his stiff shaft and then back up again, forming narrow channels of bare skin through the thick white coat, as if clearing snow from a pathway. Geoff brushed his fingers through the girl's hair as her tongue explored his hard cock.

"Ooh, baby. Lick it clean."

Patience nodded. She increased the speed of her tongue strokes, up and down, up and down, banishing all traces of whiteness. She licked it, kissed it, nuzzled on it, played with it, hoping and praying to the God Of Sex — whoever he was — that she was pleasing her man enough whilst avoiding the actual sucking of his cock.

It was then when Geoff whispered, "I want you badly."

Patience unhanded his wet but clean penis and glanced at the man. He smiled at the girl, giving her naked body an up-down examination with hungry eyes.

"And I want you now," he added.

This was it. Her moment of truth. There was certainly no going back now. It was the point of no return. Patience Hope = virgin was about to become Patience Hope = ex virgin, real woman.

Patience reached for her handbag. From it, she fished out her packet of condoms. She opened the box and handed one to Geoff. He released the sheath from its foil prison and clothed his cock with rubber.

She lay flat on the bed and opened her legs. Geoff lowered his body onto hers. He positioned his penis with his hand and rubbed his bell-end rapidly across her crack, as if masturbating. Patience squealed with pleasure as his bulbous tip collided with her clitoris and in turn buffed the rim of her entrance upon every speedy upward-downward stroke. She parted her thighs wider, inviting his big dick inside, but still he rubbed her sodden crevice with his rock hard tool. Oh, fuck, it felt fantastic. In fact, bloody amazing. Talk about working her pussy into a frenzy. Ah, but it was also a big tease. A case of so close yet so far. She wanted his cock deep inside her pussy. So why was he holding out on her?

"Fuck me, Geoff," she ordered, brusque, impatient. "Fuck me now."

She couldn't believe how blunt and forthright she'd just been. Especially to a man of higher rank. But it felt good. Really good. And judging by the glint of delight flashing across Geoff's face, he didn't seem to mind the outburst. Hmm, intriguing. He might be the big boss in the office, but he clearly loved being ordered about in the bedroom.

She tried it again. In growl talk.

"Fuck me like a bitch."

Hmm. Maybe that was going a bit too far. Quit while you're ahead, girl.

Geoff nodded and repositioned his cock. Its tip kissed the entrance to her moist tunnel, all set and in place.

He smiled and flicked an eyebrow, as if to ask, "Ready?"

She beamed up at him and nodded firmly, as if to reply, "Ooh, yes. Definitely."

He gently pushed his penis against her hole. It refused to enter. He tried again. Same problem. A sigh from the pair of them. A third try. A small portion of his helmet disappeared inside.

And then slipped out straight away.

Argh! Patience was worried, big-time. Could it be that Geoff's impressive stalk was too large for her unpractised opening? It certainly looked that way. Oh, God. If that was the case, she'd have to give every subsequent lover a length test, rather like the height restriction measurement charts found beside scary theme park attractions.

She spread her legs as far as humanly possible and used both hands to part her curtains. This was the absolute widest she could stretch. There was no room for further elasticity. To fuck or not to fuck? That was the question. Would they succeed in their quest? Who knows? They were about to find out. He straightened his dick exactly square with her entrance. He pushed a little harder and —

— they both heard the front door open and close.

"Cooee! Geoff!"

It was his wife.

Geoff's eyes widened. "Oh, shit!"

The two of them leapt off the bed, as if the sheets were red hot.

"Are you upstairs, Geoff?"

The sound of feet ascending the stairs.

In total panic, Patience looked left, looked right, and performed the scatty dance of fear, attempting to locate the clothes she'd so frivolously discarded. Oh, fuck, they were all over the place. What to pick up first? Her knickers, her blouse, her dignity, what?

"Geoff?" called his wife.

Footsteps. Getting louder. And closer.

Patience hastily pulled up her knickers. They were on back to front. Bugger. No, no, don't correct them. No time. Emergency situation, code frigging red.

"Quick," whispered Geoff, opening the window. "Through here."

She didn't like the sound of that. "You must be joking."

"Just do it. There's a ledge out there. I'll let you back in when the coast is clear."

Offering a nervous nod, she picked up her handbag. But as she reached down for the rest of her clothes —

"No time for that." Geoff grabbed her arm and steered the near-naked girl over to the window. "Get out of here. Now!"

"But I'm only in my knickers," she hissed, reluctantly clambering out onto the ledge.

"You'll be fine."

The statement failed to bestow her with any confidence.

Geoff closed the window, flung the curtains across and went about stuffing Patience's garments into a nearby chest of drawers. He looked down at himself and spotted the condom. He yanked it off his dick. It too was lobbed in a drawer. Next, he straightened the bed sheets as best as he could. He then twisted around and spotted the strawberries and spray cream.

The door opened. His wife entered.

"Geoff, I—"

She froze on the spot, stunned and confused by the sight of a nude husband with a huge boner, holding a bowl of strawberries in one hand and a spray cream canister in the other.

"What the hell is going on?"

"Um." Geoff grinned nervously. "Surprise."

She stared at him, expressionless.

It was a tense moment.

And then she smiled sweetly. "Oh, Geoff. How did you know?"

He frowned. "How did I know what?"

"This is my greatest sexual fantasy."

His mouth fell open. "Is it?"

She began to peel off her clothing. "Mmm. Too fucking right it is."

Geoff spotted Patience's shoes on the carpet. Without making it too obvious, he nudged them under the bed with his feet.

His wife kicked off her underwear and lay spread-eagled on the bed. "Spray me all over, big boy. I want to be licked from head to toe."

Geoff's face dropped, clearly unsure of what to do next. He peered at the curtained window where Patience was hidden. Then at the chest of drawers where Patience's clothes were hidden. Then underneath the bed where Patience's shoes were hidden. And finally, at his wife on the bed. Where nothing belonging to Patience was hidden. Except traces of DNA, that is.

Judging by the strained look on his face, anybody—even the most uneducated or socially challenged—could deduce that this was indeed the dilemma of the century. Or millennia. Or aeon. In fact, all of time itself.

The second naked woman to grace his bed today, the one usually least interested in his cock, namely, his wife, licked her lips and beckoned him closer with her index finger.

"Darling. I'm waiting for you."

Outside, Patience was bricking it. Here she was, a girl who might as well be naked, her bare back propped against weathered brickwork, her unshod feet balancing precariously on a thin shelf of masonry. Cold. Scared. Lonely. Exposed to the elements. And to prying eyes, for that matter.

This side of the house didn't face the road. It was a fact that came as a huge relief to the girl. But directly below was Geoff's back garden, a plot of land that stood next to a neighbouring back garden. Followed by more bloody back gardens. A whole row of them. Anybody tending to their vegetable patch or mowing the lawn in the local vicinity would be able to see her as clear as day.

Argh! Which led to the question: What if she was spotted? And the other question: What would her excuse be for being there?

"Don't worry about me. I'm just doing a spot of sun bathing."

You what? On a thin ledge? And standing up? Who'd believe a whopper like that?

"I'm playing hide and seek."

Even worse.

"You're obviously crap at the game," onlookers would say. "We can spot you from miles away."

Yes, and they'd be right. She was hardly Miss Inconspicuous. The poor girl could probably be seen from space.

If people gathered, she'd have to tell them, "There's nothing to see here."

You're joking, right? Nobody would agree with that particular statement. There was plenty to see here. Even worse, what if Geoff's wife opened the window and discovered her presence? Oh, fuck, fuck, fuck. Patience's mind was racing. A thousand thoughts and images bounced recklessly from wall to wall like demented powerballs. And then a strange but terrifying scenario began to play out in her head.

Wife: "Who the hell are you?"

Patience: "Um. The window cleaner."

"You don't look like a window cleaner. Why aren't you wearing any clothes?"

"The weather's nice."

"Where's your bucket?"

A raised handbag. "Here."

"That's not a bucket. It's a handbag."

"It's a novelty bucket. Handbag shaped. They're all the rage this season."

Oh, shut the fuck up, brain, she demanded to herself. Talk about a bloody warped imagination. The daydream was turning mental. Any more bollocks like that and she risked being sectioned for life.

A hopeless sigh escaped through her lips. There was no doubt about it. If Patience was caught, it would be the end of days for sure. No excuse could save her, no matter how ingenious. Window cleaner? Get real. Purveyors of such a trade were supposed to be outside looking in on undressed people, not getting naked outside for customers inside to look out at. Oh, God. A hard truth was staring her in the face. She was done for.

No. Don't think like that. Chin up, girl. She'd been in far worse scrapes than this. Actually, no, she hadn't. But nothing more could possibly go wrong. This was rock bottom.

From now on, the only way was up.

Right?

It was time to make her escape from the ledge. The coast had to be well and truly clear by now. She'd given Geoff ample time to usher his wife downstairs. He'd open the window for her in a moment or two. Or in a couple of shakes, to reference Geoff's quirky terminology. This would give Patience the opportunity to re-enter the bedroom and collect her clothes. Then once dressed, all she'd need to do is sneak quietly down the stairs and out through the front door. And then she'd be home and dry. Simple.

What could possibly go wrong?

The window staying closed, that's what.

She rolled her eyes and let out a huff of discontent, but decided to give him the benefit of the doubt. She was hardly an expert at adultery, so maybe it took a little longer than she thought to clear a coast.

And so she waited.

And waited.

And waited some more.

The window remained closed.

Fuck's sake, Geoff, she cursed in her head. What the hell was keeping the man? If he'd decided to take a dump before letting her in, he was a dead man.

She inched closer to the window and peered through the gap in the curtains. That's when she spotted them. Mr and Mrs Denton. On the bed. Both smothered in spray cream. Kissing each other. Licking each other. Fondling each other. And fucking each other. Like proverbial rabbits. Randy rodents with cream toppings.

Her eyes widened. Sheer disbelief. Followed by stifling disenchantment. Her face sank low. As did her heart. She turned away, stomach in knots. A heavy sense of betrayal spread over the girl like thick treacle.

"Bastard," she growled under her breath through gritted teeth.

Without a doubt, bastard was too mild an expletive for what she presently saw Geoff as being. A man who had knowingly left his bit on the side—if she could legally give herself that title—almost naked and trapped alfresco on an unsafe ledge while he happily exchanged spray cream and bodily fluids with his unexpectedly-home-early wife in a safe and warm bedroom deserved a far more scathing moniker. The C word came to mind, but as she hated the term with a vengeance, she decided not to repeat it.

So what now? She could hardly tap on the window, could she? Even if she did, what would she find to say?

"Excuse me. Mind if I step inside and retrieve my clothes?"

Hmm. Not the best of ideas.

What to do, what to do? She looked right. Nothing. She looked left. Aha. A drainpipe. And then she realised she'd been mistaken when assuming the only way was up.

From now on, the only way was down.

Patience had never scaled a drainpipe before. There was a first time for everything, she supposed, although she would have preferred to attempt it fully clothed, instead of in her current outfit of back-to-front underwear, fake designer handbag and birthday suit. She reached out and grabbed the drainpipe with both hands. A deep breath for composure. Then she stepped off the ledge and began to climb south.

A loud crack and a ping made her flinch. One of the brackets holding the drainpipe to the wall came away, making her escape route shudder. Shit. Oh, wait a minute. Plenty more brackets were still in place. A relieved smile. Relax, Patience. Continue your descent. It will take your weight.

Another crack, another ping, another bracket took flight and fell to its death.

Patience froze. And waited. Not moving anything except her eyes, she examined the remaining brackets. They seemed sturdy enough. The first two, they must have been damaged in some way. Corroded perhaps. Yes, that's what it was.

She looked down. Not far to go. Terra firma smiled up at the girl, egging her on. But should she risk further movement? Well? Decision quickly made. Yes. And she continued to clamber downward, only with more haste than before.

More cracks. More pings. In rapid succession, every bracket came away. And the drainpipe, felled like a tree, took Patience with it.

It was Geoff's ornamental fish pond that broke her fall. The relief of landing in something soft was cruelly stolen by the harsh shock of freezing cold water on bare skin. She tried her hardest not to scream, but couldn't help herself. Geoff would have heard her wails for sure. His wife too. It would take them both a mere ten seconds or so to journey from bed to window and spot the sodden trespasser. Yes. Trespasser. For let's face it, she was no longer a houseguest. She needed to make her escape from the Denton garden. And fast.

But hold on. Her handbag. Where the fuck was it? There was no way she was prepared to abandon it. The bag contained her whole life. Phone. Purse. Keys. Make up. Money-off vouchers. Coffee shop loyalty card. The remaining two condoms. Everything. She looked left, looked right, looked down, looked across, and aha! It was a miracle. The bag had missed the pond, claiming a nearby shrub as its resting place. Phew.

Handbag recovered, it was time for the girl to leave. Quickly.

With the strength and agility of a trained soldier, Patience launched herself over the wooden panel fencing and into the neighbouring garden. Where she found such nimble dexterity was beyond the realms of casual understanding. It was most probably down to the mathematical equation of Fear Of Being Caught + Nakedness = Get The Fuck Out Of There.

Dripping wet and shivering with cold, she squatted low behind the cover of a leafy bush and paused for breath. There, she worked out her next move. Phone Joe. Get him to pick her up in his car. Yes, that's what she'd do. But how would she explain her sodden near-nakedness? Ah, who cares? Joe was her best friend. An explanation wouldn't be required. It was how they were as greatest mates. No awkward questioning. No passing judgement. They accepted each other for who they were.

"Oh, Patience. What are you like, eh?" That's all he would say. And that would be the end of it, moving swiftly on to the next subject. Ah, Joe. An ideal man. Such a shame he was gay.

She produced her mobile and punched numbers. Nothing happened. Huh? She studied the phone display. Black. Argh! No power. The battery had long since drawn its swansong breath.

Great. No communication with the outside world. Now she felt even more naked.

A small boy of about four or five—still young enough to be an annoying shit, yet old enough to know how to utilise such annoyance—wandered over from where he had been playing and offered the girl a quizzical stare.

"Who are you?" he asked.

"Nobody."

"You must be somebody."

She rolled her eyes. What's the betting this kid would be harder to get rid of than an unwelcome relative at Christmas? "Look, if you must know, I'm—" Think, girl, think. "—the fairy of the—" Good start. Ending required. She thought about it, then gestured to her hiding place. "—the wotsit bush." Hmm. Not bad, but it needed work.

"You don't look like a fairy."

"We come in all shapes and sizes."

"Why are you all wet?"

A sigh. "On my travels, I thought I'd pop in to say hello to the fairy of the pond next door." It was feasible. Right?

"Where are your wings?"

"I—um—" It was all becoming too much of a struggle. Patience was in no way a child friendly person. "I haven't been given my wings yet." She racked her brains for bullshitus addendum to back up her claim. She added, "There's a six month waiting list. First come, first served."

The boy seemed disillusioned by the news. "I thought all fairies were born with wings."

Patience shook her head. "Nope. Just goes to show you shouldn't believe everything you hear when Mummy and Daddy read you bedtime stories."

"Don't care anyway. Fairies aren't real."

Patience retaliated with a broad sneer and, "Oh, yeah? If I don't exist, how come you can see me?"

The child stared at the supposed fairy in silence, unconvinced.

Hmm. A change of tactic was to be the order of the day. "Can you keep a secret?" she asked.

The boy nodded.

"In a moment, I'll be leaving your garden. When I do, will you promise you won't tell anybody you saw me here?"

Another nod, firmer than before.

"Good boy."

"It will cost you," he then informed her, holding out an expectant palm.

Patience lobbed him an aghast stare. It soon morphed into a scowl. "You're not getting anything out of me, you little sh—"

His mother emerged from the house to hang out the washing.

"Mummy," he called out as loud as he could manage. "There's a strange lady behind this bush with no clothes on."

"So much for keeping a secret," the strange lady behind the bush with no clothes on growled angrily.

The curious mother began her approach. Shit. This was getting serious. Keeping low behind her leafy sanctuary, Patience surveyed the area, searching for a way out. Aha. A nearby wooden gate. It looked like the only viable method of escape. Oh, well. Here goes nothing.

Much to the surprise of the boy's mother, Patience stood bolt upright. She covered her breasts with her handbag and marched speedily towards the exit.

"If you must know, I'm trying for an all-over tan, okay?" was Patience's lame excuse to the wide-eyed woman as she made her prompt departure.

The boy's father popped his head out of the back door of the house. "Who the hell was that?"

"A naked girl escaping from Geoff Denton's house," came the mother's reply.

The father raised his brow. "What, another one?"

Patience dashed as fast as she could along the narrow alleyway that ran parallel to the seemingly never-ending terrace of back gardens, one arm pushed against her chest to prevent excessive tit bounce. Not that she was the proud owner of prominent breasts, far from it, but any sharp or sudden movement—jumping, running, whatever—never failed to interfere with the gravity of unrestrained bosoms, no matter how big or small.

It was most fortunate that high fences flanked both sides of the alleyway. And that nobody else was using her chosen escape route at this present moment in time. Especially anybody with the profession of mugger. She could imagine the conversation:

Mugger: (Drawing a knife) "Give me your valuables!"

Patience: (Gesturing to her bare body) "Does it look like I've got any on me?"

Oh, stop it, brain! Quit creating crazy scenarios. It was bad enough that she'd accompanied Geoff to the family home in the first place. Talk about putting herself at risk. Didn't she realise? Wives always came home unexpectedly. It was one of life's unwritten laws. Had she not read enough love triangle novels to know this fact? Obviously not.

Patience had only agreed to have sex with the guy for one purpose. To lose her bloody virginity. But why go behind enemy lines to get the job done? The walk-in stationery cupboard at work would have met both their requirements. Dark. Secluded. Spacious enough. Not exactly the most comfortable of lovenests, but at least it boasted absolutely no risk of the wife killing the mood with a surprise interruption.

Ah, well. No point in fretting about the matter in hindsight. She had to look on the bright side. Well, maybe not bright. More likely fine but overcast. Patience might be ninety per cent naked, soaked by pondwater, several miles from home — oh, and still a frigging virgin — but at least she'd avoided the wrath of Mrs Denton.

Insert much-needed sigh of relief here.

The troubles of today were now far behind her. Things couldn't possibly get any worse. Right?

And then it came.

A torrential downpour.

Chapter 6
Coffee with Joe

The weatherman had been partly right. But mostly wrong. Absolutely spot on about the torrential rain, although the cloudburst happened in the afternoon, and not during the morning as forecast. It had also been mentioned that the storm would affect the whole of London. Um, no, Mr Weatherman. All that rain, every last drop, fell solely on the head of Patience Hope. Or at least that's how it seemed to her.

She recalled the question her boss had asked her during their playful frolics back at his place on the sofa.

"What would make you really wet?"

Fucking rain, that's what!

Somewhere between Geoff The C Word's residence and the coffee shop where she was due to meet Joe, Patience acquired a freshly laundered dressing gown, albeit somewhat illegally. The garment was rather tatty and frayed, and with its brown and beige tartan patterns, clearly designed for men of the over nineties variety. Not exactly her first choice of attire, but could beggars really afford to be choosers? Not in this instance.

Okay, another virtual checklist. Modesty concealed. Right? Check. Well, sort of. That was the main thing. Right? Um. Another check of the *sort of* family. Better that nothing. Right? Hmm. A sort of check, mixed with the faint shade of an *I suppose so* check. In conclusion, it was hardly the best of outfits with which to keep a low profile, but hey, this area of the city was considered pretty cosmo, renowned for its resident eccentrics and their wild and outlandish fashion tastes. She'd fit right in. Wouldn't she? Hmm. Judging by the endless double takes and eruptions of mass hysteria from the onlooker tribe, obviously not.

Whatever happened to individuality in clothing? Simple. It became extinct following the birth of hoodies, trackies and the subsequent sheep crowd.

At last. She'd reached the coffee shop. Joe sat waiting for her at the table next to the window. Oh, bloody great, she thought. Promoted from free street entertainment to an exhibit behind glass. He'd already purchased both coffees. This came as a massive relief. It saved the girl from the sheer humiliation of waiting in a long queue of pointers and starers.

Patience joined him at the table. "Hello, Joe," she greeted, fake bright eyes, equally fake smile, as if it was commonplace for this girl to be dressed for bedtime in public.

Joe made a face. And not a good one. He was clearly wondering whether this was the right Patience Hope or a somewhat asinine impostor.

"Why are you wearing a dressing gown?"

Hmm. Her head rewound to her thoughts about Joe when she had been hiding behind the bush in Geoff The C Word's neighbour's garden. You know, how she had figured that, with him, an explanation wouldn't be required. No awkward questioning. No passing judgement. And how they accepted each other for who they were.

Oh, how wrong she'd been.

Patience's plastic smile was replaced with a jaded scowl. "It was the only thing I could pinch off somebody's washing line at such short notice."

Joe opened his mouth to speak.

She cut in with, "If you want your gonads to stay intact, do not ask that question."

Dumbstruck, Joe gawped at the girl, eyes flicking between face and attire. It was obvious. He didn't know what to think. Any minute now, he'd call for the urgent assistance of men in white coats. Those guys with a soft spot for electric shock treatment.

"Oh, stop staring at me like that. You're supposed to be my best friend." She indicated the stolen dressing gown. "Forget about the outer me." Then pointed to her face. "And concentrate on the inner me."

"I am trying. But you've got to admit, that's a totally wacky outer you." Joe reached out and plucked a snippet of stray vegetation from her sodden locks. "Is this pondweed?"

She opened her mouth. No words emerged. No sounds at all really. Except for a rather lame croak. She thought about it for a second or two, cleared her throat, then dished out the first suitable reply that came to mind.

"It's good for the hair. Keeps it healthy and shiny and stuff."

"I thought it was seaweed that did that."

"Shut up, smart-arse." Patience sighed weightily and added, "If you want to laugh at me, just do it, okay? It's best you get it over and done with."

"It never crossed my mind."

She didn't believe him. "You might as well make fun of me. Everybody else has."

It was obvious. He wanted to raise a smile, the indicative sign being one corner of his mouth slightly curled upwards. But in all sincerity —

"Patience, I am not going to laugh."

"Really?"

"Really."

They looked at each other.

They shared a moment.

And then they both exploded with hilarity.

She gazed deep into Joe's dark brown eyes. His two best features. She'd told him so on many occasions. Nice smile too. Nice face all round actually. Okay, so Joe didn't exactly fit into the category of drop dead gorgeous, but he was in no way ugly. Cute was a fairly accurate observation. A boyish profile. Slightly chubby around the cheeks. In short, the kind of man a girl would love to mother.

Oh, why did he have to be gay? They could have had a future together. Or at least a chance of it. And what's more, he'd be the perfect solution to her virginity problem. She'd rather let a good friend break her in than a complete stranger. The prospect of cold unfamiliarity between bedfellows seemed a tad too clinical for her liking. But no. It was not to be. Joe preferred men. A potential husband, boyfriend, lover, fuckbuddy, whatever, he was most certainly not.

Then she had a thought. Did Joe opt for his sexual persuasion out of spite?

"Make love with Patience? No way. I'd rather bat for the other side."

Fuck's sake, girl. Stop over-analysing things. You are not the frigging reason why your best friend chose his preferred path. Got that? Good. Now, stop thinking paranoid thoughts and get on with your day.

Joe was the same age as Patience, give or take a few months. As youngsters, they lived across the road from each other. Their mothers convened for regular cups of tea and chinwags, and as such, the children became firm friends. However, the two of them hadn't seen so much of each other lately. Different jobs, different lifestyles, different calendars meant that their lives often hurtled chaotically in opposite directions. But they always made sure they hooked up for a natter over two cups of overpriced coffee every now and then. Just to catch up on the goss.

"So. What's been happening in the weird and wonderful world of Patience Hope?"

"Not a lot," she replied. "I started a new job last week. Nothing special. Just admin shit. Still, it's better than a kick up the arse. And at least it keeps me in debt."

They both smiled.

"Oh, and I'm trying to lose my virginity," she continued as casually as possible, so as not to make a big deal of it. "Tell you what, it's not as easy as I thought it would be."

Joe was rather knocked aback. "I didn't realise you were still a — well, you know."

"A virgin? Yes. I am. And it's pissing me right off."

Her friend didn't seem to understand her angst. "Why does it matter so much?"

"Funnily enough, it didn't bother me until last night."

"What happened last night?"

"It slipped out."

"What slipped out?"

Fuck's sake, Joe. Keep up. "The fact that I'm still a virgin!" she exclaimed way too loud.

Several customers twisted their heads to face the girl who had never been touched. A black cloud of narrowed-eyed disapproval hung over the room. One disgruntled mother covered her child's ears with both hands. Patience winced. Oops.

"Sorry," she squeaked, red-faced.

A few tuts sounded. Then the tutters all returned to whatever they'd been drinking, eating or gossiping about. Patience and Joe put their heads closer together. Covert. Secretive. Voices low.

"My flatmate and her boyfriend now know I've never done it before. How sad is that?"

"Doesn't seem that sad to me."

"Joe, it's sad of the saddest order. Before last night, only I knew my secret. That's it. Just me. But things have changed. Two other people know. Actually three now, because I've just told you."

Joe shrugged his shoulders. "I honestly don't see what the problem is. Okay, so you're a virgin. And?"

"Joe, I'm twenty-five years of age. I should have had plenty of cock by now."

Joe grinned, clearly not taking the convo seriously.

"What's so funny?"

"It's you," he replied. "You're making a mountain out of a molehill."

"Before last night, I would have totally agreed with you. But the whole world discovering my dark secret has changed all that."

Joe scoffed. "The whole world? It's only three people."

"Yes, but that's only the start. Today three people, tomorrow the rest of London. By next week, the whole population of the United Kingdom will know. Which makes it a serious problem."

"Why?"

"Because it's embarrassing."

"Why is it embarrassing?"

"Come on, think about it. Virgin. Twenty-five. People will ask questions. Everybody will judge me. I'll be a laughing stock."

"If you say so."

"I do say so. I want to be like everybody else. I want to fit in. That's why I've made myself a pact. I'm getting rid of my virginity as soon as possible. I don't care how, I just want it gone."

Another grin from Joe. And an incredulous shake of the head.

Patience sank, disappointed in her friend. "I thought you'd understand."

"Oh, Patience. You know I'll always be there for you. But this? It's crazy."

Patience was not letting up. "No, Joe. What's crazy is me being a virgin at my age."

Joe chuckled. Loudly. He couldn't help it. This angered her.

"Have I got "Laugh At Me, I'm A Twat" written across my forehead?"

"Don't get so worked up about it. It's really not that important in the great scheme of things."

She didn't agree. "Oh, yeah? Know any other twenty-five-year-old virgins?"

"Yes."

This had better be good. "Who?"

"Me."

Patience. Momentarily silenced by the revelation. Wow. What a surprise. Totally unexpected. She'd always assumed, with such boyish looks, Joe was inundated with propositions of an improper nature on a daily basis. Talk about learning something new every day.

"You?" she managed to croak.

"Yes. I'm a virgin too."

Patience couldn't get her head around it. "You mean you've never had it up the—" She trailed off, pointing to her bottom. "Or done it up the—" Another bottom point. "—with your—" Another trail-off whilst indicating to and mock gyrating her groin.

"I've never had it up or done it up anywhere."

Patience stared at him. He stared back. For a moment, nothing was said. Until—

"Why?" she dared to ask.

There suddenly came a loud tap on the window. It was Penny, employing the wide eyes, overblown idiot grin and exaggerated wave that everybody performed through plate glass in such a situation. She trotted through the door and joined them at the table.

"What are you doing here?" asked Patience.

"I'm dying to know how you got on with—" She quit mid sentence and frowned at the dressing gown. "What are you wearing?"

Patience was quick to change the subject with, "Penny. Meet my best friend Joe. Joe, meet my flatmate Penny."

The two of them exchanged polite greetings. It was not long before Penny's full attention was returned to Patience.

"Well? How did things go with your boss?"

"He took me back to his place."

Penny smiled. "That's great."

"Hardly. It was a total disaster."

"Why? Couldn't he get hard for you?"

"He was fine in that department. It was his wife who was the problem."

Penny made a face. "You let her join in too?"

"No way. She came home unexpectedly."

"Oh, my God. Did she catch you both in the act?" asked Penny, goggle-eyed.

"No. Geoff bundled me out of the window and said he'd bring me back in when the coast was clear. I was naked apart from my knickers. And it was bloody cold on that ledge."

Joe joined in with, "Can I assume this disaster was part of your mission to kill off your virginity?"

"You assume correctly."

"Told you all about her quest, has she?" asked Penny.

"Not this particular episode," was Joe's response. "What happened next?"

"Not a lot," Patience explained. "The bastard forgot all about me and had sex with his wife instead."

"What a wanker," snarled Penny.

"I'll say." Patience crossed her arms, sulk mode. "Typical, isn't it? I'm the one who turned him on and she's the one who got the fuck out of it."

"I guess that sort of makes you a glorified warm-up act," remarked Joe.

"Tell me about it."

Penny wondered, "So I take it he never got round to—"

"Fucking me? No."

"Which makes you—"

"Still a virgin? Yes. And back to square one."

Joe looked at Patience, grey apprehension in his eye. "Maybe it was fate telling you this pact of yours is a bit — well, for want of a better word — mental."

Patience was adamant. "I refuse to let you talk me out of this one, Joe. I see this afternoon's boss incident as a minor setback. Next time, I'll be successful in my quest. I mean, how bloody difficult can it possibly be for a girl in this day and age to get humped?"

Joe turned to Penny, seeking an alliance. "Can't you convince her otherwise?"

"Sorry, Joe," came Penny's reply. "Patience has made her bed and anybody can sleep in it."

"Only until my cherry is picked," corrected Patience. "And then I'll stop being a slut."

Joe was not happy about the situation at all. "I still don't see why you feel the need to have sex with the first guy who unzips their fly for you."

Patience touched his hand. "Joe. I know you don't approve of what I'm doing. And I'm grateful for your concern. Really, I am. It's very sweet of you. But I need to do this. It's important to me. Okay?"

Joe considered her words. Then gave in. "Okay."

"Thank you."

They shared between them another moment.

Patience then said, "All I need now is a foolproof way to lose the V word." Then an afterthought. "Hey, Joe. As we're both in the same predicament, maybe we should start helping each other out. You know, by getting together regularly and suggesting new methods to lift our curses."

Joe responded with, "I'd hardly call my virginity a curse."

Penny threw him a double take. "You're a virgin too?"

"Afraid so. Difference is, it doesn't really bother me."

Patience was still lost in her curse lifting notion. "And hey. Maybe we should seek out other virgins and help them out too."

Joe, amused by the wacky suggestion. "You mean, form some kind of club?"

A big nod. "Yeah. A club would be good."

"Aha!" yelped Penny, bright eyes animated by inspiration with a capital I. "Oh, my God. A club. That's it!"

Patience seemed a tad miffed by the sudden interruption. After all, her master plan was much more important, surely. "What are you babbling on about?"

"Something far greater that your babbling," came the reply.

Oh, yeah? Like, seriously? "That I find very hard to believe."

"Patience, I have just thought of a sure-to-work, foolproof way to get shot of your virginity once and for all," she claimed, proud beam, head held high.

"As long as it's not so tacky this time," replied Patience. "I'm sure you agree, banging the boss was a bit on the cheap side."

"This idea isn't cheap and tacky at all."

"Okaaaay. What have you got in mind?"

A big smile. "Tomorrow night—wait for it—we're going clubbing."

Patience's face dropped. "Oh, excellent idea," she moaned with a thick slice of derision. "Not cheap and tacky at all."

"Oi, you. You're the one who's begging for cock on demand, not me," protested Penny. "Think about it. The place will be chock-a-block full of hot and horny men with only one thing on their minds. Where better to bag yourself a tasty portion of Saturday Night Salami?"

Patience blew out a troubled sigh. The boss-fucking idea had been bad enough. But this proposal sounded even worse. Did she relish the prospect of being stuck on the receiving end of the cock of a total stranger? No, not really. Knowing her luck, she'd end up lumbered with a drunk total stranger. No, scrub that. A totally mashed, mullered, paralytic, almost unconscious total stranger. Ugh.

Another sigh escaped into the atmosphere. Her lifelong ambition of losing her virginity to somebody who truly loved and cared for her was drifting helplessly into the vast ocean of failed dreams. In another life, a parallel world, an opposite universe, whatever, Joe might not have been gay, and so thus would have saved her from such stifling torment. But alas, this was the world on which she existed. So Patience would just have to grin and bear it.

"I've got a bad feeling about this," she murmured, face full of grimace.

Penny rolled her eyes. "Patience. Listen to me. This plan is perfect. It's a nightclub, for God's sake. You are totally guaranteed a wil-ly-winky."

Patience didn't share such gleeful optimism. "But what if nobody fancies me?"

"Impossible. Most of those guys will be drunk as fuck."

Yes. Of course. Penny was indeed correct. Mr Average Bloke always made sure he sank several pints of strong beer before even thinking about wandering into a nightclub. After all, he needed something with a powerful kick to find the courage to strut his stuff on the dance floor. Oh, and to give him the confidence to chat up girls. Drink was the ultimate solution to the problem. Good old alcohol. This was how modern social life ticked along. Saturday night, the most active evening of the calendar week was —

Hey! Hold on an effing minute.

The concrete finger of realisation poked her in the eye. In fact, both eyes at once. Hard.

"Oi, you! Are you trying to say men will only fancy me if they're totally pissed out of their skulls?"

Penny smirked. "Only joking, babes."

"You'd better be." She thought about it some more. "Huh, knowing my luck, you're probably right."

Joe piped up with his views. "Don't you think clubbing is scraping the bottom of the barrel a bit?"

Patience nodded her full agreement. "That's just what I was thinking."

Penny said, "What do you mean? Clubs are great."

Joe's next line came in the form of, "Agreed. But you've got to admit, you get some right old desperados inhabiting those places."

Patience chipped in with, "Here, here. Right old desperados are so not my thing. Oh, and before you say it, Penny, I'm only slightly desperate, not right old."

Her flatmate made a face. "Oh, Patience. Lighten up and enjoy the flow. Tomorrow night will be your night of cock. I mean, come on, think about it. What could possibly go wrong?"

"Everything," responded both Patience and Joe in unison.

Penny shook her head. "You need to chillax, the pair of you."

The pair refused to chill, relax or partake in the amalgam of the two. Instead, they exchanged the most downbeat of uncertain glances.

"Hold on for your life, Patience," continued Penny, huge grin plastered upon face. "This Saturday night, you'd better be ready for some serious shafting."

Chapter 7

Friends and Fantasies

Patience felt relieved to arrive home and remove herself from the embarrassment of such tatty brown tartan. There the dressing gown lay in an untidy heap on her bedroom carpet while she changed into something a little more comfortable. And slightly more fashionable. A skirt. A blouse. A bra. And a change of knickers. Clothes bearing no relation whatsoever to the gown she'd commandeered just to save face. Not just face, of course. Her whole body. Sure, the garment had protected the girl from the elements in her hour of need, but on the other hand had done little to improve what minuscule street cred she'd struggled to accumulate over the years.

So what was to become of the stolen dressing gown?

Penny's suggestion: "Burn the bloody thing."

Getting rid of the evidence in such a manner certainly sounded like the most sensible option. After all, the local constabulary could be plotting a dawn raid on her place right at this very moment. At fuck-off o'clock, the front door could burst open, with a hectic storm of uniformed officers having Patience dragged from her slumber and thrown into a cold, dark cell. And oh, God, just imagine the harsh sentence imposed on her for depriving a pensioner of his nightwear. The verdict would be unanimous.

"Guilty as sin. Throw away the key."

She could get five years. Ten. Life, even. Banged up on the same wing as all the other prisoners convicted of stealing clothing from washing lines. Namely, the pervy underwear snatchers. Oh, the shame.

Patience made a snap decision. Put away the matches. She needed to return the dressing gown to its rightful owner. But first, it needed a fresh valet. She tossed it into the washing machine. Laundered it. Spun it. Dried it. Ironed it. And folded it. There. Item restored to its tatty but cleansed condition.

So what was the plan? Hmm. Take it back perhaps? No. Too risky. Aha. How about posting it? Yes. Good idea. The post office offered a next day service. By nine o'clock the following morning (or twelve o'clock if Patience went for the slightly cheaper option) the poor chap would be reunited with his gown of tartan patterns, and then he'd live happily ever after.

Of course, it meant that Patience would need to rise from her pit bright and early. No time for breakfast. Nor a coffee. Nor make up. Not even the privilege of brushing her teeth. This plan was far more important than mere eating, drinking, vanity and the fight against tooth decay. She'd seal the dressing gown in a large postal sack, head into town and send the parcel via the quickest available means, not forgetting to attach a letter to the package. A brief note. Just one word.

Sorry.

Oh. Hold on. Tomorrow was Saturday. Meaning the old guy wouldn't receive the package until Monday at the earliest. Far too long for him to wait for news of his missing garment. And besides. On Saturday mornings, Patience slept in late. Hmm. Maybe that made her sound a tad selfish. But come on. She got up early every weekday for work. Therefore, she deserved a lie-in at the weekend.

Okay, scrub the postal idea. What next? Only one valid option remained. Return it in person.

She peered through the kitchen window at the outside world. The setting sun had finally surrendered to the sullen gloom of dusk. Good. It was time to put her plan into action.

Patience popped the dressing gown into a carrier bag and glanced at the clock on the wall. Joe wouldn't be round for another two hours. At the coffee shop, Penny had informed Patience she would be out with Dave all evening. Therefore, Joe suggested bringing round pizza, a DVD and himself. What better way to spend a Friday night?

So. Two hours. Plenty of time to return the goods. Go for it, girl.

Under cover of darkness, Patience revisited the scene of the crime. Big mistake for a wanted criminal, but she was determined to right this wrong. And fast. She peered over the brick wall that helped defend the old man's home from intruders. Hah. Or at least that was its supposed purpose. As a deterrent against thieves, it was a bit on the crap side. The barrier hadn't provided much of an obstacle for Patience earlier. She'd clambered over, committed the crime and hopped back again with ease. In broad daylight, to boot.

Uh oh. The washing line. It was empty. Bugger. This meant the old man knew of the theft. He'd be angry. Upset. In fact, absolutely devastated. And forced to drink his bedtime cocoa in nothing more than the near-nakedness of thin cotton pyjamas.

Could she risk pegging it back on the line? Hmm, not sure. The victim of the robbery would be no doubt watching the locality like a hawk. He probably fought in the war, you know. She'd be caught red-handed as soon as she dipped one foot in the garden. And the old man would never believe she was genuinely returning the item. No, he'd simply assume the pirate had reappeared to plunder further treasures. He'd call the police at once and have the thieving bitch taken away.

What would they do with the washing line bandit?

They'd hang her out to dry.

Oh, here we go. Once again, she was over-thinking like a mad woman. Compulsive analytical assessment of near-lunatic proportions. A rather more subdued train of thought—pity she didn't listen to it often enough—calmly informed her that she'd be in and out of the garden within, say, twenty or thirty seconds. Ample time for the girl to return the dressing gown to its original suspended state with minimal threat of capture. Because, let's face it, an elderly gentleman would take a far longer duration of time to travel from behind a twitching curtain to the back door. This meant the plan couldn't possibly fail.

Upon deciding to listen to the part of her brain that boasted a snippet of common sense, she scaled the wall and dropped herself behind enemy lines. She tip-toed across the lawn and over to the washing line where she secured the garment with two clothes pegs.

There. Job done. See? That wasn't so difficult, was it?

What seemed like the deafening roar of a colossal monster made Patience jump out of her skin. Bark, bark, bark! Shit. A dog. A big one. She didn't hang around to identify the breed. Black and huge with razor-sharp teeth was all she needed to know.

The crazed beast chased her down to the unexplored territory that was the bottom of the garden. The wall she'd left behind — her escape route — seemed like a million miles away in the opposite direction. Tall, thick hedging dominated the perimeter of this part of the garden. Far superior protection from trespassers. Nobody could get in. Trouble is, it also meant nobody could get out.

Then aha! A small gap in the shrubbery, just about big enough for the girl to squeeze through. She dived inside, thrashing both arms in all directions, shoving aside branches and foliage, fighting her way through the leafy tunnel. The dog's head appeared right behind her, biting, barking, snapping in the darkness. The animal sunk its fangs into the material of her skirt, refusing to let go, dead set on yanking its quarry back out of the hole.

Shit. Was this to be the fate of Patience Hope? Eaten alive by a rabid, canine monster?

No way, buster. The other end of the bushy tunnel beckoned, the sanctuary of the street beyond. She could see the eerie amber glow of the streetlamps. And hear the content purr of a passing car. Just that little bit further and she'd be kissing the buttocks of freedom. If only she could free herself from the clutches of the hound.

She crawled forward. The dog pulled her back. Two knee shuffles forward. One slide back. Forward, back, forward, back, she felt like a human tug o'war rope. Then uh oh. Approaching stomps in the grass behind her. Footsteps. Human. Coming her way. Argh! It was the old man for sure. Then a voice from behind.

"What is it, boy? What have you caught?" It was definitely the raspy voice of a senior citizen.

Then came torchlight. Oh, God, that's all she needed. A thick finger of white light pierced through the branchwork, penetrating the shadowy innards of the hedging. It fanned left, fanned right, searching out the cause of the dog's excitement. It was high time to get the fuck out of there, and boy did she know it.

Patience steeled herself, grabbed the stronger, more established trunks of the hedging with both hands for sufficient leverage, then wrenched herself forward. An almighty rip could be heard as she tumbled out into the street, landing in a crumpled heap on the pavement.

She clambered into an upright position and punched the air in celebration. Yes! She'd made it. She'd escaped. She was free—

—of her skirt. Argh! The dog had torn the item of clothing from her body. And now here she stood. In a residential street. Miles from home. With no skirt. Bare legs. And underwear on display for the world to see. Again.

Then an idea. Run like buggery. And so she did. As fast as she could.

Once satisfied she was a safe distance from the crime scene, Patience paused for much-needed breath. Then another idea. Call for a taxi. Yes. That's what she'd do. One small drawback. She'd left her mobile phone charging up at home. Insert the inevitable long and drawn-out sigh here.

It took a good half hour or so (and several jeers from passers-by) to locate a public phonebox. Hardly surprising, she supposed. The half hour bit, not the jeers. Although being a woman who lacked the modesty-saving bottom half of somewhat essential clothing, she'd expected a certain amount of ribbing.

The number of callboxes had diminished considerably over the last few years. Not much call for them anymore, pun not intended. The mobile phone generation had killed off their worth to the point of extinction. Thank God, however, for the bright spark whose idea it had been to keep the odd scattering of telephone booths in service. Just in case.

Patience opened the booth door and stepped inside. Phew. Not vandalised. Things were beginning to look up. She phoned a taxi company she'd never used before. No way was she prepared to hire her regular pick-up, no matter how much discount they dished out to loyal customers. She'd never live the embarrassment down. In this case, better the devil you didn't bloody know. The radio controller promised a cab within five minutes. It arrived twenty-three minutes later. Not bad. Slightly better than average.

Good news: The cabbie didn't bang on about the price of fuel, the yawn-inducing yarn about the high-profile celebrity that Patience would never believe he picked up in the taxi last week, or the plight of having to navigate amidst the sheer senselessness of London's ever-growing army of idiot car drivers.

Bad news: The journey home was mostly taken up with the tosser behind the wheel sniggering like a snotty-nosed child at his stupid red-faced passenger; a silly girl who had somehow lost possession of her skirt. And probably her sanity.

Home sweet home. She paid the driver, but didn't hang about for change. The wanker didn't exactly deserve a tip, but there was no way she was prepared to stand beside a halted car in her underwear like some kind of desperate street hooker addressing a kerb crawler whilst laughing boy took all the time in the world to count out coinage. It was her street of residence, for God's sake. People knew her around here.

Patience closed her front door to the outside world and all its evils, then breathed what was quite possibly the longest sigh of relief known to man. Or rather, woman. Job done. It was over. She'd survived the nightmare. Time to relax. Ahhhhhh.

Her first port of call was the bathroom where she scrubbed away the ground-in dirt from her palms and knees; mess accumulated from her choice of sudden departure from the old man's garden. Next, she journeyed to her bedroom and chose herself a replacement skirt from her worryingly decreasing collection of clothes. What a day. She'd never lost so many personal possessions in such a short space of time. The odd earring, yes, but not a whole bloody outfit. A quick recap counted a blouse, a bra, a skirt and a pair of shoes at Geoff's place. Thankfully, she'd enjoy their safe return at work on Monday morning. Well, that is, if his wife hadn't discovered their hiding places. But the recent demise of her skirt was a different story altogether. She'd have to take the loss on the chin. Did it matter? Not really. It was no good to her any more anyway. Torn to pieces. And besides, the dog was no doubt using it right now to line its basket, kennel, whatever with comfort and warmth.

Finally, she wandered into the lounge and flumped herself down onto the safe and comfortable haven of the sofa. There, she poured herself a large vodka with a dash of cola. Not too much mixer, mind. She didn't like her tipple of choice drowned to oblivion by sugary blackness. Just enough to quash the bitterness, that's all that was required.

The doorbell sounded. Joe had arrived. Yay! She skipped with overblown gaiety into the hallway, but froze at the closed front door that stood between Patience and her visitor. What if it wasn't her friend? What if it was the old man and his toothy dog? Or even worse, the police?

"Who is it?" she asked, or rather, squeaked in a meek fashion.

"It's me."

Oh, great. Like that really helped.

"Who's me?"

There came a pause. Then, "Joe."

It certainly sounded like Joe. But she needed to be certain. "Are you sure you're Joe?"

Another pause from the visitor. Longer this time, clearly through some shape or form of eye-blinking, nose-wrinkling confusion, the like of which she found impossible to witness through the wooden barrier.

Note to self: Buy one of those door eye-hole thingies to peek through.

"Of course I'm sure. Patience, have you taken something?"

Patience was being stupid. And paranoid. And a little psychotic. Of course it was Joe. She opened the door and beamed brightly.

"Hi, Joe."

Joe stood at the doorway, pizza box in one hand, DVD in the other. He stepped back a pace, wary.

"How many have you had to drink?" he asked.

Eh? "None."

Joe raised a disbelieving eyebrow. "Really?"

"Yes, really. I've just this second poured out my first voddy. And you'll be pleased to know, it's still sitting there in its glass, untouched by human lips."

Joe stood in silence, hesitant, unmoving. Patience screwed up her face. What was this, bloody Let's Play Statues?

"Are you coming in or what?"

Joe nodded and entered the flat. Patience relieved her friend of the pizza box, hooked her arm in his and led him into the lounge. She plonked herself down on the sofa and patted the free space beside her.

"Don't look so scared, Joe. You should be used to me by now. Now, sit down before I pull you down."

Joe smiled and did as he was told. He then offered a puzzled frown as he reached out and plucked another snippet of stray vegetation from the tangles in her hair; the second within the space of a few hours.

"Is this a twig?"

Patience's lower jaw sank. First pondweed, now a souvenir from the old man's hedge. What was she, a walking, talking plant museum? Or a magnet for plant residue perhaps? Could she be bothered to explain the dressing gown returning incident? Hell, no. A sharp change of subject was required.

"What DVD did you rent out?"

"Bodycount 4."

You what? "Okaaaaaay. Is this film as violent and male orientated as it sounds?"

Joe nodded. "If it lives up to the first three movies, then yes."

Does not compute. "What on Earth possessed you to choose something like that for our quiet night in together?"

"I haven't seen it yet." Then taking note of her discontent. "If you want, I can go back and change it for something else."

"No, no, no, don't worry about it. It's too late now." Patience knocked back her drink and refilled the glass with happy juice. "You never know. It might turn out to be a classic."

Yeah, right.

An hour into the movie, umpteen downed voddys and one totally devoured pizza later, Patience hadn't realised there were so many ways to kill a human being; some quite ingenious, although executed a little too gory for her liking. So why had she stayed the distance? Simple. She didn't wish to move from Joe's tender arm around her shoulders.

This was how they were. The best of friends, both caring deeply for each other, and acting almost like lovers, but without the sex or stupid arguments. Patience felt content in Joe's arms. And wanted.

And loved. And adored, even. In a friend-like, platonic, companionable way, of course. The downside? This was the closest she would ever get to a proper relationship with him. And via that factor alone, a tiny piece of her heart broke away and was lost forever each time they were this close.

"Joe."

"Yes?"

"That guy. The hero."

"Flint Silver?"

"Yeah, him. Am I right in thinking he's the owner of an ice cream van?"

"That's right, yeah."

"So how the hell does he know how to kill people? And where did he get all those weapons?"

"Flint used to be a secret agent for a hush-hush government organisation. But he quit in the second movie after his wife got murdered. He couldn't handle the guilt, you see. It was a revenge killing. The man who took her life happened to be the brother of the bad guy in the first movie who Flint prevented from blowing up the White House. After that, Flint decided to get himself another job."

Patience made a face that could only mean one thing. What the fuck? "Selling ice cream to kiddies in the park?"

"Yeah."

"Why?"

"Needed the money, I guess."

"No, no, I meant why become an ice cream man? Why not use the skills he'd acquired and put them to good use in a similar career? You know, like a security man. Or a bodyguard?"

"He tried that in the third instalment. But the bad guys tracked him down and vowed to kill him. Finding an ordinary job in a sleepy town meant he could lie low."

"What bad guys? I'm surprised there are any left. We're only an hour into this film and he's already taken out about two hundred people."

"Two hundred and forty-two actually. I've been totting up the numbers in my head. Now you can see why it's called Bodycount."

She rolled her eyes to the heavens. "I had kind of guessed that."

An incredulous shake of the head. "Joe. Can I be completely honest with you?"

"Yes, of course you can."

"I mean, honest with a capital H. With bells on. And bright lights that can be seen from space. That kind of honest."

Once again, it was clear that Joe doubted her sanity, but seemed to let it pass. "Sure. Go right ahead."

Patience took a deep breath, then, "This movie is the biggest pile of horse manure I have ever had the misfortune to watch in my entire twenty-five years of existence. There. I've said it."

Joe looked at her. She looked at him. And then they both burst into an explosive fit of laughter.

"I'm sorry, Patience. I don't know what I was thinking."

"Nor do I. When you said you'd bring round a DVD, I thought you meant something a bit more romantic-comedy-ish."

Joe's face reddened. "Epic fail or what, huh?"

Patience replenished both their glasses with an overly generous quantity of vodka. "Don't worry about it. Just get this stuff down your neck."

Glasses topped up, she fired the remote at the DVD player. The tray slid open, setting the shiny disc free. Joe tore himself from the sofa and placed the DVD in its plastic case. Patience selected a music channel and hit OK. Joe returned to her side and they both cuddled into each other as the latest chart vibes filled the air.

There came an overly long hiatus in their chatter. It went on for at least ten minutes. Had they really exhausted all lines of conversation so soon? Patience had oodles of shit she could yap about. Expand on the Geoff disaster perhaps. And the dog chase was a worthy anecdote. But no. The events of today were best dead and buried.

"You're quiet, Joe. Surely you must have something to talk about."

Joe shrugged. "Not really. Just boring shit."

Patience found it hard to believe. "But we haven't seen each other for months."

"What can I say? They've been a very uneventful few months."

Patience didn't fancy sitting in monastery strength hush. She'd never taken any vows of silence. Therefore, she decided to kickstart a suitable common or garden confab.

"Still working at the same place?"

Joe nodded. "Yep."

"Still bored crapless?"

A smirk. "Yep." And then, yay, at last. Conversation. "Mind you, the company's profits are rocketing, so they've decided to expand."

Sigh. Work talk. Yawn. Time for forty winks? Tut, tut, tut. Come on, girl. He's your best friend. At least try to look interested. And don't forget. You—yes, you—were the one who prompted this particular chat.

"Yeah?" she managed.

Not bad. Relatively convincing, although not worthy of one of those film awards where an out of touch actor thanks all the people who got him that far in his sincerest form of bullshit, then spouts on about loving his dear fans. You know, those arsewipes said actor holds so much contempt for.

Joe continued with, "They're opening new branches all over the place. Even one in Scotland."

She found it difficult to hold her interest. "Really?" Oh, dear. Not quite a question, more like a grunt.

Joe sussed her boredom. "See? Told you it was boring shit."

They laughed. Cuddled closer. And watched some more music videos. In silence.

Patience's eyes gravitated to Joe's groin area. Ooh, look. A lump. Bigger than usual. Not that she studied her best friend's down-below regions too often. Actually, that was a little white lie. In fact, a total whopper. Every time they were this close, she'd rest her head on his shoulder, eyes aimed downward, wondering what he was hiding in his pants. Especially on this particular occasion where his dick looked as if it was fighting to escape from the confines of its cotton prison.

Ah, but alas, it was probably a false alarm. And equally false hopes on her part. The chance of Joe being aroused by such closeness to Patience was slimmer than slim could possibly be. Penny's Dave, in his drunken state, had often mentioned a male phenomenon known as half-hard, where the penis would reach an involuntary middling state. Not exactly erect, yet in no way flaccid. Somewhere in between. In most cases, it would happen without any prior warning. And there didn't even need to be a reason. He'd also pointed out that a flaccid penis never retained a stable and accurate size. Sometimes it would appear much longer. But in extreme weather conditions – cocks were not lovers of the cold – it would shrink to the point of embarrassing. Biology lessons at school were never this eye-opening, huh?

Diagnosis: Joe's somewhat inviting but stiflingly frustrating out-of-bounds lump was nothing more than an innocent half-hard. Safe. Non-threatening. Benign.

Side effects: Patience was now more than just a little turned on. In fact, streams were beginning to trickle down below. Bugger. There was only one solution.

It was time for a sexual fantasy.

The lounge looked different. Another world. Expensive furnishings throughout, all matching and colour-coordinated. The boring magnolia paintwork, now replaced with a sexy shade of scarlet. The sofa on which they were seated, bigger, brand new, far more comfortable. Oh, wow. This was all set to be a wonderful daydream. Or rather, evening-dream, taking into account the brilliant moon and shimmering stars that shone down on the couple via the now roofless room.

Wow! Joe's lump. It was now huge. Bursting to be free from the darkness of his underwear. Patience grappled at his jeans, unzipping his fly with voracious haste. She pulled his bottom half clothing right down to his ankles, granting freedom at last to his rock hard cock.

"What are you doing?" he gasped, uneasy. "You know full well I'm gay."

"Oh, yeah?" Patience lobbed him a wicked grin. "In my fantasy, you're into women. But not just any woman. Only me."

Joe looked pleased. "Really?"

"You'd better believe it, baby." Hmm. Bit of a naff line, but this was her dream. So it was perfectly justified.

Joe sat back, big grin, stiff cock pointed upwards, awaiting his fate. Patience knelt astride him. She hitched up her skirt, pulled the gusset of her knickers to one side and gently lowered herself onto his meat. Ooh, yeah, baby, it felt good as she took him whole.

Concern from Joe. "Shouldn't I be wearing a condom?"

The girl on the end of his cock made a face. Keep up, Joe. "No need. This isn't real life. It's my sexual fantasy."

"Oh, sorry, I forgot."

Did she really imagine that conversation? Fuck's sake, girl, stop analysing your daydream, evening-dream, whatever it is. Just enjoy it.

And so she did.

Patience slammed down upon his erect member as Joe unbuttoned her blouse and pulled it away. He craned his neck forward and explored her cleavage with an eager tongue. She unbuckled her bra and cast it aside.

"Suck my nipples," she ordered, her eyes burning with lust. "Suck them hard."

Up and down, up and down, she continued, relentless, unyielding, as he tasted her left nipple. Lick, suck, nuzzle. Then onto the right nipple. Lick, suck, nuzzle. And back to the left. Ooh, yeah, fuck, fuck, fuck, this was good stuff. She pushed his head closer to her chest, spitting wild expletives as his wide-open mouth consumed a whole breast. Down below, Joe pushed a couple of fingers into her moist hole. Ooh. Two digits and a cock, all at once. Wow. She couldn't recall any of her previous fantasies being this naughty.

Joe thrust his cock upwards as she crashed downwards. They both found their desired rhythm and gyrated in harmony. Ooh, yeah. Heaven. He pushed his fingers deeper inside, adding to the sheer electricity that sizzled all over her body.

"Fuck, fuck, fuck," she growled.

Joe pumped harder, taking her growls as another order. In turn, she quickened her pace.

"Do you like it?" Joe asked.

"Ooh, yeah," came her gasp of a reply. "I love it, baby."

Patience withdrew herself from his penis and finger combo and clambered onto all fours. "Now fuck me like a dog."

Did Joe refuse? No way. He pulled aside her gusset and plunged his dick into her dribbling pussy. Now it was his turn to be rough. He banged the girl with all his might, harder and faster upon every yelp of pleasure that escaped from her wide-open mouth.

"I'm coming, I'm coming," he squealed as he smashed his cock with haste into her hole.

"Come over my tits!" she barked, loud, aggressive, needing it badly.

"Why?"

"Because I want this sexual fantasy to be really dirty."

Patience quickly rolled onto her back. Joe knelt over the girl and wanked hard. His cock exploded, spraying hot seed all over her waiting bosoms. She smiled up at him, watching the guy squeeze out the last few remaining dribbles of come as she lathered the warm, sticky goo all over her breasts.

"What the hell are you doing?" glurked Joe, absolutely horrified.

Patience blinked a couple of times, bemused by the unexpected query. She found Joe standing in the centre of the room, fully dressed, all wide-eyed, his mouth shaped into a pained grimace. Eh? How could this be? He'd been kneeling astride her a second ago, spilling his liquid treasures. How did he pull up his boxers and jeans so fast?

She peered down at herself, lying on the sofa, naked from the waist up, both hands upon her breasts. And then she noticed something. His come had vanished. No trace of semen could be found on her body anywhere. Huh? Then she took note of her surroundings. Boring magnolia paintwork. The ceiling above exactly where it should be. The old sofa. And cheap, mis-matched furnishings. Oh, shit.

She was back in reality.

And worse still, she'd clearly been acting out her sordid fantasy in front of the real-life version of Joe. No wonder the man looked so traumatized. Bugger with a capital B.

At that moment, Penny and Dave entered the room, fresh from their evening out.

A smiling Penny said, "Hiya, we're back. I—"

Silence. Two statues. Two more aghast faces.

"Not interrupting anything, are we?" asked Dave.

Patience didn't hang around to explain. She picked up her discarded bra and blouse, then legged it out of the lounge, down the hallway and into her bedroom.

Very quickly.

Slam!

Chapter 8

Sex with a Stranger

Once again, it was the morning after the night before. And once again, Patience stepped into the kitchen, ashamed, humiliated, and not ready to face the fallout.

Penny stood by the worksurface, waiting for the kettle to boil. "Morning. Coffee?"

Avoiding eye contact, Patience responded with a rather faint and submissive version of, "Yes please."

She joined Dave at the table while Penny prepared three strong wake-up mugs. Hmm. Strange. Her flatmate was acting what could only be described as — well — pretty normal. So was Dave, all reserved and house-trained, almost husband-like, flicking through a local newspaper. It was weird. No snide remarks. No childish teasing. Nothing. Insert puzzled frown and bemused scratch of head here. It was as if last night had never happened.

Hey. Maybe it was all a mere figment of her somewhat abundant imagination. Maybe she'd dreamt the embarrassing events of yesterday evening. Maybe the Joe incident hadn't actually happened.

Not looking up from the paper, and all so casual, Dave commented, "Not a bad pair of tits you've got there, Patience."

Argh! Last night. It did happen.

Face-palm time.

Penny scowled at her boyfriend. "Oi, you! I thought I told you not to mention last night."

"Sorry, Penny. Just paying Patience a compliment, that's all. As the poor girl has been so down on herself lately, I thought she'd appreciate it."

Although scarlet with burning shame, Patience couldn't help but raise a brief, appreciative smile. "You know, Dave," she said. "In a crazy, fucked up, roundabout kind of way, that's very of sweet of you. Thanks."

Dave tipped a nod her way. "You're welcome." Then he added, tongue-in-cheek, "If you ever feel like flashing me any other part of your anatomy, just give me a call, okay?"

Penny met him with a playful slap across the back of the head. "You stop that filth or I'll grill your testicles and force-feed them to you for breakfast. Without ketchup. Got that?"

"Yes, understood."

"Good."

Patience managed another smile, but it was short-lived. She couldn't help feeling guilty about the shenanigans of the previous evening. Stripping to her waist. Getting caught with her tits out. Running away. Abandoning Joe. Locking herself in her room. Refusing to come out. And offering no explanation for her, let's face it, somewhat bizarre actions.

Patience found just about enough confidence to ask, "What time did Joe leave last night?"

Penny delivered three steaming hot drinks and seated herself at the table. "Not long after you vowed never to leave the confines of your bedroom ever, ever, ever, ever, ever again." Then an afterthought. "Have I quoted the correct number of evers?"

Dave said, "I think you'll find there were at least two more evers in her vow."

"I stand corrected." Penny then indicated to her chair. "Or rather, sit corrected."

"How did he seem?" was the next timid query from Patience.

Penny thought about it. "Confused and disillusioned are probably the best two words to describe his mood at point of exit."

Another face-palm. "Oh, God. I've lost him for sure."

"Whatever made you do such a thing?" asked Dave.

"That's what I'd like to know," said Penny.

Patience sighed. Loudly. She asked in the privacy of her head, why do you frigging think? The answer: Because, at the time in question, she was enjoying the pretty colours and tickly sensations of a sexual fantasy involving her best friend, that's bloody why. Only, she hadn't planned on performing a real-life rendition of the piece in front of said best friend. But could she tell Dave and Penny the truth? Hah, no way.

Still retaining the face-palm, Patience rasped the words, "I don't know."

A minor fib. Or major, depending on point of view. But did she care? No.

Dave appeared more bemused than he had ever been before, and that was saying something. "I don't get it. I thought Joe was supposed to be gay."

"So did I," remarked Penny. "Patience, are you sure he's that way inclined? On the two occasions I've met him, he hasn't exactly come across as a queen."

Oh, for fuck's sake, get real, Penny. "They don't all conform to that bloody stereotype, you know."

Penny raised both hands in mock surrender. "All right, all right. Hashtag, just saying."

"I told you yesterday, Penny. Joe and I have been the best of friends, like, forever. I know the bloke inside out. Stored in my head is everything there is to know about him. And I mean everything."

A grinning Dave couldn't help but quip, "Even the size of his dinkle?"

Yeah, funny, not. "Well, no, not that, obviously. But everything else, yes. And besides. Last night's disaster proves his sexuality beyond a shadow of a doubt. I got my tits out and he looked at me as if I'd clubbed a baby seal."

Penny came back with, "Maybe he thought suddenly stripping off for no reason and massaging your breasts right in front of him was a bit too full-on."

"Agreed," joined in Dave. "It's always best to start with a snog."

Patience groaned. "Put it this way," she continued, desperate to win the case. "Have I ever seen Joe with a woman? No. Have I ever seen Joe even look at a woman? No again. And have I ever found porno mags under his mattress featuring women boasting impossible tits? Yet another no. And think about it. He's got a girl as a best friend. So that proves it."

"All circumstantial evidence," said Penny.

Patience rose from her chair, tired of this madness.

Penny looked up from her coffee. "Now where are you going?"

"I need a shower."

As Patience headed for the door, Penny asked, "Got any plans for today?"

Her boyfriend replied, "Yes. Making mad, passionate love with you."

"Not you, you idiot. Patience."

Patience hovered by the door. "Shopping. I need a new outfit for tonight."

"Cool. So you're serious about tonight's sexual opportunity then?"

A loud scoff leapt out of her mouth. "I wouldn't exactly say serious is my current choice of mood."

"Oh? So what is?"

A moment of weighing up from Patience, then, "Ambivalent sounds like a better way to describe what I'm feeling right now."

"Ah, right. Well, don't forget. We're going clubbing. So make sure you don't pick anything too bloody conservative. Think fucksexy."

Patience's brow wrinkled in question. "Fucksexy?"

Penny smiled. "Yes. It's my little word for hot to trot. Short. Low-cut." Then a suggestive wink. "Revealing."

Dave looked up from his newspaper. "Half-naked with legs up to the armpits and tits almost falling out always works for me."

Patience coughed out her distaste. "Ugh, no thanks. You won't find me stooping so low."

"You should listen to Dave's advice," said Penny. "He's a bloke. As in, a man. A guy. The male of the species. The unfortunate six foot growth at the base end of a penis. In other words, your target market."

The virgin girl did not look at all won over.

"All I'm trying to say is," Penny continued, "there's no point in buying clothes just to look pretty. The only girls getting laid tonight will be the men-magnets. That is, scantily clad, near-naked tarts who will open their legs to literally anybody. Even totally minging people. So your job—actually, not just your job, your mission with a capital

M—is to make sure you fit exactly in that category. Otherwise, I'm sorry to say, babes, there will be no cock for you tonight."

Patience blew out a defeated sigh. Her mission with a capital M was depressing to say the least. And she had plenty of expletives to further describe it. Groan. How it had come to this was the mega-millions jackpot question. And so it was to be. Nightclub or bust. And that was when defeated sigh number two made itself known.

Was she heading for yet another disaster?

Most probably.

Ahhhh, clothes shopping. Every girl's dream.

The department store she currently found herself browsing boasted five floors—yes, five freaking floors—of everything a lady could ever wish for. If the female of the species desired something special, then here was the place to come. Although, saying that, not even a retailer of this excellence, one which boasted such plentiful variety, could ever supply the discerning woman a giftwrapped perfect man who could cook, provide sensuous massage and put the toilet seat down. Near-impossible feats, no. Ladieswear for all occasions, yes.

But could Patience Hope find anything she actually liked? No.

No matter what Penny said, Patience was not a prude. Well, okay, maybe just a bit of a prude. A tiny smidgen. Mind you, she'd always considered herself more sensible than prudish. Sensible was a much better way to describe her rather more conformist outlook on life. Right? And sensible was a good trait to boast.

Um. Right?

Hmm, weird. She couldn't even convince her own mind without finding herself cloaked with some form of doubt. It was official. She was going mad. In fact, totally loony.

Oh, come on, look, she argued with herself, reinforcing the loony theory. The range of party skirts and dresses on display were way too short, and not just for her liking. All she desired was a bottom hem measuring a few centimetres above the knees, that's all. Ample cut to enable a tiny flash of thigh. She'd like that. In fact, she'd wholly approve. Not revealing too much, a taster of bare leg, leaving the rest to the imagination. Just enough to get that guy interested. But no. Nothing bearing any resemblance to her wishes was in stock. All that was available averaged a measurement of just above gusset level.

Groan.

Patience checked the time. Uh oh. She'd have to get a move on. The shop would be closing soon. Typical. A whole afternoon of valuable retail therapy wasted without anything to show for it apart from sighs, tuts and rolls of the eyes. Little Miss Hope had bought absolute zilch. Except for her handbag hooked over a shoulder, which didn't exactly count, she held no shopping bags, no boxes, nothing in her hands. Talk about embarrassing. A modern woman with no purchases? Totally unheard of. People were beginning to stare. Even the security guard.

Oh, sod this for a laugh. It was time to quit. This was the last thing she wanted to do, for it meant having to instead pluck something for tonight from Penny's collection, perish the thought. Sure, her flatmate had good taste in fashion, but that wasn't the problem. So what was it that worried Patience about her threads? Simple. Everything hanging in Penny's wardrobe screamed just one line:

"Look at me, I'm a prostitute!"

Dilemma time. Patience had two choices. Borrow from Penny or wear something from her own collection. Hah, if she could call it that. In other words, look like an airhead tart or look like—

—a prude.

Plain. Conservative. Unadventurous.

Boring.

Bugger.

Patience bid farewell to Floor 5 via the lift. Good. It was empty. She preferred to travel alone in elevators. No having to avoid eye contact with absolutely everybody. No having to reply to the stick-thin old lady in a bonnet whose only purpose in life was to greet everybody with, "Nice weather we're having for this time of year." And above all, no having to pretend she couldn't smell the tubby guy's silent but violent fart.

She hit G for Ground Floor.

"Doors closing," chirped an annoyingly high-spirited, electronic female voice, far too cheerful for its own good.

Just as predicted by the stupid recorded message, the double doors swished across, blocking her view of the awful "gusset and above" range she was not sorry to leave behind. The motor came to life. The lift began its descent.

She stood alone, eyes fixed upon the floor number box thingy, or whatever it was called, and found herself almost spellbound by the digital countdown.

5.

Ooh, it'll change in a moment.

4.

Well of course it did. Fuck's sake, girl, you really need to get out more.

The lift ceased at Floor 4.

"Doors opening."

The double doors slid open. A man entered. He smiled at her. She smiled back. Out of politeness, of course. Nothing meant by the gesture at all. Mind you, she couldn't help but notice, mmm, he was kind of cute. Salon tanned skin, nice teeth, clean shaven, somewhere in his thirties. Early half of the decade, that is, not hurtling towards the morbid forty. And his attire? Hmm. Smart, yes. Then came the but. His azure—and shiny, almost to the point of metallic—suit looked a tad too much like a sweet wrapper for her liking. But could she really hold that against the guy? Especially as she'd given a welcoming thumbs up to everything else.

The man, who clearly yearned to be a candy treat in foil packaging, stood beside her. They waited in silence, both facing forward, conscious of each other's presence, yet remaining firmly incommunicado. It was weird, she thought. Human beings were supposed to be social creatures. But Patience, just like everybody else, had sailed past tens of thousands of the same species in her lifetime without so much as a word. Not even a fleeting glance. Through city streets. Across the London Underground. In bars and clubs. In fact, everywhere. So many missed friendships. Or, shit, so many unrealised relationships. Unbelievable, huh? Everybody and everybody had their story. But nobody ever took time out to stop and listen.

Conclusion: We only ever communicated if we wanted something.

Hah, such selfish animals, we were.

"Doors closing."

She rolled her eyes. No, you don't frigging say, electronic bitch.

Once more, the doors met. The motor kicked in. And the two elevator occupants watched as the countdown progressed.

4.

Go on then. Change.

4.

Change, fuck's sake.

3.

Thank you.

4.

Eh? Now what's going on?

3.

4.

3.

4.

What the f —

A loud scraping, grating noise tore through the quietness. Patience palmed her shell-likes. The lift shuddered, then ground to a sudden halt. The noise ceased. The lamp went out. For a second or two, silence and darkness. Then a flicker. And let there be light. Illumination was restored. Patience glanced at the man. He glanced back at her. They were both just as concerned.

"Shit, what's happened?" she asked.

"The lift's stopped."

"Yes, I can see that. But why?"

He shrugged his shoulders, unable to supply a suitable remedy. "How should I know? I don't work here."

Patience blew out a sigh. In fact, two sighs were exhaled. What a pointless conversation they'd just shared. The lift, yes, it had broken down. Obvious. Evident. Downright blatant. She bloody knew that. He bloody knew that. So why even debate it?

"I'm sure it will start up again in a second or two," he said.

They waited one second. Nothing happened. Two seconds. Still nothing. And thirty long, agonising seconds later —

— more of the same. That is, fuck all.

"Oh," grunted the man. "Maybe not then."

Patience pressed the intercom button. "Hello? Anybody there?"

Silence.

Another press. "Hello? Can anybody hear me?"

More silence.

A third press. "Planet Earth to the rest of civilisation. This lift has broken down. Any chance of a rescue? Pretty please."

A brief hiss of static. But apart from that, no signs of life.

Patience, unimpressed, rolled her eyes more than she'd rolled them at any point during her twenty-five year life career. "Oh, great."

So. What now? She surveyed the small metal box they stood in, searching for answers. Double doors. Shut tight. No point in prizing them open, for she'd only be met on the other side by a brick wall. Next, mirrored walls. Convenient for checking hairstyle status. Pretty useless for anything else. Then a thought. Aha. Lifts always had a hatch in the roof. Well, they sure did in movies. The elevator featured in last night's Bodycount 4 was a prime example. The hero, Flint Silver, used it as a means of escape. Just before popping yet another bad guy right between the eyes.

She looked up. No hatch.

Bugger.

An idea sprang to mind. Get noticed. Make a noise. Using both fists, she thumped on the double doors with all her might.

"Help!" she yelled amidst the bangs. "We're stuck in the lift! Can somebody come and help us please?"

She stepped back and waited for a reaction, a reply, anything. Instead, she found herself greeted by the chilly, lonesome unnoise of hush.

The man leant against the back wall. "What a bummer. We could be stuck here for hours."

"I bloody hope not."

"Nor do I. I bore very easily."

Oh, perfect. She was sharing a clapped-out metal cube with a human sweet wrapper suffering from a low attention span. Thank you very much, God.

"What will we find to do?" he asked.

"Have you got any books on you?"

"No." The man's brow wrinkled in question. "How would that help us?"

Patience groaned. Like, duh. "We'd have something to read. As in, pass the time away."

"Oh. Right. By the way. My name's Tom."

"I'm Patience."

"Nice name."

"No, it's not. It's dumb. I'd rather be called Doris. Or Bertha. Or Cecilia. Blanche, even. Anything but Patience."

They both smiled.

"A friend of mine once got stuck in a lift," said Tom. "It was the next morning before they got him out."

"What?" she gasped, anxious. "That had better not happen to us. I've got important things to do this evening."

"Like what?"

"Clubbing."

The very moment that particular C word left her mouth, she could see how frigging futile it would seem to somebody outside looking in. And right on cue —

"That doesn't sound very important."

"Oh, believe me, Tom, this will be the most significant evening ever in the whole of world history since records began. Tonight is the night I finally lose my — "

Don't say it!

Good. Sentence quit just in time. Phew.

"Lose your what?" Tom asked, intrigued.

Bugger. The aftermath. Didn't he know that curiosity killed the cat?

"Nothing. Doesn't matter. Forget I said anything."

Nothing? Hah, that was as far removed from the truth as anybody could possibly reach. She definitely wanted to lose something. The V word.

It was sad but true. Recent events had proven without a doubt that the nightclub she'd be attending tonight — if she ever bloody got there, that is — was the only place she was guaranteed a cock-shaped key to unlock her womanhood and break the curse of her virginity. Geoff The C Word had turned out to be — well, a C word. And the very sight of Patience's upper wobbly bits had scared poor Joe half to death. God knows what would have happened to the bloke if she'd flashed him her lower spongy bits. A cardiac arrest? Huh, most probably. So therefore, this girl had no choice.

If truth be told, she didn't fancy getting laid the nightclub way. There was something all too vile and debauched about the binge drinking, dance 'til you drop, fuck anybody who's willing culture. But it was the only glimmer of hope she had left to cling on to.

Oh, just imagine if an opportunity arose right now where Patience found herself one-to-one with a guy. No distractions. No interruptions. Just the two of them. Him and her. It would mean she wouldn't need to darken the doors of tonight's snakepit of shamelessness and debauchery. Instead, he'd get his dick out. She'd get her pussy out. They'd fuck. And probably fuck some more. And that would be the end of it. Out of the virgin ashes would rise the phoenix that was a bona fide woman of the sexually active variety. No more virginity. No more worries. The quest would be well and truly over.

If only, huh?

But no. Fat chance of that. The company of Tom and a suit she could see her reflection in was all she'd been blessed with. And here they were, stuck in a decrepit, packed up elevator with nothing to amuse them for God knows how many long and laborious hours to come.

Oh, my God!

This was it! Her chance. The opportunity she'd been hoping for.

But no. Surely not. Sex in an elevator? Like, seriously? The most clichéd cliché ever. Could she stoop so low? More importantly, could she take the shame?

She could imagine the future sex-talk convo:

Somebody: "So. Patience. Where did your first time take place?"

Patience: Inaudible mumble.

Somebody: "Sorry? I didn't quite catch that? Where exactly?"

Patience: "In a lift."

Insert raucous laughter here.

A shiver ran down her spine at the very prospect of such soul crushing humiliation. There would be no way to mask such a terrible secret. For as long as a girl had friends, probing questions about each other's sex lives would always pop up, guaranteed. Take the other night, for example. Penny's question. The very query that inspired her mission to lose her virginity.

"How many men have you had in your life?"

After shagging Tom, she could run away, she supposed. Kiss goodbye to civilisation. And live alone in a cave. Patience Hope, professional hermit. Yeah. Good idea. That way, she'd avoid any future girlie inquisitions of the awkward genus. But God, that would be such a sad, lonely, boring existence. She couldn't handle such monotony. She'd go mad. Even madder than she was now.

It was no good. She needed to view her latest dilemma from a different perspective. Two options. Pick up a guy in a nightclub. Or pick up this guy in the lift. The choice was hers. Hmm. It was strange. Both instances involved sex with a stranger. But somehow — and she didn't know why exactly — the latter felt less depraved.

At last, her mind was made up. She turned to face Tom, her face glowing with excitement, enthusiasm, exhilaration and a whole host of other zingy e words.

"Tom. Can you do me a really big favour?"

Tom nodded. "Fire away."

"Have sex with me."

Tom. Stunned, big-time. "What?"

"You know, sexual intercourse and stuff."

Tom pinched himself. "Are you serious?"

"Deadly."

The shiny suited man couldn't get his mind around the situation. "Is this one of those final request things?"

Eh? "Does it look like I'm about to be executed?"

"No, no, I meant, do you really believe we're both going to die in here? Is that why you're offering me sex?"

At that moment, the intercom crackled into life. "Hello?" A man's voice, the engineer. "Are you all right in there?"

"Bloody interruptions!" Patience marched over to the intercom and pressed the button. "Yes. We're both fine, thank you."

"Oh, good," said the engineer. "Well, don't you go worrying yourselves. We'll have you out of there in no time."

What? Shit. She didn't like the sound of that. Sure, she wanted to be rescued. But not quite yet.

"What amount of time are we looking at here?" she asked.

"About ten minutes."

Patience peered across at a rather befuddled Tom, then hit the reply button again. "Can you give us a bit more time? Say, fifteen?"

A pregnant pause from the outside world. Then, "Are you feeling all right, love? Is it the claustrophobia? Has it got to you?"

Patience could see the man's point, but this was an opportunity she did not wish to miss out on. Tom was there for the taking. Only, she needed time to do the taking.

"I feel perfectly fine," she assured the engineer. "What I mean is, I wouldn't want you to rush the job. Best to take your time and fix it properly, yeah?"

"No can do, I'm afraid. The store's about to close, and the boss wants it sorted pronto. See you in ten minutes."

The lonely hiss of static. The engineer was gone.

Patience rushed over to a rather apprehensive Tom. "Right, you. We've got ten minutes. Not as long as I'd originally hoped for. But I'm sure it's perfectly doable. They say sex averages fifteen minutes. So we'll need to cut some shit out. Maybe skip the kissing with tongues part and get straight down to it."

Tom backed further into the wall behind him, unnerved by the girl's overt insistence. "Not being funny, but—are you on day release?"

"Oi, you! I'm not bloody mental. I just need sex, that's all. Badly."

"But we'll be out of here in ten minutes."

"Exactly. Which means we need to get started right away."

Patience dropped her handbag and quickly stripped. Off came her shoes, her jacket, her top, her bra, her skirt, her underwear, everything. Tom swallowed hard, examining the nude woman with somewhat intimidated curiosity.

Does not compute. "What's the matter? Don't you fancy me?"

"Well, yes. It's difficult not to fancy a naked girl standing right in front of me. That's not the problem."

Impatient and raring to go, she said, "Look, come on, Tom. Stop mucking about and get your kit off. I want a fuck and I want it now."

He stood there, statuesque, unmoving. A sigh from Patience. Fine. If a job's worth doing, do it yourself. She unbuckled his belt and unzipped his fly. Tom's trousers and underwear fell to his ankles, revealing —

— oh. A totally flaccid penis.

"What the fuck?" she glurked, goggle-eyed, loose-jawed. "Am I really that hideous?"

"No. This is the problem, you see. I find it difficult to get hard."

"Oh, fucking great!" she roared, clenching both fists, frustrated.

"It's okay," he assured her. "All my cock needs is a good suck. It will rise to attention within a few minutes."

"How many minutes exactly?"

"Um. Ten."

"What? We haven't got ten minutes! Not any more. The clock is ticking. Can't you just give it a bit of a pull?"

"Masturbation doesn't work for me. Sorry."

Patience wrapped her fingers around his limp tool and massaged it gently. Sure enough, there was no oomph. It continued to hang wilted and lifeless like a long forgotten Christmas decoration. She needed to up her game. Therefore, she licked the very tip of his penis, then lapped all round his helmet. Nothing. She kissed it, bit on it, nuzzled on it. No reaction. Hmm. This was proving to be tough.

Right. In order to make this work, she had to suddenly become the greatest blowjobber in the universe. Her game plan: Raise it in record time. Pop on a condom. Bend over. And get him to fuck her from behind. Yeah. That would work. It sounded quite simple actually. There was just once small problem. She didn't actually know how to give head.

Sure, she'd munched on Geoff The C Word's stiff dick twenty-four hours previously. But all that entailed was licking off the spray cream. She hadn't sucked his cock in the true sense of the phrase. But then again, it couldn't be that difficult. Right?

Patience opened her mouth. She swallowed Tom's soft cock. And sucked. As hard as she could. Like she was sucking an ice lolly.

"Ow!" he yelped.

She spat out his penis. "What's the matter?"

"You sucked on my dick."

"Isn't that the general idea?"

"No. You don't literally suck it. Don't you know anything, girl?"

She found herself hugely annoyed by the slating. What did he bloody know? Did he give head himself? No. So how could he possibly crown himself an expert? Huh. Tosser. Any more cheek from him and she'd bite the fucking thing off.

And then it came to her in a flash. When performing the art of cock sucking, a girl's mouth should become a vagina substitute. Which meant said girl's mouth needed to act like the soft, warm tunnel of said vagina. Of course! It all seemed so clear now.

She opened her mouth and wrapped her warm lips around the sorry member. She moved her head slowly back and forth, simulating the sensual pleasures of sex. The fingers of her free hand fondled his balls as she worked his rod with her eager lips and tongue.

At last. Something rumbled down below. Tom mumbled some kind of inaudible but heartfelt appreciation as his cock began to stiffen, filling with blood, growing harder by the second. Patience quickened her pace, bobbing her head up and down, enveloping his now-erect weapon with her soft, warm mouth.

"Oh, Patience," he murmured, huge smile upon face. "You've done it. You've got me hard."

She withdrew her mouth from his throbbing tool and beamed brightly. "Now can you fuck me?"

"Ooh, yes. My pleasure."

The lamp flickered. The lift shuddered. The motor kicked in. Movement.

"No!" shrieked Patience. "Not yet! That was nowhere near ten minutes!"

Aghast, they both twisted their heads to face the countdown.

4.

3.

"Shit!" she yelped, headless chicken mode, frantically fishing for her clothes.

Tom was fortunate. All he needed to do was pull up his underwear and trousers. Patience, however, was naked. Shit. What an idiot. She pulled up her knickers. Back to front again. Argh!

2.

Bra, again relegated to her handbag. Over her head, her top. Arms through the sleeves.

1.

Skirt pulled to her waist and buttoned up.

G.

Jacket on. Both feet slipped into her shoes.

The stupid electronic voice. "Doors opening."

Patience looked at Tom. "Can I see you tonight? I'd like us to continue where we left off."

Wow. What a bold question. But an absolute necessity. After all, it was either Tom or the dreaded nightclub. And she knew which one she'd rather pick.

His face sank as the double doors swished open. "I'm so sorry. But that's not possible."

"Why not?"

It was then when Tom stepped out of the lift.

Straight into the loving and very much relieved arms of his wife.

Bugger.

Chapter 9

In the Club

Patience arrived home and wandered into the kitchen. A panting, moaning Penny sat on the worksurface in her nurse's uniform, legs wrapped tight around Dave who, with trousers down to his ankles, was happily pummelling his girlfriend to oblivion.

In normal circumstances, Patience might have been pleasantly surprised by the impromptu sex show. After all, this was one hell of a step up from her newfound hobby of late night keyhole voyeurism. But was she really in the mood to be turned on by her own private kitchen fuck theatre right at this very moment in time? No way.

"Oh, give it a rest, you two," she groaned, not knowing where to put her face. "I need a cuppa."

"Don't mind us," said Dave, taking no break from his rhythm.

"Yeah," giggled Penny with an idiot grin. "Just pretend we're not here."

Patience huffed. Loudly. "You're blocking my way to the kettle."

"Just give us another thirty seconds, Patience," Dave replied, quickening his pace. "I'm just about to shoot my load."

"And I'm about to have the orgasm of the century," squealed Penny, eyes rolled back, tongue lolled out.

Patience. Not impressed in the slightest. "Oh, for fuck's sake."

Patience left the lovers to it and entered the lounge. She dumped herself on the sofa and waited the allotted thirty seconds. Right on cue, Penny and Dave's screams of ecstasy rang out as they rode their lust across the white-water rapids of sexual satisfaction. Their cries seemed to go on forever. Followed by the ooohs of winding down. And the ahhhhs of recovery.

One quick clean up, pulling up of trousers and straightening of uniform later, the two of them joined Patience in the lounge, sporting pure and innocent faces, as if nothing had happened.

"Did you find yourself an outfit for tonight?" Penny asked.

"No. Complete disaster. Just like everything else in my life," she replied, pissed off, down in the mouth. "Oh, I tried to have sex with a stranger in a lift," she confessed without the slightest hint of fervour or conviction. "But I couldn't even get that right."

Penny chuckled. "Oh, babes. You have got such a fertile imagination."

Eh? Did it look as if she was making the story up? Oh, whatever. More importantly, did she really fancy explaining the finer details of her latest sexual disaster? No. She bloody didn't.

Ah, well. Patience needed to face the horrible truth. She had no choice. To get shot of her virginity, it had to be the nightclub. There was no other way. It was her unfortunate destiny.

"Penny, I can't believe I'm going to ask you this, but — "

Penny waited for the second half of the question. It didn't arrive. "But what, Patience?"

Go on, girl. Ask her. You'll never live it down, but things can't get any worse, surely.

"Can I borrow some of your clothes tonight?"

Penny's face lit up, as if it was an honour to serve the virgin. "Sure, you can. Tell you what, I've got some shit hot outfits in my wooden cave of many wonders that will make you look fucksexy with a capital wow."

Okay. Fucksexy. She liked that part. It sounded exciting. Exciting was good. She could live with exciting. But the capital wow bit. Hmm. The phrase kind of scared her.

"Just one stipulation," Patience said; warning eyes aimed at her flatmate.

"Go on?"

"I don't want to look too tarty. Okay?"

Penny smiled. "Okay, Patience. You win. Not too tarty."

Patience grimaced at the mammoth mirror that ran across the length of the nightclub's ladies' toilets. A cheap, half-naked slapper stared hopelessly back at her.

A critical eye examined her borrowed Saturday evening glad rags. The shortest of short skirts was a major concern, the bottom hem a millimetre higher and the world would be permanently admiring the gusset of her red lace thong. And then there was the problem of a record-breaking low-cut blouse. Were it not for the concrete rigidity of a vice-like bra pushing her cleavage together and holding everything securely in place, any sudden movement would happily spill out its contents onto an unsuspecting public.

Oh, come back, dressing gown, all is forgiven.

And what about her make up? Dear God. Penny had plastered so much warpaint onto Patience's face, she could no longer recognise her own reflection. On second thoughts, maybe total anonymity whilst dressed in such unfavourable apparel was a good thing.

"I can't believe I let you talk me into wearing this outfit," bemoaned Patience, her head shaking from side to side in a fit of self-pity, mortification, indignity, and everything related.

"What's wrong with it?" Penny asked, topping up her lipstick. "It's doing its job, isn't it? Screaming out, 'Hey, boys. I'm available.'"

"No, Penny. Get it right. It's screaming out, 'Hey boys. All I'm after is cock.'"

"I thought that was the plan."

Staring at the fallen maiden that was her reflection was making the girl go all cross-eyed. "I look like a prostitute."

"Even better. Make yourself some extra cash while you're at it."

A stern glare. "That's not funny."

The undisguised smirk from Penny thought otherwise.

Patience deflated, the whole world's problems, woes, concerns, guilt, price of bacon, everything on her shoulders. "Maybe Joe's right. Rushing headlong into sex just to get my first time out of the way is a pointless exercise."

Penny tended to her foundation as she spoke. "It was your idea."

"Yes, I know. But now I feel like a whore."

"You want my advice?"

"I'm not sure if I do."

"Ignore Joe. He's the reason you're in this predicament."

Patience shaped her brow into a quizzical frown. "And how did you reach that conclusion?"

"Isn't it obvious? If he was into women, you would have fucked him by now. Correct?"

She thought about last night's sexual fantasy. But didn't want to admit her true feelings. "Probably."

"No probably about it."

"I dare say I might have done."

"No might about it."

"Okay, okay. Yes."

"Which means, right now, you wouldn't be a desperate virgin on the lookout for somebody to pick your cherry. Correct?"

"Um. I suppose."

"No suppose about it."

"Fuck's sake, yes."

A haughty smirk from Penny. "I rest my case."

"You have got one seriously fucked up mind, Penny."

"True. But you cannot deny, I talk perfect sense." Then an idea. "Hey. If Joe's such a good mate, why can't he forget he's gay for one night and sort you out with a decent portion? Just don't scare him to death with your topless act too soon into the foreplay."

Patience rolled her eyes heavenward. "Something tells me it doesn't quite work like that. And after last night's debacle, I doubt he'll ever speak to me again."

"In that case, you've got no choice but to pick up one of those blokes out there on the dance floor. Go on. There's plenty to choose from."

A weighty sigh surged noisily through Patience's part-open mouth. "Do I have to? It doesn't seem right, begging for sex."

"Make your mind up, girl. You're like a bloody human yo-yo. Yes please, no thanks, yes please, no thanks. Do you want to kick your virginity's arse out the door or not?"

"Yes. I do."

"Like, as soon as possible?"

A firm nod. "Too bloody right."

"Then get out there, girl, and seduce somebody."

Patience hesitated, still in two minds. It was as if the desire to kick her virginity's arse out the door had never been realised.

"Now what's the matter?" asked Penny, hands upon hips, one eyebrow arched.

"Maybe I should just find myself a boyfriend to lose it with."

"That could take years."

Patience's lower jaw headed south. "Oh, thanks a lot. Do you think I'm minging or something?"

"No, of course not. All I'm saying is, don't waste your time trying to find that elusive relationship when there are plenty of easy willy-winkies out there for the taking."

"I think I'd be happier if the person who broke me in loved me."

Penny sighed. Loudly. "Patience. Listen to me. Don't run before you can walk."

"What's that supposed to mean?"

"The last thing you want to do is get seriously involved with the first guy who shows you any proper attention. Yeah, yeah, so he might be nice looking and treat you well. But what if he's crap at sex? You'll be buggered." And then an afterthought. "Of course, I don't mean buggered as in plugging the wrong hole. I mean —" The second afterthought of the sentence kicked in. "Actually, that could be the case if he's really shit at it."

"Penny," interrupted Patience, tired of her friend's insane drivel. "How about you get to the point?"

And so she did. "Sex is like shopping for clothes. You need to spend plenty of quality time window shopping, checking out all the latest fads and styles. Some you try on for size. Some you take home. Some you return for a full refund. And some you throw back on the rail straight away without even trying on. The best look good on you. The worst you wouldn't be seen dead with ever again. But the point is, you will never find exactly what you're looking for first time round. You've got to rummage through several mountains of useless jumble before you uncover that perfect outfit."

Patience smiled without humour. "How very poetic," she thought not.

Penny tossed her make up into a handbag the size of a suitcase — funny how everything else in life was forever shrinking, yet handbags seemed to grow larger every day — and struck the kind of pose usually reserved for topless models.

"How do I look?"

"Like a cheap tart."

Penny smiled. "Excellent. Let's find you some cock."

They journeyed from the solitude of the toilets to the near-thunderous din of the main room. The evening was in full swing. A wall-to-wall carpet of revellers bounced fervently to the deafening vibes delivered by the shaven-headed, stick-thin dude behind the turntables. Loud was an understatement. Nobody could hear what was being said to them, even by their closest neighbours. Unless the words were bellowed out, of course. Which would result in involuntary sprays of saliva distributed in a most unsolicited fashion.

Oh, how everybody wished tissues were provided as standard.

The two girls walked onwards until they reached the part of the room furthest away from the DJ booth. Several million decibels continued their relentless eardrum collisions, but at least shouting to the person next to you without allowing spittle to take flight could just about be achieved at this distance from the music. It was a result of sorts.

A twenty-something lass, blessed with cascading spirals of natural — and no doubt envy-inducing — auburn hair hovered by the edge of the dance floor, alcopop bottle in hand, head bopping to the rhythm. A younger female whose face screamed, "OMG, barely eighteen," but with the world-weary eyes of somebody pissed off with flashing her ID to endless sentries in monkey suits stood by her side.

Penny nudged Patience and pointed in the direction of the redhead. "Hey, look, it's Felicity down the road."

Felicity's face illuminated as the girls approached. Big eyes, bigger smile, a flap-handed finger-wiggle greeting.

"Oh, wow. Penny. Patience. What are you two doing here?"

"Same as you," came Penny's response. "A bit of a dance, a bit of a flirt, way too much alcohol. We'll all regret it in the morning, but hey, ho. One day at a time, that's what I always say."

"Cool." Felicity gestured to her accomplice. "This is Chantelle, the girl I was telling you about. My grandfather's carer."

Chantelle flung out her hand, flaunting a huge gemstone on her finger. "Fiancée actually," she boasted, smug grin used to full effect.

Patience took a closer look at the rock and gave a smirk. It was an oh-so-obvious glass replica with ambitions of being a diamond in the next life. Had a dodgy market trader sold it to Felicity's grandfather? Definitely. Was the old man aware of its lack of authenticity? Another definitely. Did Chantelle's blatant bimboism prevent her from knowing the difference between absolute genuine and downright bogus? Yay. Three definitelys in a row.

"Ah, yes," said Penny. "We heard you were getting married."

"It's so romantic," gushed Chantelle, her empty head already soaring through the clouds at break-neck speed. "I am such a lucky girl."

Patience frowned and indicated to the dance floor. "Am I seeing things?" she asked Felicity. "Or is that really your grandfather?"

Sure enough, the man in question was slap-bang in the thick of the dance floor, hands waving, hips wiggling, feet stomping. He was currently being accosted — though far from against his will — by a somewhat inebriated hen party troupe all dressed in pink fairy costumes. The sweat-soaked elderly gentleman looked rather out of place amidst the frantic crowds of drunk or high (or both at once) partygoers in his tweed blazer, beige slacks and trilby hat, but one fact couldn't be denied. He was having the time of his life.

Penny was equally surprised to see the old man strutting his stuff. "Bloody hell, you're right. It is him."

"Chantelle insisted on my grandfather joining us," explained Felicity. "He was hoping for a quiet night in on his own, but she can be very persuasive at times."

"Why the hell shouldn't my hubby-to-be come here?" asked Chantelle, vexed by where she thought the conversation was leading. "It's a free country. And eighty-seven is just a number, you ageist freaks."

"True," replied Penny. "But should a pensioner of that age really be exerting himself like that?"

"I agree," joined in Patience, concerned. "Especially with his heart condition."

Chantelle didn't take too kindly to their observations. "Leave him alone. He's enjoying himself." And in addition, "You're just jealous."

Patience and Penny rolled their eyes in unison. Repeatedly smashing the stupid tart's skull against the nearest available wall seemed like an enjoyable hobby to take up. But no. Self-control was to be the order of the day. Or rather, night.

Keep calm and buy more booze.

Chantelle was not done yet. "If the love of my life wants to boogie on down all night," she lectured, the acid tone in her voice signifying a virtual middle finger fitted with, "Swivel on this, bitches!" as standard, "far be it from me to stop him. So there."

"Fair enough," conceded Penny. "But don't forget. You're not married to him yet."

Chantelle screwed up her face. "What's that got to do with anything?"

"It means," was the response, "if he drops dead on that dance floor tonight, you won't get a single penny."

The face of Felicity's barely-out-of-nappies and soon-to-be step-grandmother iced over with impending horror. Her eyes flicked rapidly from side to side. Her mouth fell open. Her complexion lost its colour. A hard swallow. And then a decision. Chantelle flung herself into the chaos and plucked the old man from the clutches of the intoxicated hens.

"Time for us to head home, darling," she ordered, dragging him towards the exit. "It's way past your bedtime."

And they were gone. And then there were three.

Penny figured it was time to return to the plan that had brought them here. "Seen anybody you fancy yet, Patience?"

Patience scoffed, offering a pained expression.

"Why the funny noise and even funnier face?"

"Why do you think? This club, it's like a bloody cattle market. I mean, look at those two." Patience pointed to a young couple on the dance floor, groins buffing, lips pressed together, tongues swapped like phone numbers. "They might as well be having sex."

"They probably are." A wink. "It's called being intimate. Which incidentally, my dear Patience, is why we're here. It's the best place for you to bag yourself some guaranteed pussy-filling."

"I've got nothing against intimacy, but must they be so full-on in public? Is it really too much to ask for those—those dogs on heat to wait until they're behind closed doors?"

Penny smirked. "You prude."

"I am not a prude. I just think a little discretion and self control wouldn't go amiss, that's all."

Penny chuckled. "What did you think it would be like in this place, huh? A romantic dinner for two?"

A curious Felicity entered the conversation with, "Are you looking for a boyfriend, Patience?"

It was Penny who answered the query. "No. She's after an emergency fuck."

A quizzical look from Felicity. "What's the emergency?"

"She's desperate to lose her virginity."

"Oh, thanks a lot, Penny!" If looks could kill, her flatmate would be dead ten times over. "Let the whole bloody world know, why don't you?"

It was bad enough that Penny and Dave had discovered her lack of sexual achievement, but now Felicity had won herself a golden ticket to join the We Know Patience Is A Virgin Club.

Penny shrugged it off with, "She's our friend. She won't blab."

Patience was having none of it. "You promised me you wouldn't tell anybody. And now look what you've done. You've told somebody."

"Are you absolutely sure you're a virgin, Patience?" asked Felicity.

Patience threw her a double take. No, scrub that. She tossed across a triple take. An umpteen take, even. What the fuck? Was she absolutely sure she was a virgin? What had happened to the world? Strong doubt was cast whether or not she was still in the proverbial Kansas.

"Of course I'm bloody sure!"

Felicity backed away. "All right, all right. There's no need to take it out on me just because you've never felt a stiff one between your legs."

Oh, how wrong she was. Well, sort of. Patience had technically felt a stiff one between her legs yesterday afternoon. Geoff's stiff one. Trouble was, between her literal legs had been its final destination. His wife's unexpected return had prevented the train from bursting through the curtains of paradise and into her tunnel. So near yet so frigging far. And now, here she was, still a bloody virgin.

The path of true lust never ran smoothly.

"Don't worry, Patience," assured Penny. "When you wake up tomorrow morning, the dreaded V word will be a thing of the past. Look around you. You've got your pick of men tonight, all under one roof, all begging for pussy. This plan of mine is brilliant. It can't possibly fail."

Patience didn't share so much confidence. "Penny. I'm sure you'll agree, we've seen countless TV shows where one character says to another, 'It can't possibly fail.'"

"Yeah, so?"

"What usually happens in the end?"

"Um. Everything goes tits up."

"Exactly."

"Yeah, but that's fiction. This is real life."

Patience gave a tut and followed through with a sigh. No answer for that one.

"Right, Patience. Listen to me and listen good." Penny placed both hands upon her friend's shoulders and looked her straight in the eye, like a boxing coach giving the fighter a quick pep talk between rounds. "Catching the attention of men is not exactly difficult. But there are rules."

Patience's brow wrinkled in question. "Rules?"

Felicity found herself equally bemused. "I didn't think rules came into it. I thought it was a simple case of meet a guy, back to his place, open legs wide."

"Okay, maybe not rules," self-corrected Penny. "Think of them more as rough guidelines to make sure things run as smoothly as possible. Firstly, blow out any guys with girl's names. Example, Ashley or Lesley. They are always complete wankers. Probably their upbringing. You know, being forced to wear dresses as kids or something."

Patience could feel herself going all cross-eyed again.

"Sweaty blokes are also a big no-no," continued Penny. "Especially the ones you can smell before they come into view. And push away men who crowd you too much and invade your personal space. They'll be the clingy types. You definitely don't want that kind of hassle. Oh, and never, never, never go for a crappy dancer. If he hasn't got rhythm, he'll be totally shit in bed. Fact."

A weary Patience intervened with, "I am not two years old, Penny. I'm sure I'll be perfectly able to weed out the tossers, thank you very much."

Penny cast a dismissive flick of the hand. "Fine. Don't listen to the pearls of wisdom I've accumulated over my long and distinguished sexual career."

Patience and Felicity exchanged incredulous glances. Was this girl for real?

"And above all, don't be too choosy," was Penny's concluding advice. "You can't afford to be."

A young, skinny lad, eighteen or nineteen at the most, possibly partaking in his clubbing debut, made himself known to Penny. A courageous move, Patience figured, for her flatmate could effortlessly eat this boy for breakfast and still have enough appetite left for corn-flakes. Or was he simply too naïve and inexpert to read her somewhat supercilious demeanour? Only time would tell. Say, ten seconds at the most.

"Hey. What's a nice girl like you doing in a—"

Penny cut short the boy's cliché claptrap by groping his pelvic package. Was she impressed? No way. It stuck out a mile. Her dissatisfaction, that is, not his wotsits.

"Go away, little boy. Take your maggot elsewhere."

Ouch. Even Patience could feel the sting, and she was far from being on the receiving end. The lad's mouth fell open in a fusion of shock and disappointment. Then came the gritted teeth of resentment, closely followed by the indifferent sneer of somebody who pretended not to care too much about the knockback because he had a girlfriend anyway.

"Lesbian," he growled, stiffening his middle finger in Penny's direction before storming over to the bar to no doubt drown his sorrows.

Patience grinned. Okay, okay, so she'd been way too ambitious with her ten second estimate. The poor baby hadn't even lasted five. Of course, it came as no surprise. Especially after his delivery of a chat up line that predated the invention of being chatted up.

"Right. Here's the plan," came Penny's revisit to the matter in hand, namely, the reason they were all present and correct at this particular waterhole. "Patience. Get your arse on that dance floor. Me and Felicity down the road will find a vacant table and watch from afar."

They always called her Felicity down the road. Even to her face.

Then Patience realised, "You're leaving me on my own?"

Penny nodded. "It's a necessity. Guys hate approaching groups of girls together. They have this weird notion that we'll gang up on them and make them look stupid."

"I don't know where they get that idea from," chuckled Felicity, tongue firmly pressed against cheek.

"Nor do I," said Penny. "They're perfectly able to look stupid without our intervention." A grin, then, "But what they simply cannot resist is a girl dancing on her lonesome. It's every man's dream. An available prize for the taking. All you need to do is wiggle your hips and wobble your wibblies. Guaranteed, you'll have men circling round you like vultures to a carcass."

Oh, great. Compared to dead meat. What a lovely thought.

"Flutter your eyelashes at the bloke you fancy the most and he'll come a-running right on over to you. It never fails."

"But what do I say to him?"

"Doesn't matter. He won't be listening anyway. He'll be too busy working out how best to get you back to his place."

"You make it all sound so easy."

"That's because it is."

"You also make it all sound so dirty."

Her flatmate giggled. "The dirtier the better, if you ask me."

Patience froze on the sidelines like a would-be swimmer refusing to dive in for fear of freezing water. Penny spotted such stubborn apprehension and nudged the nervous girl onto the dance floor.

"Time to shine, Patience Hope."

Chapter 10

Sex on the Dance Floor

Patience shuffled with trepidation over to the nearest available clearing on the dance floor. She turned around and peered at her flatmate who seemed the greatest of distances away now. An uncomfortable shrug. What now? Penny stood on the sidelines, egging her on. Dance, girl, dance. Patience took a deep breath. It was now or never. No turning back. She composed herself. And then began to move to the music.

She was hardly the dancer type—such moves would never win her any trophies—but at least she was making the effort. Sort of. In technical terms, the girl was swaying from left to right and back again, with a scattering of random arm motions thrown in for good measure. Although, surveying the area, she found most of her peers doing the same thing, give or take a few extra arm shakes. So did it matter that Patience was one of many rather awkward owners of two left feet? No. Not at all. And besides, her mission was not to impress all and sundry with her dancing skills. There was only one true reason for her presence on that dance floor.

Man-bait.

"You go, girl," called Penny from the floor's edge, like she was cheering on her favourite football team.

Patience smiled at her friend, glad for the encouragement. Being amongst this army of alcohol-fuelled floor dwellers was a nerve-racking experience. She felt alone. Isolated. Naked, even. And not just because she was wearing next to nothing. But then it all started to change for the better. It was weird. The more she lost herself in the music, the less self-conscious she felt. Dancing had never been anywhere near the top of her list of priorities, yet here she was in the thick of it all, actually beginning to enjoy herself.

Another shout from Penny. This time, a warning. "One word of advice. Well, six words actually. Watch out for the grinding guy."

Patience made a face. Eh? "Who the hell is the grinding guy?"

Penny smirked. "You'll find out." And then she disappeared into the shadows with Felicity.

Patience shrugged off such a bizarre caution and continued to dance. Her simple left to right swaying quickly evolved. Her moves became bold and imaginative as she immersed herself in the music. Buttock wiggles, hip circles, bosom jiggles, the lot. The girl found herself overwhelmed by the atmosphere. Engaged by the basslines. Controlled by the beats. She raised both arms. Closed her eyes. And smiled to herself.

She was jolted back to reality by a sharp collision from behind. What the fuck? She twisted her head to investigate. A rather plump man, late twenties perhaps, with a chubby face that had no doubt felt many a cheek tweak from Great Auntie Maureen as a child, had latched onto her, drilling his groin into her buttocks. He wrapped both arms around her waist and gyrated harder, as if the girl's alarmed grimace was an invitation to use her body to simulate sexual intercourse.

And then she realised. It must be him.

The grinding guy.

From then on, things went from bad to worse. The grinding guy slobbered at her neck like a rabid dog as he pushed his trouser-bulge harder against her bottom. Grinding was too kind a word for this type of assault. Chafing, more like. Or eroding. One clammy hand discovered the soft flesh of her right thigh, his fingers exploring just beneath the bottom hem of her skirt. The other headed upwards towards her left breast, cupping it with his palm. This idiot seemed to be enjoying himself, but for Patience, it was nothing short of a nightmare. Enough was enough. Such unsolicited filth had to stop.

Patience twisted around, grabbed his testicle region and squeezed as hard as she could.

"Argh, you bitch!" the grinding guy squealed, knocking away her hand and stumbling back a few paces.

"Oh, I'm sorry," growled Patience, narrowed eyes, wrinkled nose.

"I thought you were into the rough stuff."

"Fucking lesbo," were the final words before his swift departure.

Strange how girls who said no were always deemed gay by rejected males. After all, it couldn't possibly be that the girls simply didn't fancy them.

Undeterred, Patience eased back into it all and submerged herself in the rhythm, the sounds, the lights, the elation. As she boogied, she scanned the locality, on the look-out for talent. What she found was a considerable amount of competition. All around her, youthful females with peroxide locks, bright warpaint and legs up to their armpits paraded themselves to the hilt. Most were donned in miniskirts and low-cut tops that made Patience look way too overdressed in comparison. Nothing was left to the imagination. Everything was on display, and there for the taking, no holds barred, a meat raffle of sorts. Naturally, buzzing around them like flies to fresh dung were floods of young crisp-shirted males — undeniable fact, their mums still did their ironing — with puppy-dog eyes and salivating chops, all hoping for a winning ticket.

It was then when Patience realised. She appeared to be the oldest person on the dance floor. No wonder nobody had taken any notice of her. Apart from the recently rejected grinding guy, of course, who was probably nursing his wounds in a dark and secluded corner of the club. And then she thought about it. Why would blokes go for an old stale sandwich when silver platters of fresh volly-vonty thingies were on offer, left, right and centre? Oh, God. This was bad. At twenty-five, she was already a has-been. And this was before her sex life had even reached first base.

Then she caught his eye. A rather handsome chap of, say, the same age as her. She smiled sweetly at him. He smiled back. Cool. The first move had been well and truly made. She looked away in the coy manner she'd seen done in chick flicks, then returned her sights to him. There he was, not five feet away, still smiling at her. Wow. Was he to become her first sexual partner? A proper sexual partner, that is, where actual penetration was a possibility? She certainly hoped so. He was kind of cute.

The man headed her way. Patience froze on the spot, unable to move or speak, an idiot smile permanently etched on her rigid face.

As he approached, his smile widened, his eyes sparkled. This was it. The beginning of something special. And then—

—he sailed right past. Into the arms of a woman who was dancing directly behind her.

Patience's heart, face, shoulders, her whole body sank as the couple's mutual familiarity revealed the very bombshell she didn't want to learn. The two of them were obviously an item. Bugger. He hadn't been smiling at her at all. She'd practically been see-through enough for the lovers to gaze at each other. God knows how. She was a mass of carbon just like everybody else. A barrier of skin, muscle, bone, blood and slimy, wobbly bits. Bugger again. In fact, bugger and double bugger. A sigh of despair launched the official announcement. Patience Hope was nothing more than a human window.

Masking her disappointment as best as she could, she jumped back aboard the bus that was the music and returned to dancing. Another man, a little older, late twenties, early thirties perhaps, glanced across at her. Patience smiled at him. He tipped his head and beamed back. Cool. A fish was biting on her line. Time to reel him in. Oh, hold on. She checked behind her. No hidden woman this time. Good. Which meant one thing. This guy was smiling at her. Just her. Nobody else. Excellent. Now, what was it that Penny had advised? Ah, yes, that's it. Flutter your eyelashes and he'll come a-running.

And so she did. She fluttered them, big-time.

The man literally hurtled in her direction. Patience's face lit up. Wow, it worked. It was then when he examined her eyes, pulling apart eyelids with thumb and forefinger.

What the fuck? "What the hell are you doing?"

"You must have something in your eye," he replied, concerned.

Eh? Was this guy mad or what? "No, I haven't."

The man looked a little foolish. "But—you were blinking so rapidly."

"Could you please unhand me?" she requested, not too happy about her eyelids being stretched to breaking point.

The man let go. "It's all right, I'm qualified. I'm a doctor."

Ooh. A doctor. Renewed interest. Instantly forgiven for the rather impromptu medical procedure.

"A surgeon?" asked Patience, swaying her body to the music as she spoke.

The doctor danced in close proximity and responded with, "No, no. Just a GP."

"Yes, but it's a sexy profession, right?"

"Hardly. All I seem to treat are bouts of flu, sprained wrists and haemorrhoids."

They both laughed.

Okay, so maybe they'd got off on the wrong foot. Or rather, the wrong eye. But this doctor could be the one to turn her into a fully-fledged woman. Her first fuck, a career man. Mmm. It sounded good. Penny would be so jealous when she heard about it. Bedding a doctor was a sordid fantasy straight out of a steamy romantic novel. Penny hadn't even managed it and she worked at a hospital. But it looked like Patience's luck was well and truly in. She just hoped his stethoscope wouldn't be too cold.

Patience drew herself closer and boldly wrapped her arms around the doctor's neck. Only, he didn't seem to respond too well to the gesture.

"What are you doing?" he asked.

"What does it look like?"

"Um. I'm not sure."

"I'd like you to give me a full body examination." A wicked grin soon followed.

"Sorry. The surgery's closed."

Patience broke the embrace, taken aback by his response. This was a joke, right? Then it came to her. He was playing along. Yeah, that's what he was doing. Teasing her.

"Stop acting so innocent, Doc." A wink. "You know exactly what I'm after."

The doctor looked horrified. "Are you drunk?"

"A little. Aren't you?"

"No. I've only had a couple of beers."

It was all becoming rather annoying. The scenario didn't seem to be playing out in the way she'd hoped. Why was her doctor not taking the frigging hint? Was he too dim to realise what was going on? Only one option remained. Spelling it out in words of no more than one syllable.

"Look, just take me back to your place," she blurted out with heavy insistence, embracing him once more.

The doctor swallowed hard, momentarily speechless. Then he just about managed to croak the words, "I can't."

Patience's face dropped. "Why not? Don't you like me?"

His face turned apologetic as he freed himself from her clutches. "I'm happily married. Sorry."

Oh, for fuck's sake. "Oh. I see."

"I don't usually frequent places like this, but my wife insisted on it. It's her friend's birthday, you see. There's a whole party of us here."

"Do I look as if I want to hear your life story?" A nasty line for sure, but she was seriously pissed off with the man.

The doctor made his excuses and left to rejoin his wife and party. Patience stood motionless at the heart of a ring of movement, staring blankly into space. She tried her hardest not to let the rejection affect her, but couldn't help herself. She was not fortunate enough to be co-cooned in a thick skin like Penny. At times like this, she wished she was.

Argh! This was getting serious. Where the fuck was the guaranteed sex? It was a nightclub, for God's sake. The epitome of debauchery. Action of the fumbling kind was always on offer. So why not tonight? It was like visiting a supermarket and finding no groceries. Watching a comedy with no jokes. Or being trapped in a bar with no beer.

It. Was. Seriously. Not. Happening.

"Hi."

Patience turned in the direction of the latest male voice. To her surprise, it was the young lad with the maggot of a penis who Penny had turned down earlier. He didn't look too bad. Quite cute actually. Penny hadn't really given him a chance. The girl had spat him out without even tasting the flavour. So therefore, Patience decided to offer him a fair crack of the whip. After all, she was fast running out of suitors. Small cock, yes, but if he knew how to use it, he'd be serving her breakfast in bed tomorrow morning. Just one fuck was required to set her free from the prison of virgins. And that's all that mattered.

"Hi," she greeted back. "I'm Patience. What's your name?"

The boy smiled. "It's Lee." Then he came out with, "What's a nice girl like you doing in a—"

"Shut up," she interrupted, abrupt, in control. "Dance with me."

Patience held out both arms. The lad moved forward and embraced her, beaming from ear to ear, as if his birthday, Christmas, Easter and Pancake Day had all come at once. As they danced close, his hands brushed up and down her back. His breathing became heavy. And she could feel a strong heart ready to burst free from his chest. Was this the first time he'd held a woman in his arms? Possibly. Then she had a thought. What if he was a virgin too? Ooer. Two virgins in one bed would be twice as awkward. A double disaster. Ah, well. He'd have to do. Now, what was it they said about beggars and choosers?

One of Lee's hands found its way onto her bottom. Tut, tut, she thought. A bold move, but at the same time rather mischievous. They'd only been dancing for a minute or so. It was too early for such intimacy, surely. She then reminded herself of why she was here. A quest to find a suitable mate. So therefore, during her selection process, some dance floor foreplay wouldn't go amiss. And let's face it. Arse touching was hardly the crime of the—

Without warning, that same hand journeyed over to the front of her thighs and shot up her skirt. His fingers grappled at the gusset of her underwear, eager to bag a touch of her pussy.

"Oi," glurked Patience, shocked by such heavy audacity. "Don't you think that's a bit forward?"

Lee bowed his head, full of remorse. "Sorry." And then the guilty hand instead cupped one of her breasts. "Is that any better?" he asked, as if a grab of tit was a lesser crime.

Patience pulled away, annoyed, angry, exasperated. Were tits, arse and pussy all men saw in a woman? Whatever happened to being wooed? Like, gradually.

Lee looked confused. "What did I do wrong?"

"Sorry, Lee. This isn't working."

Sod this for a laugh. She didn't feel like dancing any more. Between them, the man who walked right through her like a ghost through a wall, the married doctor who took his job far too seriously and small-cocked demon groper Lee, they had taken the fun out of it all. And who could possibly forget the grinding guy? Dear God, what a freak.

Sure, Patience had arrived at this establishment to find herself a fuck, so why hadn't she accepted either Lee or the grinding guy's somewhat dubious advances without question? Simple. These two men were far from ideal. They couldn't even be classed as factory seconds. Why? Because they were too selfish. All that groping and buffing had been for self-gratification only, and not part of the shared experience she'd hoped for. Everything for them, nothing for the girl.

Major frigging turn-off.

Yeah, yeah, okay, so searching for a quick sex session with anybody willing to donate their genital organs to the cause was hardly a reliable method to uncover the best sex ever, and would undoubtedly attract the kind of male who saw a woman as a mere hole to come inside, but did it really have to be that way?

Patience was not exactly fussy with her demands. She'd hardly sent a ransom note. Dual satisfaction, that's all she desired. To feel just as much pleasure as the man. Two orgasms, one each. His and hers. Was it really too much to ask?

Clearly, yes.

Time to leave the dance floor.

Patience steered herself through the hectic disorder of drunken revellers and past the saddo sideliners waiting by the floor's edge. Sideliners were men, usually of the short and weedy variety, who lacked the confidence to hit the dance floor, so instead populated the sidelines, drinks in hand, hoping in vain for women to approach them. Hah, fat chance. Not even Patience felt like bothering with them. Therefore, success would probably not be smiling down on those idiots tonight.

She wallowed without too much zeal into the seating area. She found Penny and Felicity occupying a table. Two men of around twenty or so were chatting them up. She plonked herself down on the nearest available chair and blew out a long-trailing sigh of despair, desolation, despondency and anything else closely related, especially if the prefix was des.

Penny glanced across at her. "I assume you didn't pull."

"Total washout."

And with a smirk, Penny added, "Grinding guy?"

Patience emitted a strange sound as a reply. A cross between a scoff, a cough, and the kind of throaty grate men always made when clearing out their passages of mucus just before spitting out those horrible green globules of snot. It probably meant, "Yes, met him, got rid of him, what a wanker."

Penny chuckled. "On the dance floor, a girl is never three feet from a grinding guy."

Patience shook her head in a moment of disillusion. "They warn us not to accept sweets from strangers, and to never get into their cars, but the first time we hear of the dangers of the grinding guy is when he's smashing into our posteriors like a battering ram."

"It goes with the territory." Penny then indicated to the two lads. "Oh, by the way. This is—um—what did you say your names were again?"

"Will."

"Matt."

They both tipped nods of greeting.

"Hello," Patience muttered in a half-hearted fashion, not wishing for too much involvement.

Matt returned his attention to Felicity. "So. What do they call you, gorgeous?"

"Felicity down the road," she replied.

Matt screwed up his face. "That's your name?"

"That's what everybody calls me. Even people who don't live up the road from me. It started off as a nickname at school, but it's kind of stuck. How insane is that, huh?"

Matt had no answer for that, so he advanced the discussion. "Has anybody told you, Felicity down the road, you've got the most beautiful ginger hair?"

"Auburn, Matt. Auburn," sternly corrected Felicity. "You can't say ginger any more. It's racist."

"Oh, right." A couple of confused blinks from Matt, clearly unsure whether the girl was joking or deadly serious, then a recovery. "I've always wondered. Are you, like, ging—um—sorry—auburn down below too?"

Felicity grinned. "Buy me another drink and you might find

out."

Like a shot, and even more like a sucker, Matt made a frantic bee-line towards the bar.

At the lonely end of the table, Patience sat in silence, studying the activity going on around her. People everywhere. Drinking. Chatting. Laughing. Canoodling. Everything. She was right in the heart of a so-cial jungle, yet she didn't feel part of it at all. She saw herself more as an outsider. An onlooker. An observer of sorts. Like a tourist peering through the bars of a lion's cage. Only, in this particular zoo, it was mating season all year round.

Except for Patience Hope.

She rose from her seat, head hung low. It was no good. Time to concede. She'd tried. She'd failed. Miserably. If she couldn't even pull in a nightclub, then what hope did she have? It was obvious. This girl was destined to remain a virgin forever. And then an afterthought begged for attention inside her brain. Was never having sexual inter-course really so terrible? Nuns seemed to manage it. And they never complained. In fact, didn't they spend all day singing? So what was she fretting about? A pure and virginal life wouldn't be so bad after all.

That's when she spotted him standing by the bar. An attractive specimen, well groomed, nicely dressed. The man took note of the scrutiny bestowed upon him and threw across a warm smile. This was followed by a friendly wave. Patience returned both gestures. The ob-ject of her interest smiled once more and drained his glass.

It was then when he beckoned her to join him.

Chapter 11

Back to His Place

Patience's face shone like a full moon on a clear night. OMG. Finally. Male attention at last. As she approached the handsome man beside the bar, butterflies fluttered in her stomach. Actually, it felt more like a swarm of bees buzzing around in there. He was most certainly a striking example of a male. In fact, no doubt about it, he was the most attractive man she'd ever laid eyes on.

She rested her butt on the bar stool next to him. The most attractive man she'd ever laid eyes on introduced himself as Nathan.

"Pleased to meet you, Nathan," she greeted in her finest telephone voice. First impressions and all that jazz. "I'm Patience."

"Nice name."

"You reckon? I think it's awful. My parents, what were they thinking?"

"Maybe they didn't want you to pop out so soon." And then he tittered at his own quip.

Patience giggled. Just for show. She didn't really get the joke. Had it been a joke? Cue the virtual uncertain shrug of her mind's shoulders.

Nathan held up his empty glass. "Drink?"

"Yes. I do. A bit too much sometimes."

"No, no, I meant, would you like a drink?"

"Oh, I see." Nervy giggle. Playful roll of eyes. "Sorry, Nathan. I'm not always this scatty." Liar. "I'm just a bit nervous around you, that's all."

"Why? I'm nothing special."

Patience begged to differ. Although house points were deserv-

119

edly awarded to her prospective suitor for not acting like a Billy Big Bollocks and thinking he's all that and everything.

Drinks were duly purchased. The two of them migrated away from the bar and found a lone table in the far corner of the room.

Nathan commented, "I don't think I've ever seen you in here before."

"Nightclubs aren't really my thing. Too sleazy for my liking."

"So why grace this—" Open air quote fingers. "—seedy joint—" And close air quotes. "—with your presence tonight?"

"My flatmate Penny, she reckons it's the best place for me to lose my—" Patience suddenly realised. She zipped herself, then stumbled onwards with a half-arsed recovery in the form of, "Um. To lose my—self and have a good time."

"And are you having a good time?"

Cue the coy smile. "I am now."

They shared a moment.

Nathan pointed to the dance floor. "Would you like to dance?"

You what? And risk losing the newly acquired Nathan to her rivals. No frigging way was she prepared to let him anywhere near those bottom-wiggling, scantily clad, prepubescent tarts. Tonight, he was her property.

"How about we stay right here?" she suggested. "And, you know—talk and stuff."

Nathan smiled. "Okay. If that's what you want."

Good boy. "So. Nathan." Important question coming up. "Do you have a girlfriend at the moment?"

"Nope. Young, free and single."

Fucking yes! "Aw. Such a shame."

Nathan shrugged it off in a that's life kind of way.

"So how come you're not taken?"

"I guess I haven't met the right girl yet."

He has now. "I'm sure she'll turn up some time."

Nathan nodded. "I hope so."

Patience felt good inside. Her confidence was growing. The convo was going well. In fact, brilliantly. This was it for sure. Nathan was destined to be the taker of her virginity. All she needed to do was keep him interested.

Note to self: Seriously, girl. Do not fuck this up.

"Do you still live with your parents, Nathan?" She bloody hoped not.

"No way. I've got a place of my own. It's only a rented bedsit, but it beats being told what to do by my folks."

Fucking double yes! No girlfriend. And a roof over his head. Things were certainly on the up. Her chosen penis — um, man — had somewhere private for the pair of them to retire. Excellent. A bachelor pad, all ready and waiting for the surgical removal of her virginity. Come sunrise tomorrow morning, she'd wake up a fully qualified woman.

"I'm guessing you're about twenty-three," Patience surmised. "Am I right?"

"Close. Twenty-two. How old are you?"

Oof! Didn't he know it was rude to ask a woman her age? Sure, she was only three years older than he was, but three years in nightclub terms was a decade. Eek! The truth could scare him off. And that was a disaster she had to prevent at all costs. It was time to get clever.

"How old do you think I am?"

Yes. Brilliant idea. Avoid the actual answer by suggesting a guessing game. Nathan would flatter her for sure by taking a few years off his estimate. He'd probably say twenty-one. Men always did in this type of situation. And then she would congratulate him on getting her age exactly right. Yep. Twenty-one. Full marks, Nathan.

Yeah, yeah, so it was a little white lie. But completely valid and necessary in context.

"Um. Twenty-five?"

Bastard. "Good guess. Exactly right."

Nathan's eyes glinted. "Cool. I've always had a bit of a thing for the older woman."

Older woman? Older frigging woman? Patience's smile dutifully shone, yet inside, a large chunk of her soul died a horrible death.

"Lucky me," she managed to say.

"Funnily enough, saying that," Nathan continued, "I've only ever gone out with teenagers. Probably my downfall. They're more trouble than they're worth. Way too childish. But talking to a mature woman like you is a breath of fresh air."

Mature? Only wine, cheese and whisky matured well, and as a result, tasted divine on the palate of society. This rule, however, did in no way apply to women. The Department Of Cutthroat Social Acceptance only ever saw mature in human terms as old. Ancient. Overripe. Wrinkled. Crumbling. And dispensable.

Mature woman? Hah! Thinly veiled as a supposed compliment, yet in truth, a polite way of saying old hag.

Oh, why was she fretting about it so much? Nathan was still here, sitting opposite, talking to her, looking at her, smiling at her. This meant he was interested. So bloody sort yourself out, girl.

A young lady, barely of legal drinking age, floated past in possibly the tightest denim shorts ever worn. The contours of her slender legs were complimented by close-fitting black leggings and her black bra was clearly visible under a semi-transparent top. She caught Nathan's eye. They exchanged smiles. He gave her an up-down glance of lip-licking approval. She loved every second of it. He followed her with his eyes. She offered him an extra fleeting look, coupled with a cheeky grin as she headed for the bar.

Bugger. Patience had assumed Nathan and his man-bits already had her name stamped on them. But now she realised the stake she'd claimed faced the threat of younger flesh. Multi-bugger. It was no good. She needed to up her game. Be more direct. And usher the man away from this ruthless pit of temptation as soon as possible.

Patience delivered a polite cough. Ahem! Nathan's attention — and eyes — returned.

"Take me back to your place. Now."

The sheer bluntness of her statement astonished Nathan. His mouth opened wide, releasing a family of vague croaks.

Patience grimaced. Oh, God. Had it sounded too much like a direct order? Too demanding? Too blunt? Too desperate, even?

"What's the matter?" she dared to ask.

Nathan peered at his wristwatch. "It's only eleven. This place doesn't shut up shop until four in the morning."

Patience made a face. This guy had to be frigging kidding. "A girl asks you to take her home and all you want to do is stay for more drinks?"

"No, I — um — "

Paranoia reared its most hideous head. "Don't you like me? Do you think I'm a monster or something?" Then jealousy tried its luck. "Or do you find Miss Black Bra more appealing?"

"It's not that."

"Then what is it?" Oh, God. Could it be the Patience hormone? "I'm not a virgin, you know." Argh! Why bring that up? Idiot!

"I didn't say you were."

"Good." Let that be the end of the V convo. "Because I'm not. I've had sex loads of times." Shut the fuck up, girl!

"It's just—I'm a bit surprised, that's all. You don't seem the type who would be so—" A struggle for an apt word. " —easy."

Patience placed her hands upon his. "I'm not. But every now and then, a girl has needs. You know, of the bouncing up and down on somebody's cock variety." God, did she really say that? Not like her at all, but, ooh, it felt so liberating. What did she have lined up for an encore? "So are you taking me home or not?" Wow. Talk about bringing the house down.

A muted Nathan stared at her for a moment. A delighted smile then made itself known on his face. "Okay. Let's go."

They both stood up and headed hand in hand across the room.

"Oh. Would you excuse me for a moment?" said Patience. "I need to speak to my friend."

Nathan nodded.

Patience plucked Penny from her chair and steered the girl away from Felicity and the two admirers. "Boardroom. Now."

The boardroom in question was the ladies' toilets. This was where all discussions, strategic planning and whatever else, concerning males had been held since the beginning of time. The very reason why women always visited the loo in pairs.

See, guys? The pair thing was not because they had lesbian tendencies. Shame on you for thinking that.

"I think I've cracked it," Patience squealed excitedly. "His name's Nathan and he's well fit."

Penny was pleased for her. "Good on you, girl. Are you heading back to our place or his?"

"His." And then a curious frown. "Why do you ask? Are you and Felicity down the road planning on taking those blokes home?"

Penny shook her head in a like hell we are kind of way. "We'll get them to ply us with a few more drinks, then blow them out, big-time. I've had a much better offer from Dave." Penny wiggled her eyebrows. "He just texted me. Reckons he's got an unexpected erection he needs assistance with."

For the duration of the taxi ride to Nathan's bedsit, an ecstatic beam spanned across the entire width of Patience's face. Excited was an understatement. Keyed up to almost bursting point, the swarm of bees in her stomach had now evolved into a herd of rutting stags. So this was what going home with somebody was like, huh? Maybe she'd been missing out on all the fun of one-night stands by being a —

Now, what was it that Penny had called her? Ah, yes, that's right. A prude. Hah! Penalised for being sensible enough not to open her legs for every Tom, Dick and Nathan. What was the world coming to?

Empty sex, promiscuity and all their sleazy cousins had never floated her boat. Patience had always hoped for more romantic gestures. Having doors opened for her. Wooed gently by candlelight. And not pressured into a first date fuck. She'd always favoured the getting to know each other first approach before taking any kind of genital plunge. If such views and preferences made her a prude, then so be it.

Hold on a minute. If she detested the one-night stand and all that it stood for, why was she so keen tonight to slip out of her clothes and straight into Nathan's duvet? A five minute conversation with the guy and the subsequent cab journey back to his place hardly constituted getting to know each other properly first. It was against everything she believed in. Then right between the eyes, the reason why suddenly hit her. And as a result, everything became crystal clear.

Minute by minute, second by second, grain by grain, the hourglass of her virginal status was losing its sand.

Nathan's humble abode was part of an old and somewhat run-down converted house. Judging by the number of doorbells jostling for space in a mismatched column, there were at least another nine neighbouring bedsits. The building boasted an intercom security system, albeit mega-ancient—its heyday estimated at around the time of Christ—but the lone brick that permanently held the main door open for all and sundry to freely come and go as they pleased seemed to defeat the object.

They both entered a narrow communal lobby. Nathan slotted his key into the first door they arrived at. Patience was relieved to learn that his place was on the ground floor. Just one look at the dilapidated staircase at the end of the hallway forewarned her of the dangers of feet plunging through rotten woodwork. Top floor tenants no doubt risked their lives with every ascent or descent on a daily basis.

"Ah, home shit home," joked Nathan as he ambled into the bedsit and switched on the light.

Patience followed him in. She surveyed the vicinity with pleasant surprise as Nathan closed the door behind her. All predicted fears of having to endure a typical single man's squalid bachelor pad were betrayed in a flash by the shocking cleanliness of the place. The far side of the bedsit doubled up as a kitchen. Well, a cupboard, small worksurface and sink, to be exact. And shock horror. Not one food-encrusted plate in sight. A portable TV, a DVD player and a decent-sized stereo all took pride of place on some kind of fancy media stand. The carpet was in good condition, irrefutably vacuumed on a regular basis. And a sofabed, the dominant feature of the room, was readily pulled out and graced with two pillows and a duvet. Patience deduced from all gathered evidence that the plan of action upon arriving home drunk in the middle of the night was to simply fall straight into bed.

Good thinking.

"Do you employ a cleaner?" she asked.

He gave a chuckle. "Why, what did you expect? Piles of washing up, dirty socks and empty beer cans everywhere?"

She had to admit, everything Nathan reeled off had been on her worry list prior to entering the bedsit. Only, she'd also predicted countless screwed up wank tissues scattered across the floor, a mere lob distance from a laptop or a prized DVD porn collection.

"Something like that," was all she could think of to say.

He took it all in good spirits. "Believe it or not, some of us lads are perfectly house-trained."

Nathan relieved himself of his footwear and retired to the so-fabed. He made himself comfortable on top of the duvet. And then he suggestively patted the vacant half.

"Don't be shy. Come and join me."

Patience beamed with glee. She kicked off her shoes and rested herself beside him. There, she gazed into his eyes. He peered into hers. Her heart began to beat faster with the anticipation of what was about to happen. This was it. Her virginity would soon be nothing more than a distant memory. Her time had finally arrived.

He drew his head forward. Their lips said hello to each other. Soft, sporadic pecks at first, soon promoted to full-on volatile passion as their mouths held onto each other for dear life. She wrapped her arms around him, grasping fervently at his back muscles through the thin cotton barricade of his shirt. He placed a hand upon her stomach. Discovering bare skin, he explored beneath her blouse where eager fingertips caressed the soft, warm flesh of her torso.

Nathan's lips bid farewell to her mouth and journeyed slowly downward, planting hot kisses upon her cheeks, her neck, her shoulders, until finally reaching the point where collar met bosom. Patience moaned with elated approval as his hungry tongue burrowed deep into her cleavage.

Oh, God, she thought. Absolute heaven. It seemed as though Nathan knew exactly which buttons to press to turn her on, as if he'd digested the Patience Hope operating manual, word for word. She could feel herself becoming moist down below. Dripping wet, in fact. Oh, wow. Never in a million years did she think her pussy would be crying with happiness over the prospect of sex with a nightclub dragback. But here she was. Loving it.

One by one, he unfastened the buttons of her blouse. She did the same with his shirt. He impressed the girl by unhooking her bra with one hand. Party trick apparently. She yearned to ask how many women he'd undressed to reach such a pinnacle in his talent, but decided against it. She was probably better off not knowing.

With all above-the-waist garments discarded, Nathan lay upon the girl, kissing her, touching her, licking her, biting her. Patience slid both hands inside the seat of his trousers and squeezed his buttocks as he nuzzled hungrily on her nipples. She then manoeuvred one such hand to the front where she discovered his hidden treasure. Wrapping her fingers around his hard cock, she began to masturbate him. Judging by the murmurs he emitted whilst sucking on her tits, she was doing a grand job.

Nathan grappled with his trousers and underwear, yanking them down to his knees. This gave Patience more room to play with his erect dick. She pumped his shaft with vigour as he went about hitching up her skirt. Everything was moving so fast now. Unbridled passion had firmly taken a foothold. Parting her legs, he didn't bother to remove her thong. Instead, he pulled aside the gusset, revealing moist, pink lips.

"Ooh, yeah," he murmured, smiling. "Nice looking pussy."

Aw. What a lovely compliment. "Thank you."

He took control of his cock back from Patience's hand and aimed it towards her vagina. She pushed him away.

"Ah, ah, ah." Out of her handbag came a condom.

Nathan's face sank. "Do I have to?"

"Yes," she responded in no uncertain terms.

He nodded, then rolled it over his dick. And play resumed. She opened wide, allowing him to guide his penis between her legs. His swollen tip slid effortlessly along her wet crack until it met her inviting, pouting entrance.

Patience's heart was all a-flutter. Her time had finally arrived. There would be no wife coming home unexpectedly this time. Nothing could possibly stop what was about to happen. This was her one true moment.

There came a knock at the door.

"Shit," cursed Nathan under his breath.

With both hands, Patience held onto his penis, preventing the man's planned retreat. "Ignore it," she whispered sharply. "We're busy."

Nathan glanced at her in silence, considering her suggestion.

Another knock. Louder this time.

"Don't answer it." She hoped her request didn't sound too much like a desperate plea. "It's Saturday night. Pretend you're out."

Nathan seemed unsure of his next move. "What if it's important?"

She indicated to the hard cock that rested against her pussy. "Believe me, Nathan. Right now, nothing is more important than this."

The knock evolved into a succession of urgent fist thumps.

"Open up, Nathan!" It was a girl's voice. "I know you're in there. Your light's on."

There was a look of alarm on his face. "Fuck, it's her."

WTF? "Who?"

The man who owned the penis that Patience needed so badly blew out a weighty sigh. He pulled away from her clutches, stood up and restored his below-the-waist attire to original factory settings. He then headed in the direction of the disturbance.

"Oh, for fuck's sake," growled Patience, disappointed in him.

Another frigging wasted condom. Two had now bitten the dust in the same way. Rolled on. Aimed. Bloody interrupted. She only had one left.

She sat up, donned her blouse and proceeded to button the garment as quickly as she could. The discarded bra, relegated to her handbag.

Nathan opened the door to a young bubblegum-chewing filly in a skirt even shorter than Patience's borrowed effort. The girl took note of his bare chest and threw him a scornful sneer.

"Not disturbing anything, am I?"

Oh, God. That line again.

Nathan was in no way pleased to see her. "What do you want, Aimee?"

The girl addressed as Aimee floated past him, uninvited. She smirked at the now-standing Patience and her clumsy attempt at straightening her skirt.

"Who are you? Latest girlfriend?"

Patience tried her hardest not to appear intimidated by the brash teen. "My name's Patience. I only met Nathan tonight."

"Looks like I arrived just in time. Before any permanent damage was done."

Patience. A quizzical frown. "What's that supposed to mean?"

Before Aimee could reply, Nathan cut in with, "Get lost, Aimee. You're not welcome here."

Aimee scoffed. Loudly. "You didn't say that on the night you bedded me."

It was obvious. Aimee had no intention of departing just yet. She lobbed Nathan a middle finger salute, then returned her attention to the girl she clearly saw as her successor. The smile she offered was almost sympathetic.

"I was just like you," Aimee explained. "In a club. Minding my own business. Then along came Nathan, giving it all the chat. Straight away, I was hooked. And why wouldn't I be? I mean, look at him. Fit as fuck. Anyway, he invited me back here. One thing led to another. And we fucked like rabbits. Excellent, I thought. I'd found myself my dream man." Her demeanour then changed. Little girl lost. "But that's where the dream ended. Next morning, he totally blanked me. Couldn't get me out the door fast enough." And back to the original headstrong Aimee. "So don't go expecting a lovey-dovey relationship. That bastard doesn't do commitment."

"I'm not expecting anything." It was the truth. Well, except the taking of her virginity.

Aimee smirked and shook her head, unconvinced. "Oh, Patience. I can see it in your eyes. You want so much more than just one night of empty sex."

Nathan held the door wide open. "I think it's time you were leaving."

Aimee headed for the exit. "No need to worry that handsome little head of yours, Nathan. I'm not staying a moment longer." Aimee disappeared into the lobby. A moment later, she returned, pushing a pram into the bedsit. "You can look after your kid tonight. I'm going clubbing."

Patience's face didn't just drop. It fell to its death. Talk about the bombshell of a lifetime. Aimee was not just a fellow one-night stand. She was the mother of a child. Nathan's child. A snippet of his life he'd conveniently forgotten to mention.

"There's no way I'm bloody babysitting," snarled Nathan, greatly annoyed that his plans had been scuppered by a former bedfellow.

"Oh, yes you are. It's about time you took responsibility for your actions."

Patience didn't know what to think. "Nathan, you said you were single."

"You really think I'm with this bitch?"

Aimee said, "When I told him I was pregnant, he didn't want to know. Not his problem, that's what he reckoned. That's the kind of bloke he is."

Nathan blurted out, "You said you were on the Pill!"

"That's right, put all the fucking blame on me!"

"It's probably not even mine! There's no way I'm only bloke you've slept with!"

"Are you calling me a slag?"

The escalating ruckus disturbed the baby. The infant's piercing screech filled the room. It was amazing what a tiny pair of lungs was capable of achieving.

Nathan huffed, eyes burning, teeth gritted. "Now look what you've done."

Aimee grinned, loving it. "I do believe that's my cue to say good-bye."

The father of the tiny human looked horrified, volleying his sights back and forth between the baby and his mother. "What the hell am I supposed to do with the snivelling brat?"

"Look after him, that's what. It will do you good to bond with the boy. He is your son, after all."

And then Aimee left. In a hurry.

"Shit," was all Nathan could muster.

The baby continued to blare. Nathan loomed over the pram, panic-stricken, clueless. A bite of his bottom lip. A shrug of his shoulders. A wipe of a palm across his face. He picked up a rattle and gave it a shake. It didn't do the trick. He discovered a half-consumed bottle of milk and inserted the teat into the child's mouth. Refused. Spat out. He turned to Patience for answers.

"Don't look at me," she said, disapproving of his manner. And as she walked towards the door, she added, "This is not my problem."

"Oh, Patience, please don't go," appealed Nathan. "We can still have sex. Just help me shut this kid up and we'll get down to it, okay?"

She opened the door, sneering at such a callous suggestion. "I don't think so."

Sheer desperation flickered in Nathan's wide eyes. "Wait! Please.

You can't leave me on my own with a screaming baby."

Patience glanced at him with pity. It soon morphed into ugly resentment. The beautiful person she'd met at the club no longer existed. He'd been replaced by the helpless, pathetic wreck of a man who now cowered before her.

The final words she uttered to him were, "It's all you deserve."

Chapter 12

Four Play

Patience arrived home and fixed herself a tomato sauce sandwich. Why? It was quick. And convenient. Oh, and she couldn't be bothered to actually cook something. The bizarre snack acted as comfort food for times when she felt depressed. Or angry. Or lost. Or all three at once. Tonight, she was the unfortunate bearer of said trio.

And so, here she sat at the kitchen table. In the middle of the night. Feeling a little tipsy. With smudges of ketchup around her downturned mouth.

Still. A. Bloody. Virgin.

Bugger.

Yet another epic frigging fail.

This time, the reason for the total collapse of her plans for genital penetration hadn't been the unexpected return of a wife. Instead, she'd come face to face with just another silly girl who had fallen for Nathan's charms. And then fallen pregnant with his child.

She truly felt sorry for the girl. What was her name again? Ah, yes. Aimee. Funny, that. She knew a lot of teenagers in the area with that particular forename. Not the more traditional spelling of Amy, it had to be said. One i, double e, the far more common of late variant. It seemed as though all their mothers had opted to be cool and different at the time when naming the newborns — mm, yes, commendable — but had then gone on to totally copy each other, letter for letter. What was the point of that? Insert world-weary shake of the head here. It must have been weird for the lass at school. A whole classroom full of namesakes.

"Aimee."

"Yes, Miss?"

"Not you. That Aimee."

"Yes, Miss?"

"No, no, no, the girl sitting behind you. That Aimee."

"Yes, Miss?"

"Oh, for—" A jaded exhale. "Maybe I should stick to surnames."

And back to the present, poor little Aimee; this one, the girl Patience had met tonight, not that one, nor that one, nor the girl who had sat behind the other one in the classroom—I'm sure you get the point—a blossoming young lady, barely introduced to adulthood, doomed to the gloomy prison of serious commitment. A dark and lonely void where escape was futile and fun was just another fading memory from the carefree life she used to lead. Nothing but an abandoned pramface, her only company: soiled nappies, sleepless nights and leaky nipples. And what for? One single night of passion with a "well fit bloke" whom she'd no doubt boasted about the following day to her equally silly friends.

Patience sucked all fingers clean of ketchup and mopped away the scarlet smudges from her lips with a tissue. She loved the way her favourite stupid o'clock nibble refused to be tamed, dripping its blood all over her. It also granted the girl a wicked sense of mischievous satisfaction by letting the snack do its thing whilst showing blatant disregard for the inevitable messy outcome.

She left the table and placed the plate in the kitchen sink. It was filled with freezing cold, rather discoloured water where, several hours earlier, vibrant suds, dancing wisps of steam and sparkling window-lit bubbles had reigned. The plate shared the neglected pool with its crockery and cutlery brothers and sisters. It has been Penny's turn to do the dishes. This chore was supposed to have been completed long before they ventured out for the evening. Okay, so her flatmate had squirted ample quantities of washing up liquid into a cascade of hot running water. And she'd placed all dirty items into the sink to soak, thus preventing the dreaded food-weld. But she'd missed out the doing the dishes part of doing the dishes. Typical. Ah, well. The contents of the sink would now remain submerged and unloved until at least late afternoon the next day. Or when the first of the hangovers subsided. Whichever came soonest.

As she turned and left the chaos of the sink, Patience took note of more used but not cleaned cookware on the kitchen worksurface. Namely, a plate smudged with a Pollock-like mess of brown sauce and, next to it, a fatty frying pan. Both hadn't been there earlier. A late night snack, clearly. From the charred remains in the frying pan, it looked like somebody — more likely Penny — had fried the last of the prawns. Ooer. Risky. The seafood in question had been several days past its eat-by date, yet nobody had thought to dispose of the expired foodstuff. More fool Penny. Why she couldn't have rustled up a sensible snack like a tomato sauce sandwich was the ultimate question.

Patience headed down the dark corridor that led to her bedroom. It was then when it hit home to her that not bedding Nathan had been a lucky escape. Phew. Ah, but alas, it presented the girl with one niggling problem. Right at this very moment in time, she felt hornier than she'd ever been before. Talk about fizzy, fuzzy sensations on overdrive. Yeah, so Nathan could easily qualify for the coveted Wanker Of The Year award. And not to mention pride of place in the Total Bastard Hall Of Fame. But one fact couldn't be denied. He certainly knew how to stimulate a woman. Sigh! What a dilemma. Absolutely flooding down below with no penis available to plug the gap. She could feel the insatiable appetite of sexual frustration eating away at her body. Why, oh, why couldn't she find a man to do the actual eating?

"Ooooh, yes."

The cry came from Penny's bedroom. But it didn't sound like Penny. She knew her flatmate's pleasure murmurs off by heart through listening in umpteen times on the couple's amorous antics from the comfort of her own bed. In fact, she could identify the girl's sex screams blindfolded in a voice identity parade. So who the fuck was Dave servicing in there? And where was Penny? More importantly, did she know about the affair? And hold on. How come Dave was using Penny's bedroom for his illicit liaison? It didn't make sense. There was only one way to seek and find enlightenment.

The Forbidden Keyhole.

She crept over to Penny's bedroom door, stooped low and took a peek through her very own personal peephole. Her eyes widened. Both eyebrows headed north. Her lower jaw headed south.

Oh. My. Fucking. God.

Dave was naked on the bed, knelt behind a girl on all fours. His hands clasped her hips as he rammed his stiff cock into her pussy. In and out, in and out, he gyrated. The girl squealed with delight upon every forward thrust, accommodating his hard meat with relish. But who was she? Patience couldn't make out her identity. The girl's head hung low, her face obscured by shoulders and arms. Dave then quickened his pace, burrowing his stiff dick deeper inside her hole. She yelped loudly and tilted her head back, wild eyes, massive grin. Aha. At last. Her face. Revealed. The mystery woman was —

Oh. My. Fucking. Fucking. Fucking. God.

No. It couldn't be. Yes. It was.

Felicity down the road.

Yep. That's right. Felicity down the fucking road.

Only, she was most definitely not down any form of street tonight. Right now, she was playing a dog on heat on Penny's bed. Being fucked to oblivion. And absolutely loving it.

But where the hell was Penny?

Oh, my God, then her flatmate came into view. Penny was naked too. She knelt in front of Felicity, her pussy close to the girl's face. Felicity lolled out an eager tongue and lapped hungrily around Penny's clitoris. Her eyes slammed shut and she beamed from ear to ear, moaning loudly with pleasure as Felicity pushed her mouth into her groin. Penny parted her wet lips with both hands to allow the redhead easier entry into her crack. Felicity graciously accepted the offer and ran her tongue up and down her moist crevice. As it all played out, Dave continued to pound the girl hard from behind.

Behind the keyhole, Patience's body tingled all over. She was turned on, big-time. She'd never seen a threesome before. Hell, it was only recently she'd witnessed her debut monogamous sexual relationship, for God's sake, let alone adding extra players to the mix. It was as if she'd enrolled in a voyeuristic crash course, with each lesson covering a peepshow far more daring than the previous titillation. What stage would it reach by the end of next week? Roman orgy?

Patience unbuttoned her borrowed low-cut blouse and cast it aside, exposing her bare, bra-less breasts. She tweaked a nipple. Ooh, yeah, it felt good. She hitched up the equally borrowed shortest of short skirts—not that it needed much of a raise—and dived a hand inside her underwear. Her fingers did the talking, rubbing her clitoris and stroking her lips as she observed the action taking place on the other side of the keyhole with the keenest of eyes. She watched Felicity munch on Penny's pussy and wondered what a female tongue would feel like across her own genitals. Like a man's, she guessed, but hitting the right zing spots far more often. After all, women knew what they liked themselves, licky-licky-wise, so all they had to do was emulate the moves.

The watcher's juices flowed freely. As a result, her undies were soaked. They needed to come off, pronto. She pulled them down to her ankles, lifted one leg and attempted to yank them over her shoe. No joy. The elastic, it got caught round the heel. A tut. A curse. A sigh. She pulled again. Still stuck. She tugged as hard as she could. The elastic pinged back and stung her ankle.

"Ow!"

She wobbled. She stumbled. She grabbed hold of the door handle for balance. It twisted. The door opened. She fell through. And she landed in an ungainly heap on Penny's bedroom carpet.

Three gasps from a shocked threesome. Three pairs of widened eyes, all aimed at a fallen Patience. She peered up at the naked figures and offered a pained grimace. Then she took note of the fact that she was topless. Again. Shit. And registered that her thong was still wrapped around her ankles. Fuck. This would require a bloody good explanation.

"Patience, what the fuck are you doing?" asked Penny, lower jaw sagged.

"Um." Patience thought about it. All she could think of to say was, "Just wondered if any of you three fancied a coffee."

Argh! What a dumb line.

Penny narrowed her eyes, both hands resting upon naked hips. "Were you spying on us through the keyhole?"

Patience pulled her most convincing—or so she hoped—disgusted expression. "Don't be so absurd. What do you think I am, some kind of sick pervert?"

Penny smiled. "It's all right. I don't mind if you were watching. It's quite a turn-on actually."

Felicity seemed to agree. And so did Dave. A huge nod from the guy. Total conformity, complete with animated eyes and idiot grin. Patience emitted a long trailing sigh. The game was up. Time to confess her sins.

"Okay, so I might have had a quick peek. But that's all. I heard a noise. I was—" A quick search through her brain for an apt word. "—curious."

Penny's smile broadened. It was as if being observed during sex had been one of her greatest ambitions, fantasies, whatever. Knowing her flatmate, it probably was.

Patience yearned to learn, "How long have you lot been having— you know—" She was so thrown by the revelation, she couldn't even complete the sentence.

Penny responded with, "Threesomes? Oh, ages."

"We love it. It's so much fun," chipped in Felicity.

Another firm nod and another idiot grin from an almost dribbling Dave.

Patience blinked a number of times. It was her way of getting her head around things. She knew Penny and Dave were fanatically open-minded. But this? A bloody threesome? Wow. And with Felicity? That was something else. She would never have guessed in a million years. For sure, the usually more reserved redhead was certainly a dark horse.

"What I don't understand," queried Penny, "is why you needed to get off on the three of us fucking. Didn't Nathan satisfy you enough?"

Patience screwed up her face. "Nathan didn't happen."

"Why not?"

Patience sat herself up on the floor and kicked off her thong. The underwear flew through the air and hooked onto one of the knobs on Penny's chest of drawers. She then rose to her feet, wearing only the skirt.

"Long story. But I can sum it up in just two words. Fucking tosser."

Penny seemed genuinely sorry for the girl. "Aw, Patience. I really thought he was the one."

"So did I." A regretful exhale. "Oh, sod it. I've had enough of trying to lose my virginity. I must be jinxed. Every time I get close to actual penetration, disaster strikes. I might as well face facts. Sex is never going to happen for me."

Dave's face glowed with inspiration. "Hey. Why don't you join us?"

Penny looked at him. And then grinned. "Great idea. Let's make it a foursome."

"Always room for one more," said Felicity, well and truly up for it.

Patience stepped back, the suggestion making her a tad uncomfortable. "I'm not sure," she murmured shyly, covering her bare breasts with her hands.

Penny excitedly added, "I don't know why we didn't think of this before. It's perfect."

Patience didn't look too convinced by the offer.

"Don't be shy," assured Felicity. "You're amongst friends."

"Yeah," contributed Dave, his tongue half sticking out. "Why search for a dickhead stranger to pick your cherry when you can get the job done with people you know?"

"Exactly," said Penny. "Good friends who love and care about you."

Patience regarded their words. Dave's effort somehow felt more like a contrived opportunity to screw an extra woman, rather than a selfless favour from a buddy. Typical male. But maybe the three of them were right. Friends with benefits. No complications. Sex with no strings attached. Lots of people got laid that way these days. It was a growing trend. And she had to admit, if Joe were not of the gay variety, she and him would have been fuckbuddies for sure. So why was she so hesitant about sharing some fun and frolics with a flatmate and boyfriend combo, plus a girl from down the road whom she'd known for ages?

With the careful scrutiny of a jeweller checking out the authenticity of a gemstone, she examined her three previous near misses. Or fortunate non-hits, depending on points of view.

Firstly, Geoff, her boss. Or rather, Geoff The C Word. Had they successfully consummated their lust, would she now be able to handle the awkward eye avoidances at work, the knowledge that she'd assisted him in cheating on his wife, and not to mention the status of being just another office conquest? No. Probably not.

Then there was Tom in the broken lift. Had the engineer not fixed the elevator in time, they would have fucked each other's brains out. But again, she would feel the eternal guilt of knowing she'd screwed somebody's husband.

And finally, good looking, well fit Nathan. Had Aimee not shown her face — and her child — when she did, Patience would have absolutely no knowledge of his selfish ways. Or at least not until it was too late. And would she really enjoy the prospect of being just another nightclub conquest? No. Definitely not.

Conclusion: Sex with strangers was probably not the way forward for Patience Hope. So maybe sex with friends was.

Ah, fuck it. In more ways than one.

Patience smiled, her mind made up. "I say, let's do it," she squealed, leaping onto the bed.

She unzipped what was left of her clothing, namely, Penny's skirt, and yanked it free, revealing her knickerless vagina. Her sudden total nakedness felt oh, so bloody liberating.

"Lay down, Patience," said Dave. "Let's get you lubricated."

Patience did as she was told and lay flat on her back. Dave parted her legs and dived right in, sliding his hungry tongue up and down the length of her crevice. Ooh, yes, it felt good. She knew it would. After all, she'd witnessed the extent of his talented tongue-play on Penny through the keyhole and since then had yearned for a piece of the action. And look. Now her wish had come true.

Penny and Felicity flanked either side of Patience, kissing and licking the smooth skin of her neck and shoulders. They slowly worked their way down to her breasts and claimed one nipple each as their own, sucking, biting, nuzzling. Patience was buzzing. Three tongues, all doing their thing on different parts of her body. Wow. She reached out to the two girls' bosoms and stroked them, squeezed them, fondled them. Her actions urged the pair to suck harder on the bullets that were her erect nipples.

Patience barked in unbridled ecstasy as Dave rolled his tongue across her clitoris, setting it on fire. Juices trickled, poured, cascaded from her pussy into his waiting mouth. He inserted his middle finger into her hole and worked it hard and fast. Then two fingers. Then three. Fuck, he certainly knew what he was doing.

"Swap places, Dave," ordered Penny. "We want to taste her now."

Dave shuffled upwards, lay beside Patience and stroked the warm skin of her abdomen. Penny and Felicity moved down between her parted thighs and began to share her pussy. Patience shrieked, eyes shut, teeth bared as both tongues made contact with her soaked crack. Ooh, fuck, yes. No doubt about it, two tongues were definitely better that one. Fuck, fuck, fuck, it felt good! Felicity sucked on her clit. Penny tongued between her pussy lips until she discovered the rim of her hole. Dave peppered her neck with kisses as he cupped both breasts with fervent palms. As it all played out, a massive smile stretched across Patience's face. She was in sexual heaven.

Patience ran a finger along Dave's inner thigh and cupped his balls. Dave offered a murmur of approval as she caressed his sack. He looked deep into her eyes and gave her a small peck on the lips. Then another kiss. And another. His tongue found its way into her mouth. This pleased the girl. Their lips pushed together, not letting go. Patience wrapped her fingers around Dave's monster of a cock and wanked it hard and fast. She tightened her grip, pretending the hand was her tight pussy, dreaming he was fucking her right now. Oh, God, she wouldn't have long to wait. The way he grunted and groaned, he was sure to beg for pussy any second now. And tonight, this magnificent beast of a shaft was hers for the taking.

"Ladies and gentlemen, it's time to fuck," quipped Penny, licking her lips.

They all stopped what they were doing and stood up.

Patience walked over to her handbag and produced her last condom. A symbolic notion cropped up in her head. Maybe the final rubber in the box was always destined to be the successful one. And that its two predecessors were simply sacrificing themselves, making way for the glory of the chosen one. Hmm. What weird shit she'd think up sometimes, huh?

She placed the sheath in Dave's hand. "I practice safe sex," she said, giving him a peck on the cheek.

"Okay, babes," said Dave, tearing the foil.

Penny returned to the bed and opened her legs, ready for action. Felicity lay to her right, thighs also parted. The redhead smiled at Patience and patted the vacant area of the bed.

"Lay here next to me, Patience. You're third in line for the fuck-o-thon."

As Patience rested herself, she asked, "What's a fuck-o-thon?"

"Sex with the three of us in rapid succession. Dave fucks Penny, crosses over to me, then on to you and back again. We get thirty seconds of his cock each time, back and forth, back and forth. You could say it's a kind of a stamina test for Dave to see how many times he can do the circuit before either coming his lot or passing out. Do you get what I mean?"

Patience nodded. And blinked a few times. "Yeah, I think I understand."

"Put it this way," continued Felicity with a wink and a smirk. "In one minute's time, that virginity of yours will be preparing to say goodbye. In a minute and a half, the V word will be a thing of the past."

Oh, God, it was actually on the cards. Her big night. Her moment. All she needed to do was wait patiently for sixty seconds. Sixty short seconds until Dave's penis hopped over to say hi to the pussy of Patience Hope and set about turning the virgin into a bona fide woman of experience. Wahey!

Dave mounted his girlfriend, ready and waiting. Penny produced a stopwatch — from where exactly was the jackpot question — and held it aloft.

"5. 4. 3. 2. 1. Go!"

Penny clicked the timer into action. Dave's stiff dick disappeared inside her pussy. He began to gyrate furiously. Upon each upward thrust, Penny pushed down with her pelvis, creating harmonious rhythm. Patience watched in awe as the girl's tunnel swallowed his massive cock whole, only for it to re-emerge during the latter end of each cycle and then dive back in again. Soon, it would be her turn. She couldn't wait.

"Time's up," yelled Penny, eyeing her stopwatch. "Felicity down the road's turn."

Patience looked stunned. My, how time flew by, she mused.

Dave withdrew and clambered onto Felicity. She grabbed his penis and guided it towards her hole. It slipped inside with ease. He pounded her with all his might, in and out, in and out, as if his life depended on it.

"Hey, slow down, Dave," ordered Penny. "Don't forget, you've got a third pussy to satisfy this time."

Dave threw her a mock salute as he lessened his pace. "Yes, Miss."

Patience couldn't take her eyes off Dave's rigid weapon as it pumped in and out of the redhead. The thick film of lovejuice donated by the two girls made the rubber over his cock glisten. The sight was almost hypnotic.

How fast the first thirty seconds had rushed past greatly astonished her. And any moment now, the second allocation of time would be spent. Oh, fuck. It was her turn next. Her first time. Was she ready for this?

"All change," commanded Penny.

Dave pulled himself out of Felicity and climbed aboard the good ship Patience.

"Make sure you give it to her good, Dave," Penny stressed. "This shag is special."

Patience trembled as Dave pointed his dick towards her waiting entrance. She was oh, so frigging nervous. Oh, God, she hoped her sudden fear wouldn't close it up. Please, please, please allow the penis entry. Yes, I know it's fucking enormous, and you're only a small and virginal pussy, but Dave's got a ticket to ride, so for fuck's sake let him in.

Dave pushed. His penis missed the hole and slipped to the right. He straightened up and tried again. This time, it slipped to the left. Oh, fuck. This was so embarrassing. Patience grabbed his shaft with both hands and held it exactly in place. All Dave needed to do was move it forward. She heard a squelch as his penis kissed the rim. The girl was evidently wet enough, so it was sure to slot in. Right?

His swollen bell-end greeted the opening. He pushed gently this time. Yes, she thought. Easing it in gradually should do the trick. And success—sort of. Part of his helmet slipped inside. Not much. Just the very tip. A few millimetres at the most. But at least it was a start. One more decent push and it would officially be inside.

"Thirty seconds are up."

Patience lobbed Penny her most widened eyes. "What? I haven't even started yet!"

"Rules are rules, Patience."

"Fuck's sake."

Penny grinned. "Only joking. I'll start the stopwatch again."

Dave smiled at Patience. She returned the gesture.

"I've always wanted to fuck you," he admitted to her. Then he glanced at Penny and checked himself. "Not that I'd ever leave Penny for you, or anything like that. But, you know, I reckon you're good for a fuck or two." Then an afterthought. "Actually, that makes me sound like an arsehole. Hang on. Let me start again."

Patience placed two fingers over his lips to stifle such slapdash mumbling. "How about you just shut up and get on with it?"

Dave smiled and gave a nod. "Good idea."

Penny cocked the stopwatch, thumb over button. "Ready, Patience?"

Dave peered down at the naked girl below him. "Ready?"

Patience blew out some air. It was all so overwhelming. She was about to enjoy sex for the first time. And finally lose her bloody virginity. Yay! She felt like screaming with joy at the top of her voice, but soon changed her mind. She needed to save her voice for her forthcoming come cry. It was all set to be a loud one.

"Ready as I'll ever be," she said.

Penny began to count her down. "5."

Oh, God.

"4."

This is it.

"3."

No turning back now.

"2."

I fucking hope I don't just lie there like a sack of potatoes.

"1."

Goodbye, dear virginity. It's been nice knowing you.

"Arghhhhh!"

The scream came from Dave. He rolled off the bed and crashed onto the floor. Everybody leapt to their feet and found the man doubled up in agony.

"Arrrrghhhhhhh!" he roared, louder than before.

"What the fuck is going on?" asked Felicity.

"Looks like Dave is in pain," responded Patience.

Penny scowled at the virgin. "What did you do to him?"

Who, me? "Nothing."

Penny prodded him all over. "Can you tell me where it hurts, babes?"

Dave clutched his abdomen for dear life. "Isn't it fucking obvious?" And then he covered his mouth with a clammy palm. "Oh, fuck," he mumbled through the cracks between his fingers. "I feel bloody sick as well."

Penny pointed at Felicity. "You. Fetch a bowl, a bucket, anything."

It was an attempt by the trainee nurse to act all calm and collected under stress like characters from her favourite TV medical dramas. However, such bravado didn't look too convincing at all.

She added, "The last thing I need is vomit on this carpet."

Felicity nodded and flew out of the room.

Penny indicated to Patience. "You. Call for an ambulance."

Patience opened up her handbag, grabbed her mobile and punched some numbers.

"Have we got any painkillers?" was Penny's next line.

Waiting for her call to be connected, Patience rifled once again through the chaos of her bag and held aloft a packet of medication. "Will headache tablets do?"

"Not for this, no."

At last, Patience was through to the emergency services. Out of fire, police and ambulance, she chose the latter, then waited to be redirected. At the same moment, Felicity burst through with a bucket and placed it beside Dave. The timing was impeccable — and bloody fortunate — for the man immediately hoffed up a rather gruesome part-digested mess.

A male voice on the other end of the phone. "Ambulance."

"Yes, hello," said Patience. "Ambulance please to — "

"There aren't any."

"What?"

"No ambulances. Sorry. There's been a massive motorway pile-up. And any units not attending that crash are sorting out the usual Saturday night club fights."

"But this is an emergency!"

"I'm sure it is, love. But I can't help you. Sorry."

Patience shut off her call. "Bollocks!"

Penny looked across. "What's happening?"

"No free ambulances."

"Shit."

Patience shrugged her shoulders, awaiting further instructions. "What now?"

Penny looked left, looked right, then down at Dave. Her bravado began to falter. In fact, it was in tatters. Even though the girl was in the medical profession, she was clearly not cut out for emergencies.

"I don't know," was all she could think of to say.

Dave, anxious, perspiring, fearing for his life croaked, "Penny. What's wrong with me?"

"I don't mean to alarm you, babes." Penny swallowed hard. There was no easy way to say it. "But I think you might be dying."

Chapter 13
Patients and Virgins

"Any luck?" Penny asked, anxious, fearful.

Ten minutes had passed since Dave's agonising collapse. Patience and Felicity, now dressed, mobile phones pressed against ears, scurried around the bedroom in all directions for no particular reason like a pair of confused ants trekking the finger of a curious child.

Bad news from Patience. "No taxis for at least another hour."

"Same here," said Felicity, killing her phone. "Nightclub chucking out time, you see."

"Fuck," responded Penny. "No wonder it's so crazy."

A nude Dave was still doubled-up in pain on the carpet. Penny knelt beside him, also naked. No time for clothes just yet. Right now, priority one was to tend to her boyfriend, patting his burning brow with a damp flannel.

"Oh, God," the sick man groaned. "I need to get to the toilet."

"Just use the bucket, babes," advised Penny. "Best to conserve your energy."

Dave was most adamant. "No, no, you don't understand. I really, really, really need to go. Like, number twos and stuff."

Now Penny got it. "Oh. Right." She indicated to Felicity. "Help me get him to the bathroom."

The two girls wrenched the deadweight to his feet. How they managed it could only be described as a heavenly miracle. Hooking one of Dave's arms over each pillar's shoulder, they led the patient out of the room.

"What do you think is wrong with him?" Patience asked, following them into the hallway.

Penny looked back, eyes awash with concern. "I don't know."

Patience suddenly felt helpless. It was a horrible feeling. "What shall I do?"

"Keep ringing those cab companies."

"But Penny. I've tried them all."

"Shit. In that case, do you know anybody with a car?"

Patience fell silent. And hesitant. Yes, of course she did. Whether she wanted to disturb him at this hour was another story.

"Well?"

"Yes."

"Who?"

A pause. Then, "Joe."

As Penny disappeared into the bathroom with Dave and Felicity, she begged, "Patience. I know you've both got your differences. But call him. Please."

Patience froze, alone in the hallway. Bugger. What a dilemma. The last time she'd laid eyes on Joe was Friday night. The infamous breast flashing incident. They hadn't spoken to each other since. Well, they had, sort of. But only through the impersonal wood of her firmly shut and locked bedroom door, moments after she'd fled from the lounge like some kind of demented topless Cinderella.

That very conversation came flooding back to her.

"Oh, come on, Patience. Let me in," Joe requested.

Patience sat on her bedroom carpet, bare back against door, eyes welling with the salty tears of hurt, humiliation and everything related. "Go away, Joe. I don't want to speak to you."

"Please. Let's talk about this."

She shook her head, disillusioned, even though Joe couldn't witness the gesture. "What else is there to say? You're my best friend, yet my body repulses you. Which means everybody else will feel repulsed by it. So what's the point of me even fucking trying?"

"Don't say that. I think you're beautiful."

Patience scoffed. Noisily. "Yeah. You certainly proved that."

"Look, Patience, I—"

"Fuck off! Go on. Piss off out of it. I don't need you. Hear that, Joe?" Then she repeated the last four words, loud and clear, devoid of sentiment, in no uncertain terms, "I don't need you."

Silence from the other side of the door. Her damning statement had certainly hit home for sure.

One long moment later, a clearly upset Joe whispered, "Goodbye, Patience."

Patience sat alone in stubborn silence. She heard the front door. Somebody was leaving.

Joe.

At that, the topless girl had burst into tears.

Patience. Suddenly jolted forward to the present night by Penny and Felicity vacating the bathroom and closing the door. She looked down at the phone in her hand. Should she call him?

Strange noises emanated from the bathroom.

Penny called through the door, "Are you all right, Dave?"

Dave's reply came in the form of, "It's coming out of all orifices. I don't know what to point at the pan most. My mouth or my arse."

"Try to alternate between the two, babes," was Penny's advice. "Mouth, arse, mouth, arse, mouth, arse. Get a good rhythm going and you'll be laughing." An afterthought. "Well, not literally laughing, but I'm sure you catch my drift." She then turned to Patience. "Have you called Joe yet?"

Patience shook her head.

"For fuck's sake, girl, sort yourself out," the flatmate snarled, more out of alarmed concern than of heated anger. "Get your act together. Now."

Yes. Penny was right. She did indeed need to sort herself out. Getting said act together was priority one. She selected Joe from her contacts and hit the call key. The ringing tone purred on for a while. Well, it was late, after all. He'd be tucked up in bed. Then a connection.

"Hello?"

"Joe. It's Patience. Please don't hang up on me."

She paused for a response. Good. No harsh click and a purr. Still connected. He hadn't cut her off. Phew. That was a good sign. She swallowed hard. And took a deep breath. It took all her strength to utter just three words.

"I need you."

The car pulled up just as Penny, Patience and Felicity escorted Dave to the roadside. Joe clambered out of the vehicle and opened the back door for them. Felicity dived in first and watched as Joe and Penny helped Dave onto the back seat. Penny seated herself next to him. Joe closed the door behind her. Patience opened the passenger door and glanced across the car roof at Joe on the other side.

"Thanks for doing this," she said softly.

They looked at each other. Shared a moment. And both entered the vehicle. Joe eased off the handbrake and they were off.

Through the pain, Dave managed a sickly beam and stared cross-eyed at his girlfriend. "I love you, Penny. I love you more than words can say."

"Oh, God," Penny groaned. "It's worse than I thought. The poor sod's delirious."

"But I do love you. With all my heart." He was almost acting as if he was drunk.

"Yes, of course you do, babes," she humoured.

"So what exactly is wrong with him?" asked Joe.

"I wish I knew," said Penny, cuddling her groaning boyfriend.

The driver looked puzzled. "I thought you said you were a nurse."

"Trainee nurse. Big difference." And off everybody's funny looks, she added, "What can I say? There's a lot to take in. I haven't got to mystery stomach illnesses yet."

Stomach illness. Hmm. The very mention of the ailment nudged something deep in Patience's memory. But what exactly? It was something she'd seen earlier. But where? And when? Think, girl, think. This could be a life or death situation.

Then aha! Patience's face suddenly glowed with inspiration. "Oh, my God! The frying pan."

Penny scowled. "Now is not the time to have a go at me for not washing up."

"No, no, what I mean is, when I rolled in earlier, I noticed the pan contained charred remains of prawns."

Penny shrugged, not following too well. "Yeah, so? Dave was hungry. So I rustled up my world famous Prawn Surprise."

Patience. Detective mode. "What exactly is Prawn Surprise?"

"Fried prawns in a sandwich, smothered with brown sauce."

"What's the surprise?"

"I usually make it with tomato ketchup."

"Penny. Those prawns were off. You shouldn't have used them." Then a new thought. "Hold on a minute. Who else ate this meal?"

"Nobody. Just Dave."

"But that means—" Patience's jaw sagged low. "Oh, my God."

"Oh, my God," gasped Joe.

"Oh, my God," equally gasped Felicity in turn.

And the penny dropped for Penny. "Oh, my fucking God."

Dave didn't quite get it. "Hello? Can somebody please explain to me why everybody's throwing around all these oh-my-Gods?"

"Tell him, Patience," requested a worried Penny.

Patience passed the buck. "Tell him, Joe."

"Joe peeked in his rear-view mirror and said, "Tell him—um—what's your name?"

"Felicity down the road."

Frown time. "Felicity down the road?"

"Long story."

"Okay. Pleased to meet you, Felicity."

"Pleased to meet you, Joe."

Then Joe said to Felicity, "Oh, just one more thing."

"Yes, Joe?"

"Tell him, Felicity."

In turn, Felicity said, "Penny. It really is best if the bad news comes from you."

Penny groaned, then turned to her man. "Dave. Darling. Honey. Babes. Please don't take this the wrong way." A struggle of conscience, then, "But there's a very small chance—well, quite a big chance actually—that I might have poisoned you."

"What?" he yelped, eyes popping out of their sockets, almost cartoon-like. "Oh, fuck, am I going to die?"

Penny didn't have a clue how to respond, so she settled with, "Look, just relax, okay?"

"How can I relax?" he glurked, trembling. "You've just admitted you've killed me!"

"Dave," she said sternly. "Don't you think you're getting a bit ahead of yourself? I haven't actually killed anybody. Not yet."

The stress of such a horrific revelation brought on the return of Dave's pains.

Penny shouted to Joe, "Can't this thing go any faster?"

"It's thirty along this road."

"So?"

"I don't want to exceed the speed limit."

Patience rolled her eyes. She'd forgotten how much of a goody two shoes her best friend was. "Joe, this is an emergency. And besides, who's going to know? There's nobody else about. See? The road's empty."

Joe mumbled something inaudible as he took the car to forty. He was no doubt moaning about being coerced into breaking the law. His flawless behaviour was of no surprise to Patience. Her friend had never done anything wrong in his life. He'd never scrumped apples. He'd never accidentally on purpose packed a hotel towel in his suitcase. Oh, and he'd even offered to pay for the complimentary biscuits that came with cups of coffee. Something about feeling guilty about obtaining goods for free.

Behind them, sudden blue flashing lights. And the wail of a siren.

"Shit," cursed Joe, eyes wide open, mouth curled into a worried gurn.

Patience turned around and peered through the rear screen. Police patrol car. Oh, fuck.

"Sorry, Joe."

Joe pulled over to the side of the road. The patrol car slowed to a halt behind them. A uniformed policeman stepped out and slowly approached the target vehicle.

"Oh, God, I've never been in trouble with the law in my life," whimpered Joe, somewhat in distress. "I'll get points on my licence now. All thanks to you."

Patience was having none of it. "Oh, shut up. I never forced you to speed."

"I think you'll find you did."

"Oh, so I pushed your foot down on the accelerator pedal, did I?"

"You said it was an emergency."

"Well, it is."

The poker-faced policeman peered into the vehicle, shining a torch across their faces. They all stared at the officer, nervous, tense, mute.

"Step out of the car please, sir."

Joe swallowed hard. He climbed out, his head tilted forward in shame.

"Do you realise you were doing forty miles an hour in a thirty limit?"

"Um. Yes. Sorry about that. Thing is, my friend Dave, he needs to get to a—"

"Speak when you're spoken to, lad." The copper produced an object from of his pocket. "Would you mind blowing into this for me?"

"I haven't had a drink."

"Just do it, sir."

The policeman handed him the object. Joe looked at it. His face contorted with sheer disbelief. What the fuck?

It was a party blower, complete with a multi-coloured feather on its tip.

"You have got to be kidding."

The copper, adamant, resolute, unyielding. "If you don't do as I say, sonny, you'll be spending a night in the cells. Now blow. As hard as you can."

In the car, a concerned Penny said, "Excuse me, officer. We've got to go. It's my boyfriend. He's very ill."

The policeman peered through the window at the trainee nurse. "Do you want to blow into it as well?"

"No."

"Then keep quiet." He returned his attention to Joe. "Go on, sir. Blow. I haven't got all night."

With heavy reluctance, he did as he was told. One big puff. The blower squeaked, its tube unfurled, the feather quivered.

The lawman chuckled. "Oh, that's priceless. It never fails to amuse me."

Joe glared at him. "Can you please stop humiliating me now, Uncle Pete?"

The car occupants all threw startled double takes. Uncle Pete?

"I'm sorry, Joe, but an officer's got to have his perks. I get bored very easily, you see. Everybody else has been called away to a big motorway pile-up. But what have they given me? Local traffic duties. In the middle of the night. When there are hardly any cars on the road."

Joe looked at him. "Can I go now please?"

"Be my guest. But no more land speed record attempts. Got that?"

Joe entered the vehicle. "Loud and clear."

He drove away, leaving the copper standing alone in the road.

"I'm bored again now," Uncle Pete said to himself.

They pulled up at the hospital car park as close as they could to the front entrance. Penny leapt out of the car and trotted over to a loitering nurse and porter both enjoying a crafty cigarette break. After a quick briefing, they hastily commandeered a trolley.

"Penny," cried Dave as he was helped out of the vehicle and onto the waiting trolley.

His girlfriend held his hand tight. "I'm here, Dave."

"I forgive you, baby."

"That's a relief."

"Oh, and Penny.

"Yes, Dave?"

"If I die, I'd like you to donate my penis to medical science."

"Let's hope it doesn't come to that, hey?"

"Don't you think they'll want my cock?"

"No, I meant—" A disregarding flick of her hand. "Oh, never mind."

"Oh, and Penny."

"Yes?"

"I can't get down on one knee at the moment, but—" A pause for dramatic effect. "—will you marry me?" he asked her in all sincerity.

Penny and Felicity exchanged shocked glances. Then all eyes back on the patient.

"What did you say?" asked Penny, making sure.

"Marry me, Penny. Please."

"Dave. Stop talking. You need to rest." A tactful reply.

But her boyfriend was adamant. "Yes or no, Penny? Yes or no?" he asked — or rather, insisted — as he was wheeled towards the building. "I need an answer. Yes or no."

Joe opened the driver's door, ready to get back in. Patience stood nearby. They peered at each other, both still a little self-conscious about Friday night's events.

"Aren't you coming in?" Patience asked.

"Sorry, no. I've got an early start tomorrow," replied Joe. "I need to get back to my beauty sleep," he coyly quipped.

Patience offered a thin smile. "Well, you certainly need it."

Another shared moment.

"You will be all right getting home, won't you?" he asked, concerned.

"Yes. I'll be fine. I'll have Penny for company. Nobody will try to mug us with her around." Her smile faded as she added, "Look. Joe. I'm sorry about the other night. I don't know what came over me." Although she knew exactly what — or rather, who — came over her breasts in her sexual fantasy.

"Forget about it. Water under the bridge."

"Thanks. But I do know one thing," continued Patience. "I was wrong." Totally sincere face coming up. "I do need you. And I always will."

Joe looked away, conflicted. Then eyes back on the girl. "Patience. There's something I need to tell you. It's about work."

Waiting by the hospital entrance, Penny called out, "Patience. Are you coming or what?"

Patience looked across at Penny. Then back at Joe. Apologetic face. "I've got to go."

Joe nodded. "It's okay. My news will keep. See you later."

"Bye."

Patience kissed him on the forehead. And then she cantered away.

Hospital waiting rooms during the first cold light of day — the stark moment where the final breath of Saturday night tipped its hat to the initial yawn of Sunday morning — were never that much fun. Patience, Penny and Felicity had missed most of the action. The staff had patched up and kicked out the last of the bloody noses, blackened eyes and bruised egos half an hour ago. All who remained were two homeless drunks camped out by the drinks machine, both hoping for a kind soul to buy them a hot beverage. As long as it was most definitely not the gnat's piss tea option.

The three girls sat in silence. Counting empty plastic chairs (including two damaged upturned seats in the far corner) and then counting them all over again just to make sure had become the only pastime worth pastiming. Desperate, yes, but anything beat trawling through out of date fashion magazines for the second time around.

Such eyelid-heavy boredom forced Patience to ponder over yet another failed attempt to lose her virginity. It seemed as if Dave would rather be struck down with a potentially life-threatening condition than have sex with her. Typical. It didn't exactly do her self esteem a lot of good. He could have at least waited until he'd done the business and turned her into a been-there-done-it-now ex virgin before doubling up in excruciating pain. Just a few seconds of cock inside her would have been sufficient to tell her virginal status to piss off. Right? Or technically, was a girl still a virgin right up until the messy orgasm stage? In her mind, she lobbed herself an imaginary shrug of the shoulders. Who knows? Certainly not her.

One thing was sure. Here sat Patience. In morbid non-speak.

Still.

A.

Frigging.

Virgin.

Oh, what was she bloody thinking? How could she be so fucking selfish? Shame on you, bitch. Her self-complaint about the penis no-show paled in comparison to the seriousness of the situation. Upon arrival, Dave's illness had been treated as an emergency, and as such, the poor man found himself whisked away for immediate prodding and poking. This had happened well over an hour ago, no word since. No news was good news, she supposed.

It was Penny who brushed aside such grey hush with, "I hate hospitals."

Patience tossed her a confused double take. "But you work here."

"Doesn't mean I have to like the place." She blew out a sigh and crossed her arms. "I only joined up because I thought it would make me look sexy. Instead, what happens? I arrive home wearing a memento of each tiring double shift on my uniform, that's what. Vomit. Blood. Sometimes even the contents of a beer bottle commandeered from an intoxicated patient. Shortest-straw shifts in the Children's Ward are never plain sailing."

Patience smirked, but it was short-lived. "Do you reckon Dave will be okay?"

"Yeah. Food poisoning is pretty serious shit. But he'll live."

Patience glanced at her flatmate. Although the girl was doing a good job of holding her own, she could tell deep down she was pretty shaken up by the whole affair. Penny frowned, noticing such overt scrutiny.

"What?"

Patience said, "You really love Dave, don't you?"

Penny opened her mouth. No words emerged. She quickly changed the subject with, "I know. Let's play I Spy. I'll go first. I spy with my little eye, something beginning with—" She searched far and wide for inspiration, then, "—C."

Patience and Felicity looked around. All that could be seen were—

"Chairs?" guessed Felicity.

"Correct," said Penny. "Your turn."

While Felicity sought out the subject of her I Spy, Patience said to Penny, "Hey. Out in the car park, did I hear Dave propose to you?"

Penny grinned. "Yep, you sure did. He only did it because he thought he was a goner. He demanded an immediate yes or no, just in case he suddenly popped his clogs."

"What was your answer?"

Penny grinned. "I said I'd think about it."

Mass laughter from her audience ensued.

Chapter 14

Monday Morning Blues

Monday morning arrived way too soon for Patience Hope.

After the seemingly endless shenanigans of Saturday night, she slept through the remainder of the weekend, right up until late Sunday evening, when the only option left available was to return to bed. Did it really matter? Yes. Of course it did. Yeah, yeah, so Sundays were typically boring, but at least they provided a whole day's grace between play and work. A time for reflection, rest and relaxation. Oh, and ample time to recover from weekend hangovers.

There was plenty of available seating on the bus to work. The weatherman had promised clear blue skies and an absolute scorcher of a heatwave. Um. No, Mr Weatherman. The sky was instead heavily overcast with grey and off-white fluffy cloudiness and the temperature could only be described as moderate. Hardly solaris tropica. Saying that, however, it was a dry morning, mild enough to tempt the walkers back to using their feet instead of merely seeing the bus as convenient insurance against the elements. This came as a huge relief to Patience, for she didn't exactly relish the prospect of her bottom having to say hello again to Old Rumble-Shaky, the seat of doom. The last hindrance she needed right now was something that made her feel mega-horny.

Saturday night's two offers of sex, the one-on-one and the subsequent one-on-three, both of which had collapsed just before the initial penis poke, had left her feeling a strong desire to satisfy herself the DIY way. Again. And then again. And then again. And then again. It was all becoming rather tiresome. She would come, then think, "That's better, I've got it out of my system now." But within half an hour or so, her pleasure bud would scream out for more finger action.

She guessed it was her body adjusting from no chance of sex to several sudden offers on a plate, pumping out gallons of whichever hormone it was that made girls crave hard cock. Whatever the chemical was, she'd had quite enough of it. Patience had rubbed herself so many times late last night and early this morning, both hands ached to the point where she found it a painful struggle just to hold a coffee cup or use her phone; two absolute essentials for the modern woman. Furthermore, she'd secreted so much juice over her digits, her fingertips were beginning to prune.

There was good news on the Dave front. He was on the mend. Penny hadn't killed him off—albeit accidentally—with her late night Prawn Surprise after all. Speaking of whom, Penny had practically set up camp at his bedside since his admission. This surprised Patience. She'd always seen her flatmate's relationship with her boyfriend as nothing too serious. Just a non-committal laugh. A bit of the other with nothing much else included. Now she saw her in a wholly different light. Maybe lust alone was not what made the couple tick. Perhaps there was a slim chance that love had made an appearance somewhere along the line. Needless to say, neither Penny nor Dave would ever admit to such a damning allegation. Fact.

Patience stepped off the bus and decided to give Penny a quick call, aching fingers permitting—just about. She could have easily contacted the girl whilst sitting in comfort on the bus, but had decided against it. Even though mobile phones had been an integral part of everyday life for years, it was still socially illegal for anybody to use their handset on public transport, especially if accompanied by a loud and irritating voice. People who broke this law were considered wankers by everybody else around them.

She promised Penny she'd pop in on Dave as soon as her working day was done and dusted. Of course, that was more than eight hours away. Eight long and laborious sixty-minute clusters. Still, the hospital visit was something to look forward to. Sort of. Better than the seemingly endless piles of paperwork she would be struggling through all day. Oh, and not to mention, the one work-related issue she'd been dreading since Friday afternoon. Coming face to face with Geoff The C Word Denton.

Just as she was about to throw her mobile back into its handbag home, it burst into song. Its loudness turned heads, and not in a good way. Ooer. She really needed to change that ringtone. The track had fallen out of the UK Top 40 Singles Chart months ago. The music was out of date. Practically dead. This made it unfashionable. Highly inappropriate for a twenty-first century, upwardly mobile, cool as cucumber chick like Patience Hope.

Oh, who was she kidding? Patience Hope was quite simply Patience Hope, twenty-first century ordinary chick. Ah, sod it. Who cares if the tune was of ex chart status? She liked the song. Every time she heard the track, it made her feel all warm and happy inside. So why delete it from her listening pleasure?

Keep the ringtone. It didn't matter what other people thought.

She stopped dead in her tracks. The statement echoed through the tunnels of her mind like a yodeller doing a spot of pot holing.

It didn't matter what other people thought.

Yes. Exactly. It echoed one more time, just for good measure.

It really didn't fucking matter what other people thought.

This included her virginity. Yes. Her bloody virginity. She shook her head at her own stupidity. Who the hell was she trying to impress anyway if said virginity was lost? Nobody. And were members of the outside world really judging her? No. And even if they were, why bow down to what other people expected her to do, say, like, want, be, whatever? This was her life. Her decisions. Her everything.

There was absolutely no reason for Miss Patience Hope to rush into losing her virginity, having her cherry picked, being broken in, popping her penis pocket, loosening up her love tunnel, or any of her crude and juvenile euphemisms. Why? Simple.

It. Just. Didn't. Matter.

"You dumb idiot," she whispered to herself about herself.

"Are you going to answer that bloody phone or what?" barked an irate passer-by.

Patience recoiled. Blinked rapidly. Tumbled back to reality. And realised her handset was still begging for attention. Oops. She punched the green key — ouch, sore fingertip — and put it to her ear.

"Hello?"

"Patience, hi. It's Joe."

She smiled. "Joe." And then she frowned. "Why are you calling me at this ungodly hour?"

"It's almost nine."

"Exactly. It must be an emergency."

"Actually, I was wondering if you'd like to go out to dinner with me tonight."

Free food and wine. You try and stop me. "Sounds good. What's the occasion?"

A pregnant pause. Then, "I'm leaving."

"What?" Her face dropped. She quit walking. "What do you mean, leaving?"

Joe's tone changed. Uneasy. Hesitant. "I tried to tell you the other night in the hospital car park. I'm going away."

Patience. Confused. "Away? Where?"

Silence.

"When will you be back?"

More silence.

Totally bemused, she continued with, "Have I missed an episode or something? You're not making any sense. I demand catch-up, and I demand it now."

"Remember the other night at your place when you yawned all the way through the news that my employer was expanding?"

"Yeah, what about it?"

"I've agreed to transfer to another branch. In another town."

She smiled, although she was unsure why. "Well, that doesn't sound too much like going away. I mean, you've got a car and every-thing. So travel's not exactly a problem."

"The branch. It's in Scotland."

The mystery smile, erased from her face in an instant. "Scotland? But that's miles away." And with more emphasis, "Hundreds of thou-sands of millions of miles away."

"That's a bit of an exaggeration, but yes. I know."

This was one hell of a blow to Patience. Her mind was racing. So many questions. "But—what—" She was having trouble getting them out. "This job. Is it, like, a promotion? More money? Is that why you're leaving?"

"No. It's the same shit dosh as what I'm earning now. Same role, in fact."

"So why even bother?"

"Because I have to. There's nothing here for me any more."

"Is there something there for you in Scotland?"

"Probably not, no."

"Then don't go." She was almost begging.

"I have to."

"But Joe. You're my best friend."

"Yes. And you're my best friend too. This move won't change that."

"What about our chats?" Patience was snatching at anything now. "Our coffee shop catch-ups."

"We hardly see each other these days as it is. Different locations won't make any difference. And there's nothing stopping you from coming up and visiting occasionally. Or me coming down to you."

Patience had to agree as she got back to walking. Joe did have a point there. And let's face it, he was hardly moving to the other side of the world. A few hours on a train and she would be in his company, coffee in hand, chatting about how crap her life was.

So stop being so selfish, bitch.

"That's why," continued Joe, "I thought it would be nice to see you tonight."

She raised a faint smile. But inside, ambivalence on the brink of sorrow reigned supreme. "The last supper, eh?"

"Something like that."

She snapped out it. "Right. Got to go, Joe. Work beckons. Text me later, okay?"

"Sure."

Patience killed the phone and entered her place of work. She dreaded bumping into Geoff, but at the same time needed to see him. She wanted answers. An explanation. And her clothes and shoes back.

For the first two hours of the shift, Geoff mostly played the hermit behind the firmly closed door of his office. When he did occasionally emerge, he avoided eye contact. Post-sex awkwardness, she guessed. Oh, hold on. How could it be? More like post-non-sex awkwardness, as they hadn't actually done it.

Another forty minutes ticked by before she finally managed a brief conversation with the man. Patience entered the walk-in stationery cupboard to find her boss, trousers pulled down to his knees, fucking Sheila, she of severe acne, slightly more fat cells and bad breath fame. The woman faced the other way, bent over a small free-standing shelving unit, skirt hitched up to her waist, knickers keeping her ankles warm. Geoff stood directly behind the woman, both hands clutching her wide hips as he plunged his weapon in and out.

"Ah. Um. Good morning, Patience," he mumbled, throwing across an embarrassed grin upon being discovered. "What can I get you?"

Patience rolled her eyes. Tosser. "A ream of paper. If that's not too much trouble."

"Certainly." Keeping his cock firmly planted inside Sheila's pussy, Geoff reached for the paper and handed it over. "There you go. Anything else?"

"I need to see you in private. Urgently."

"Right. Wait in my office. Let me — erm — finish up here and I'll be right with you."

Patience nodded. She closed the door and did as she was asked. Geoff made his appearance in the office about five minutes later. He was met with a disapproving scowl from the girl.

"Sheila?" Repugnance. "Again?"

Geoff looked ashamed. "What can I say? She asked for a pay rise."

"Yes, but even so. She's a nice enough woman, but—that acne. And the bad breath."

"Why do you think I took her from behind?" He passed her a plastic carrier bag. It contained her belongings. "There you go. Everything's there. Skirt. Blouse. Bra. Shoes."

"Thank you," she said, although her tone lacked any trace of gratitude.

"Take a seat, Patience."

"I'll stand, if it's all the same to you."

"Fine. Have it your own way." He seated himself behind his desk. "Now, what did you want to speak to me about?"

What do you think I want to speak to you about, you wanker? Of course, this was not what she actually said.

"You left me stranded on a ledge," she hissed, narrowed eyes, wrinkled nose.

Geoff swallowed hard. Nervous. Apprehensive. "Yes. Um. Sorry about that." And then in a firmer tone, "You owe me a new drainpipe."

Patience's mouth flopped open. Her expression said it all. You're fucking joking, right? She then gnashed her teeth and delivered arguably the scariest angry face ever known to mankind. It seemed to do the trick, for Geoff began to falter.

"Um. On second thoughts, forget about the drainpipe."

"You promised you'd let me back in once the coast was clear. But you didn't."

"I couldn't. Something came up."

"Yes. I know. Your cock up your wife! You forgot all about me and screwed her instead." And off his surprised alarm, she added, "Don't try to deny it. I looked through the window and saw you."

Her manager's defence was, "How was I supposed to know strawberries and spray cream would turn her into a crazed nymphomaniac?"

"Because she's your wife, Geoff. You should know her inside out."

Geoff bowed his head, remorseful. He then cast aside his regret, lobbed her a plastic smile and attempted to diffuse the situation with, "Look. Patience. Let me make it up to you. I'll book us a fancy hotel, no expense spared. That way, we'll be able to fuck all night, totally undisturbed. If you like, we could even call room service half way through for refreshments. The finest champagne, of course. What do you say?"

Patience scowled at him like he was shit on her shoe. "You really think I still want sex with you after what happened?"

Yes. Clearly, he did. "You were well up for it last Friday."

Patience couldn't believe the gall of the man. "That was before you left me stark naked on a fucking ledge."

"Stark naked? That's not entirely true, is it? You had your knickers on."

Patience shook her head, livid. Was there really any point in arguing the toss with this man? Probably not. Geoff was a seasoned love rat, and as such, highly trained in the art of wriggling out of awkward situations.

"Is there anything else you'd like to get off your chest?" he asked her.

"Yes. Those women out there. Your workforce. The poor bitches you've fucked."

"What about them?"

"Have you actually taken the time to get to know them? Properly, I mean."

Geoff frowned. "I'm sorry, I don't follow."

"Do you know anything about them? Birthdays? Hobbies? Hopes and dreams? Kids names, if any? Whether or not they're married? Anything like that?" And off his uncomfortable hush, "No. I didn't think so."

"I'm the boss, they're my employees. It's the them and us divide. You get it in every workplace."

Patience didn't buy into his bullshit. "All they are to you are vaginas waiting to be filled whenever you feel the urge. You don't treat them like real people at all."

"Come on, Patience. You know the score. It's tit for tat. They want something from me, they've got to earn it. It's always been that way and always will be. Not just here. Everywhere. In offices up and down the country." And then an afterthought. "What the hell has made you take the moral high ground, all of a sudden?"

She considered his question. Her reply consisted of just one word.

"Enlightenment."

Nothing more was said. Patience bid farewell to the manager's office and returned to a desk laden with towering piles of paperwork.

Three hundred years later, or at least that's how long it felt, saw the end of the working day. She grabbed her things, not forgetting the plastic bag of Friday's clothes, and left the building. Out she emerged into a street alive with five o'clock people, all pushing, shoving, dodging, scurrying like crazed ants. Their only purpose, to get home as fast as possible.

As she walked along street after street, she realised how lucky she'd been. Her boss could have easily sacked her for such a rude outburst. But he hadn't. Why was that? Maybe he saw Patience as a loyal, dedicated, and as such, indispensable employee. Either that or he'd decided to save her job on the off-chance that he might one day be fortunate enough to get his cock wet inside her. The latter was in all probability closer to the truth.

Hah! Geoff The C Word didn't stand a chance. Not any more. Nor did anybody else. Not unless she met a man who really floated her boat. From now on, Patience Hope would be socially known as Patience Choosy As Hell.

She took a short cut through the recreation park. It was the quickest route to the hospital. Much more sensible that slogging it all the way to the roundabout at the top of the hill and then literally doubling back on herself.

"Don't say hello then."

The voice was female. And strangely familiar. She turned to face a young lady who smiled up at her, seated on a park bench, pram by her side. It was Aimee, as in Nathan's ex.

"Hi." Patience sat down beside the girl. "How are you?"

"Not too bad, considering I've been so stupid."

Patience offered a knowing nod, recalling in her head the events of the past few days. "You and me both." She indicated to the pram. "How's the little one?"

"Fine. The clever boy kept Nathan up all night. When I went round there Sunday morning to pick him up, the twat looked like a zombie."

They both laughed. There then came a brief hiatus where both parties strove for something else to say. It was a rather sullen Aimee who broke the silence.

"You probably think I've been round the block a few times. But I'm not a slag."

"I never said you were."

"How many men do you think I've had in my life?"

She tossed Aimee a double take. It was more or less the same question Penny had asked Patience during the night of her birthday.

The question that had kicked off her quest to kill off her virginity. Weird. Talk about full circle.

"Go on," prompted Aimee. "Guess."

Patience hated being put on the spot. Today was no exception. "I don't know. Three? Four?" She'd been told it was the average for a girl of Aimee's age.

The teen's nose wrinkled and her eyes narrowed, not best pleased by the estimate. Oops. She'd obviously been told an incorrect average.

The snap correction came in the form of, "Two?"

"Wrong. The answer is in fact—"

Patience was sure she could hear a drum roll.

"—one."

She was gobsmacked by the young mother's answer. "But that means—before Nathan, you were—"

"A virgin? Yes."

"Oh, my God." Talk about a coincidence.

"Hard to believe, huh?"

"No. Not hard to believe at all."

Aimee smirked. "Liar." And then the smirk was lost, replaced by a wave of morose self-pity. "And now look at me. Soiled goods. No self-respecting guy will take on somebody with a child. One stupid, unprotected shag. That's all it took to completely fuck up any chance of getting a ring on my finger."

It was certainly a reality check for Patience. Had she not already decided to give up trying to kiss goodbye to her virginity, this would be the pivotal moment where she'd see the error of her ways and close her legs to the general public forthwith. Sure, Patience would always insist on a condom—that's if she ever got round to the actual sex part of sex—but it still made her think.

"I am so lonely," the girl continued. "Yeah, so I've got my little boy. But it's not the same. There's no man on the scene. I hardly go out any more or do anything. And my friends have all deserted me. Basically, I've been reduced to a pramface nobody."

Patience looked at her. Thought about it. And then said, "Give me your phone number."

Aimee's brow furrowed in puzzlement. "Why?"

"So we can arrange something together."

"Like what?"

A shoulder shrug. "Anything you want."

Aimee struggled to put two and two together. Although she reached the sum of four, she was still not too sure if she'd calculated it correctly. "Are you saying you want to be my friend?"

Patience smiled. She certainly was. "Yeah. Why not?"

Aimee tried her hardest to get her head around it all. "But what's the point? I can't afford to go out that much."

"So we'll stay in. Rent out a girlie DVD. Sink a few voddys."

"What about the baby?"

"Way too young for alcohol," Patience quipped. "He'll have to stick to milk."

They both giggled. It was probably the first time Aimee had laughed like this in a long time. The two girls swapped numbers. Patience then said her goodbyes, kissed the baby's head and continued her journey to the hospital, warm and fuzzy in the knowledge that she'd made somebody happy today.

Around a quarter of an hour later, she reached the hospital. Upon sailing into the correct ward, she discovered a fierce debate raging between Penny and Dave.

"You asked me to marry you and I said yes. You can't back out of it now."

A worried Dave responded with, "All I heard you say was, you'd think about it. At no point did you officially accept my proposal."

Penny wound him up further with, "I know what I said, Dave."

The trembling man looked to Patience for an alliance. "You were there. Tell her I'm the one in the right, I'm begging you."

"Sorry, Dave. I definitely heard Penny say yes," she lied.

Dave rubbed his sweaty face with both palms. The noises that came out of his mouth sounded like constipation cries. This was a true audio-visual example of a man in distress.

"Oh, God, I'm way too young for a death sentence."

Penny and Patience exchanged conspiratorial smirks.

Dave continued to attempt saving himself. "I didn't know what I was saying. I was delirious. At death's door. I thought I'd never see you again. That's the only reason I proposed."

Penny feigned a warm smile. "It was very sweet of you, Dave." She turned to Patience. "Will you help me choose a wedding dress?"

"Yes, of course."

Dave's eyes widened. "Penny. Please. I'm sorry. I can't go through with this. I'm not a commitment person."

Penny's face dropped. "Are you saying you don't want to marry me now?"

Patience was hugely impressed by the girl's acting skills.

Dave grimaced, not knowing what to think, do or say. It was a case of damned if he did, damned if he didn't. He eventually arrived at, "No. Sorry."

Penny then smiled, relieved. "Thank fuck for that. You really think I want to tie the knot at my age? Oh, God, no."

The two girls erupted.

"Oh, very funny," Dave groaned, realising he'd been set up, but taking it all in good spirits. "Look at my sides. They're splitting." He then glanced at Patience. "Sorry about the other night. If I'd known I was going to be struck down with food poisoning, I'd have fucked you first."

Patience smiled. "Really, it's not that important. You just concentrate on getting better."

Penny piped up with, "Don't worry, Patience. We'll bag you some hot sex, and that's a promise. I've already thought of another foolproof plan. All we need to do is contact every broad-minded person we know and invite them to the flat for a mass orgy. That way, if one bloke is taken ill before they get inside you, there will be plenty of spare willy-winkies ready to take his place. This has got to be my finest idea to date. It can't possibly fail."

Patience waved down her overt enthusiasm. "Before you get totally carried away with your dead-cert sex schemes, I've made an important decision. I'm not going to rush into losing my virginity after all."

Penny, taken aback. "Why?"

"Because it's just not worth it."

It did not compute for the flatmate. "Wow. Talk about a sudden change of heart. You said it was your quest. Your mission. Your destiny. Something you had to do."

"Yes, I know. What was I bloody thinking, eh? It all boiled down to what I thought other people would think or say if they discovered my secret. So I figured if got rid of the V word, there would be nothing for them to mock me about. I'd fit right in. But it's all so clear to me now. Nobody gives a shit. They're all too busy living their own lives. So what the hell am I worried about?"

Penny shrugged her shoulders. "Fuck knows."

"Okay, so I'm a twenty-five-year-old virgin. So what? It doesn't make me a bad person. Or a twathead. Or a stupid freak. It's my life. Nobody else's. It's up to me what I do. Or don't do." Big smile alert. "It is so frigging liberating to finally realise. In the great scheme of things, it really doesn't matter at all."

Dave clapped. "Here, here. Speech of the century."

"Thank you, Dave."

Then Dave realised. "Hey. Does this mean I'll never get a chance to fuck you?"

Patience smirked. "Probably not, no."

"Oh. Shame." Then came the joking wink.

Penny asked, "Patience, are you absolutely sure about this?"

A firm nod. "Dead sure. Sex will happen for me when it happens. With somebody I love who loves me back. I don't care whether it's tomorrow, next month, or in twenty year's time."

"Well, it's your life," said Penny. "But don't come running to me if you're on your deathbed and you still haven't bagged your first bonk."

They all laughed. Loudly.

Patience and Penny emerged from the building. Felicity stood waiting by the entrance.

"Hey, look," squealed Penny. "It's Felicity down the road."

They greeted each other with air kisses. "How's Dave?" asked Felicity.

Penny responded with, "Getting better by the minute. He'll soon be pounding our pussies to oblivion again."

Felicity smiled. "Cool. Looking forward to it. I bet you are too, Patience."

Before Patience could reply, Penny cut in with, "I doubt it. Patience has decided to be a virgin again."

The redhead said, "Oh. Right." Then a grin. "By the way, girls. I've got shocking gossip."

"Excellent. Spill the beans."

"All in good time, Penny." She tapped her nose. "All in good time."

The three girls strolled across the car park, heading out of the hospital grounds and beyond.

"Fancy hitting a bar for a couple of quick voddys?" suggested Penny.

"Count me in," was Felicity's contribution.

"Good idea," said Patience. "After everything that's happened over the past few days, I think I deserve a drink."

Penny looked pleased. "Excellent. Game on."

"I'm only stopping for one though," afterthought Patience. "The last thing I want to do is turn up at the restaurant totally out of my tree."

Penny, intrigued. "What restaurant?"

"Joe's taking me out to dinner tonight."

"Woooh. It's all right for some. So the sight of your scary tits didn't frighten him off for long then?"

"No, Penny. They didn't."

Felicity's mobile phone sang to her. "Aha. This is the shocking gossip I promised you." A tap of the green key. "Hello?" For the benefit and subsequent amusement of Patience and Penny, she put it on loudspeaker.

"Hi, Felicity. It's me. Chantelle." Her grandfather's young fiancée didn't sound at all in the best of moods.

"Oh, hi, Chantelle. What's up?" As if she didn't know.

"I've got some bad news," Chantelle began to explain, "I'm moving back in with my parents. Me and your grandfather have split up."

All three women felt a strong, almost overpowering urge to laugh. Loudly. In fact, they found themselves all set to explode into hysterics. Somehow, however, they managed not to succumb to their desires.

It was Felicity who deserved an award for her beautifully convincing portrayal of friendly concern. "Oh, no, Chantelle, I don't believe it. I thought you two were made for each other."

Patience screwed up her face. Hmm. Maybe that was taking faux affability a little too far.

"What happened?" Felicity asked next.

"He took me out shopping. Said he wanted to spend his money. I thought, great. Diamond rings and designer clothes, here I come. But do you know what we came back with?"

Felicity shrugged, even though her ex step-grandmother couldn't see the action. "I give up. What did you come back with?"

Chantelle's voice sounded as though the girl was baring the teeth of anger. "A loaf of bread and pint of milk."

Muffled giggles all round. These girls were almost pissing themselves.

"That's it?" Felicity managed to ask.

"Yeah. That's it. He did it to prove a point."

"What point?"

"That it was all he could afford. He didn't have any money after all. He's just another skint pensioner. The wrinkly bastard's been using me all this time. So I dumped him."

Exactly how these girls were continually able to keep almost straight faces was beyond the realms of human comprehension.

"Oh. Right. What did he say to that?" Felicity asked.

"He thanked me for all the sex and helped pack my suitcase."

Then boom! A vivid explosion of unbridled hilarity. Not even Felicity survived this particular giggle-bang unscathed.

Chantelle couldn't understand the need for such an eruption of belly laughs. "Felicity? Are you making fun of me?"

Wisdom amidst the mirth from Felicity. "You've got to understand, Chantelle. A relationship isn't determined by how rich somebody is. There's so much more to it than that. For starters, you need mutual love. And trust. And plenty of give and take."

The girl who was no longer destined to become Felicity's step-grandmother scoffed. "Yeah, yeah, as if."

"Money isn't everything."

A long pause. It seemed as though the young carer on the other end of the line was regarding such wisdom with merit and understanding, and that the advice was actually sinking in.

But Chantelle spoilt the moment with, "Yes, it is." And she hung up. Abruptly.

Felicity shook her head, a tad disappointed. "What a stupid bitch. For a moment there, I really thought I was getting through to the girl."

"Don't worry about it, Felicity," said Patience. "There will always be stupid cows like Chantelle who will never change. Not everybody can be helped."

"Hey, girls," giggled Penny, keen to lighten up the mood. "Race you to the nearest bar. Last one there smells like rotten eggs."

It was childish. In fact, totally and utterly infantile. But it didn't stop them taking Penny up on the challenge.

Chapter 15

The Road to Sex

Never mind Patience not once having sex. The girl was a restaurant virgin too.

Sure, she'd enjoyed late-night curry house craziness with Penny, Dave and Felicity. And she'd attended some kind of middle-of-nowhere posh carvery for last year's Christmas works do. But she had never before accompanied a man for a romantic candlelit dinner. Not that this particular meal could be considered romantic, of course. Joe was just a friend. Oh, and gay. Still, she supposed it would be good practice for when she eventually did find—by some strange miracle, divine intervention, fate, whatever, delete as appropriate—a proper boyfriend to take her out on a real date.

"Do you really have to go to Scotland?" she asked, eyes lost and cheerless. "I mean, it's hardly a promotion or anything, so it doesn't seem worth it."

He placed his hand upon hers and looked squarely into her despondent eyes. "This is something I have to do. Nothing will make me change my mind, no matter what anybody says. Just like you and your quest to lose your virginity."

Patience scoffed. "Oh, that."

The waiter made himself known and passed them each a menu. The couple thanked him and began to browse through the goodies on offer.

"Wine?" the waiter asked.

"I will if the bill's too high," she joked, one corner of her mouth curling upwards into a cheeky smirk.

The waiter stared at the girl, unresponsive, expressionless. Patience's smirk melted to nothing. Hmm. Either the man in the penguin suit had no sense of humour, or she was a crap stand-up—um—who was actually sitting down. Maybe that's why the gag bombed.

Joe saved the situation with, "We'll order drinks with our food, thank you."

The waiter nodded and left.

Patience shook her head, embarrassed. "God, some people just can't take a joke."

Her dinner partner changed the subject to blanket her disquiet. "Hey, I was wondering. Did Penny's nightclub plan work out for you?"

Another scoff from Patience, only louder this time. "Total frigging disaster. I'll tell you what, the sex fairy doesn't like me at all. Every time I get this close to actual penetration—" She positioned her thumb and forefinger a few millimetres apart from each other. "—something always buggers it up."

"Oh. So I take it you're still—"

"A virgin?" She gave a nod. "Full marks, Einstein."

Joe was rather surprised by the news. "But you went to a nightclub. Where there's—"

"Guaranteed sex? Yes. I know." A weighty sigh escaped from her lungs. "I did manage to go home with a guy. But it didn't work out." Another noise left her mouth. Stranger, this time. Some kind of throaty growl. "It's official. I must be the most unfuckable girl in the world."

"Oh, I wouldn't say that."

Patience fired an appreciative smile at her best friend. "Thanks, Joe. I know you're only being kind. But it's true. I've got more chance of growing a penis than getting laid. So I've reached a momentous decision. I'm abandoning my quest for ex virginity."

"You mean, you're turning celibate?"

Patience made a sucking on a lemon face. "Ooh, no, I won't go that far. Never say never and all that bollocks. I'm just fed up to the eyeballs with chasing it, that's all. From now on, men can do all the hard work." Then her face sank. "Not that anybody will bother, of course. As far as the world's concerned, Patience Hope is a no-fuck zone."

She really needed to steer away from this subject. Or at least divert the limelight over to Joe. All this talk about her non-existent sex life was far too depressing.

"What about you, Joe? How come you're still a virgin?"

By the speed that Joe delivered his riposte, it seemed as though he'd been expecting the question. Talk about being prepared.

"I decided to wait for the right person."

She gave the man a sympathetic shake of the head. He was just as wet behind the ears as she was.

"That's exactly what I've been doing all these years," she told him. "And after all that effort, Mr Right never bothered to make contact. I always checked my phone. No missed calls." A long-trailing exhale. "Complete waste of time. In hindsight, it was all a bit pathetic really."

"Ah, but I've always had somebody specific in mind."

"Really?"

He nodded. "I've been waiting for this person to notice me for years. But for some weird reason, it hasn't quite happened in the way I'd planned. Worst thing is, this person is bound to meet somebody one day. Fall in love. Settle down. And yes, I know this might sound a little selfish of me, but I don't think I could handle standing on the sidelines. All by myself. Watching their happiness." A lost stare, but only brief. "So that's why I've decided to cut my losses and try my luck with a new life in Scotland."

Patience. Astounded by the speech, confession, waiting in vain anecdote, whatever it was. "Wow. Must be one hell of a special person."

Joe wore the kind of expression that asked the Pope's choice of religion. "You're not wrong there."

Patience was hugely intrigued. In fact, the suspense was killing the girl over and over again. "Look, sorry, I'm dying to know. Call me a nosey bitch if you like, but that's just the way I am. It's confession time, Joe. Who exactly have you been waiting for all this time?"

Joe gazed at the girl.

There followed the longest hiatus in all of human history. Until —

"You."

It didn't quite sink in at first. Then came the confusion, the surprise, the gobsmacked simpleton face. She didn't just throw across one double take. A bombshell of this magnitude warranted several in a row.

"What do you mean, me?"

"You. As in, Patience Hope."

She pulled a strange, contorted, difficult to describe face. "What the fuck are you smoking? You can't fancy me."

"Why not?"

"It's impossible."

"Why is it?"

"Because—" Go on. Say it. Set the guy straight. "—you're gay."

Joe leaned back in his chair, his brow all folds and creases. "First I've heard of it."

What the frigging hell? "You must be."

"I can assure you I'm not."

Patience stared at him, confused, dumbstruck, trying her hardest to make sense of it all. "So you're not a—?"

"Homosexual? No. I'm one hundred per cent heterosexual."

The three millionth puzzled frown. It was making her go all cross-eyed. "Why the fuck did I think you were gay?"

Joe shrugged, no answers to offer. "I have absolutely no idea."

She looked right. She looked left. She looked down. She looked back up. Then she stared straight at him. "So how come you never told me you didn't bat for the other side?"

It was Joe's turn to pitch across a double take. "Because I was totally unaware that you thought I did."

"Oh, my God." Patience didn't look at all happy about the shock revelation. "You mean to tell me I've had to endure all those idiots during the past few days, and stumbled through all those disasters in the name of attempting to lose my bloody virginity, when I could have easily asked you to sort me out for no hassle at all?"

Joe thought about it, then, "That's about the size of it, yes."

"Well, thanks a lot, Joe! I thought you were my fucking friend!"

Joe was flabbergasted by what he was hearing. "Are you actually blaming me for the false belief that you—yes, you—held about my sexuality?"

"Yes!" She then reconsidered. "No." More uncertainty. "Oh, I don't know."

"Unbe-fucking-lievable," he remarked, not best pleased.

Patience was determined to get her point across. "This is all irrelevant anyway. You've never shown any signs that you fancy me, so what's the point in even continuing this discussion?"

It was all getting pretty heated.

"I've never shown you any signs because you've never shown any to me!"

"I've never shown you any signs because I thought you were gay!"

"Well, if I'd known what you thought you knew about me, I would have set you straight a long time ago!"

And they crashed headlong into an awkward silence.

They both stared at each other in disorientated non-speak for what seemed a hundred years. A thousand, even. It was Joe who finally found the courage to break the hush.

"Oh, Patience." His tone was soft. Low. Almost a whisper. "Where do we go from here?"

Patience stared at him. Good fucking question. Where should they go from here? Like, duh. Wasn't it obvious? She knew exactly which way she yearned to head.

She found herself overwhelmed by the whole situation. Her mouth didn't know whether to continue hanging loose or smile. So it volleyed between the two options. Hang loose. Smile. Hang loose. Smile. Hang loose. Smile. Another smile. A fucking great big smile.

"Joe. All my life I've wanted you to be my boyfriend." Frigging hell, girl. Did you really say that?

The reply. "And all my life I've wanted you to be my girlfriend."

More smiles. And big eyes. To passing observers, they probably looked like a pair of dribbling loonies.

"Oh, my God," she gasped, elated.

"Oh, my God, as well," he responded.

Patience's face glowed brilliant white with happiness. She'd finally got her man. Yay! And what's more, he was the man she'd always desired. Wow with one hell of a capital W.

And then she said it.

"I love you."

Then he said it.

"I love you too."

OMG! Patience's smile was so broad, it was in danger of falling off the sides of her face.

"Does this mean you're not moving to Scotland now?"

"Too fucking right. Patience, don't you fret, I am staying right here with you."

It was no good. She could hold back no longer. The girl craned her neck forward and planted a kiss upon his lips. He did the same to her. This was followed by two more smiles. Then their lips met once more, only this time not letting go.

The waiter made his return and offered a polite cough. The two brand new lovers parted company of each other's mouth.

"Sir? Madam? Are you ready to order now?"

They glanced up at the waiter. Then back at each other. A chair scraped back. Patience stood bolt upright.

"If it's all the same to you," she said to the penguin, "we'll skip the meal and fast-forward straight to the sex."

She pulled Joe to his feet and steered him quickly towards the exit. This left the now-lonesome waiter staring blankly at two empty chairs, pencil and pad in hand, nothing to scribble.

They both emerged from the restaurant and made a hasty bee-line across the car park towards Joe's vehicle.

"Patience. Are you sure about this?"

"If you're sure, yes."

Joe unlocked his car. They both climbed in.

"If I'm sure?" he queried. "Are you only doing this for me?"

"No way."

"Are you sure?"

"Of course I'm sure."

Joe didn't quite get it. A quick check was in order. "Does that mean you're sure you're not just doing it for me, or you're sure you do want to do it with me?"

Oh, for fuck's sake! "Joe. Stop over-analysing things. That's my job."

He nodded. "So you're absolutely sure?"

Argh! "Yes! Dead sure. In fact, I've never been so sure of anything else in my life. I want to go to bed with you. I want to make love with you. I want to sleep with you. I want to have sex with you. I want to fuck you. I want to screw you. I want to shag you. I want to bonk you." She paused for a quick breath, then, "If I've missed out any other synonyms, include them too. But most importantly—I love you."

"I love you too."

"Good. Glad that's settled."

Joe. Absolutely delighted. "I've always wanted to say this. Your place or mine?"

"My place. There's nobody home. And besides, I don't think your parents would appreciate all the racket."

Joe grinned. "Are you one of those girls you hear about?"

"What girls?"

"Screamers."

"How should I know? I haven't had a chance to find out yet. Now, for fuck's sake, just drive."

Patience's face shone with happiness. OMG. At last. It was finally going to happen. With somebody who had been right under her nose all along. OMG again. Why had she assumed he was gay? She racked her brains again and again, but couldn't uncover the answer. Something in the dim and distant past must have given her that idea. A conversation perhaps. Or one of Joe's quirky effeminate mannerisms. Or quite simply a false assumption on her part. Whatever the inciting incident had been, it would almost certainly remain buried forever. But did it really matter? No. At this moment in time, just one goal needed to be scored. That is, for the two of them to get home, get naked and wiggle a lot.

Of course, it wasn't just a sex thing. Not this time. Patience Hope's lifelong dream and ambition was about to come true. Her first time would be with somebody she loved who truly loved and cared for her. Oh. My. Fucking. God. Yes, yes, yes!

Joe turned the ignition key. The engine struggled to turn over.

And failed to fire up.

They exchanged concerned glances. Uh oh. He tried again. It still didn't start. Instead, the mechanics of the bloody thing groaned with a low, throaty, slowed-down yawn which sounded uncannily like Patience attempting to rise too early in the morning.

"What's the matter?" she asked.

"I think the battery's dead."

Bugger and double bugger. "Oh, great!"

Was a broken down vehicle destined to be the next barrier in a long list of obstacles designed to prevent the taking of her virginity? It certainly looked that way. But why Patience? What had she done to deserve such bad luck? She couldn't recall smashing any mirrors. And she'd never once walked under a ladder. Argh! Typical. Her brain had reached the point where silly superstitions were as real as trees. Or bushes. Or blades of grass. Or those nodding dogs found on the parcel shelves of cars driven by Geography teachers. Oh, God. Now she'd reminded herself of cars. Or rather, this particular non-starter.

"Don't worry," he assured her. "There is a solution."

"And what's that?"

"We can bump start it."

"Bump start it?"

"Yes. All we need to do is roll the car down a hill. When it builds up enough momentum, I'll shove it into gear and the engine will fire up."

"Joe. There aren't any hills around here. Look out the window. Nothing but horizontalness as far as the eye can see."

His face slumped. "Ah. In that case, you'll have to get out and push."

You must be frigging joking. "Me?"

"Well, it can't be me, can it? I need to be in the car. Unless you want to do the gear shoving thing."

"Joe, I can't drive." She cursed herself inside for not taking lessons. "Knowing me, I'd steer it into a brick wall." And then she found inspiration. "I've got a much better idea. Sod the bump start. We'll thump start it."

A puzzled frown from Joe. "Thump start?"

"Yeah. This." She made a fist and thumped the top of the dashboard. "Bloody!" Thump! "Start!" Thump! "You!" Thump! "Stupid!" Thump! "Heap!" Thump! "Of!" Thump! "Metal." And as calm as a gentle breeze, she concluded with, "Try it now."

Joe turned the key. The engine burst into life. He looked totally dumbfounded by the miracle. Patience threw him a smug grin.

"The power of a woman. Now, put your foot down and step on it."

Joe responded with, "I can put my foot down, but if I step on it, I'll hurt my toes."

A stern glare from Patience. "You've been cracking that same joke ever since you bought your first car. I laughed the first time round, probably out of sympathy, but since then, I have failed to find it funny. So shut up and drive us back to my place. Like, pronto."

At once, Joe drove out of the car park and down the road.

Patience was surprised to notice something familiar on the roadside up ahead. The dressing gown. The tatty brown tartan thing she'd stolen off the washing line the other night. Only, this time, it was draped around the old man. He was using it as a jacket, walking his dog along the pavement, big beam upon face, clearly glad of its safe return.

She smiled to herself. The hassle of returning the garment, followed by her subsequent sharp departure and loss of her skirt had been worth it after all. Old man and dressing gown, reunited. What a beautiful —

The dog barked loudly at the car as they passed. Patience gasped. Shit. Spotted by a toothy canine with a photographic memory. She covered her face from window view.

Joe frowned. "Do you know that bloke?"

"No." It was the most unconvincing no ever.

"Are you sure? His dog seemed to recognise you."

She narrowed her eyes in Joe's direction. "If you don't drop this line of questioning right now, somebody won't be getting their willy wet tonight. Is that understood?"

An interruption. Patience's mobile phone played her song again. Glad that she'd decided earlier not to change the ringtone, she offered it ten more seconds of airtime, and even sang along to it, before accepting the call and putting it to her ear.

"Hello?"

"Hey, you. It's Penny. Just to let you know, surprise, surprise, I'm in a bar." Hospital visiting hours had obviously expired and Penny hours had just begun. "If you're at a loose end after your dinner date, come and join me. I've got some shots lined up with our names on them."

"Your offer sounds very tempting, Penny, but I'm heading back to the flat with Joe to fuck his brains out."

A moment of bewildered silence. Then, "I thought he was gay."

"So did I." Patience giggled like a naughty schoolgirl. "But it turns out he's not. Isn't that great? Looks like I made a bit of a blunder on the assumption front."

"Oh, my God."

"Double oh, my God, more like."

"Cool. That means after tonight, you'll no longer be — "

"A virgin? No."

Penny cheered. "You go, girl. In the meantime, I'll sink these shots, find myself some fun in the city and give you two some privacy for a while."

"Thanks, Penny. Very much appreciated."

"That's what friends are for." Then she added, "Oh, and Patience. Losing your virginity only happens once in your life. So make the most of it."

"I will."

"And that thing I said the other day. You know, about the first time being awkward and painful and a total disaster."

"What about it?"

"It usually is. But it doesn't have to be that way. Especially as yours will be with somebody you really care about."

"I'll do my best."

"I'm sure you will. Right. It's time for me to sign off. But here's one final piece of advice." A pause for dramatic effect. "Make it special."

"Oh, don't worry." She gave a wink, even though Penny was blind to it. "I intend to."

Patience shut off the phone and threw it into her handbag. She peered out of the window to find her bearings. Hmm. Still a long way from home.

"Joe. Why are you driving so slow?"

"Thirty limit."

"So what? I want to get home and jump into bed with you. Like,

ASAP."

"Relax. We're only ten minutes away."

"In ten minutes, it might be too late," she stressed, anxious and impatient. "My vagina is on pout overdrive. I've never felt so turned on in my life. And me being shaken about in this seat isn't helping matters." Oh, come back Old Rumble-Shaky, all is forgiven.

"It's not my fault this road is full of potholes."

Bouncing about, Patience ordered, "Just get us home as fast as possible."

"I'm not speeding again. Not after what happened last time."

"Put it this way," she said in no uncertain terms. "If I reach my orgasm before we get there, all you'll be fucking tonight is your hand." It was not just a statement. It was a warning.

Joe made a face. "Do women actually suffer from premature orgasms?"

"Do you want to find out the hard way?"

Joe bit his bottom lip. The whirrs and clicks of the man weighing things up in his head could be heard loud and clear. Then, a desperate decision. He took the car to forty.

Patience beamed from ear to ear. "I am so excited about this," she gushed. "I can't think of anything that could go wrong. You're not married, so there won't be a wife coming home unexpectedly. You haven't got a child, so there's no chance of a sudden family reunion." She then thought about what happened to Dave. Uh oh. Major concern alert, beep, beep, beep! "How's your general health? Any aches or pains?"

"I feel fine."

"Have you eaten any dodgy prawns?"

Joe. Seriously concerned for her sanity. "Stop spouting rubbish and pull yourself together."

Patience nodded and composed herself. "You're right. I must stop worrying. Everything's going to be all right. You and I, we're destined to have the best sex ever in the whole history of naughtiness. Nothing—and I mean nothing—can possibly prevent our first time from happening tonight." Her face then froze over with horror. "Oh, my fucking God!"

Joe looked equally worried. In fact, panicky. "What's the matter?"

"I haven't got any condoms!" she cried, end of the world style.

It was true. She'd purchased a three-pack the other day, yes. But those same three condoms had each died a very uneventful death. Sure, they had been used. Well, if you could call it that. They'd been put on at least. And that's as far as they'd got. So near yet so bloody light years away.

"Shit. Nor have I. I've never needed them."

Patience had an idea. "Oh, I know. You can come over my tits."

Joe grimaced, face almost green with disgust. "For God's sake, please tell me you're joking."

Eh? "I thought blokes liked that kind of thing."

Joe shook his head. "Not all blokes."

"Yeah, but think about it. It's safe sex in a way. My tits are miles from my baby-making bits."

Joe was in no way won over. "What on Earth made you suggest such a thing in the first place?"

Patience thought about it, then, "Promise you won't laugh."

"Depends what it is."

"No, please. Promise."

"All right. I promise I won't laugh."

Patience drew a deep breath for composure. "Friday night. When we were watching music videos." Should he be told? Yeah, you go, girl. Well, here goes nothing. "I had a sexual fantasy."

Joe's face lit up with delight. "Yeah? What about?"

Patience made a face. Isn't it obvious? "About us two having sex, of course."

Joe looked puzzled. "But back then, you thought I was gay?"

"Yes, I know. But that didn't stop me wondering what sex with you would be like."

"Oh, right." He smiled smugly, liking the sound of that. "So let me guess. In this sexual fantasy, I came over your tits."

"Correct."

Her friend was getting it now. "Ah. Which is why you—" With his free hand, he lifted his shirt slightly.

She completed the sentence for him. "Inadvertently whipped off my top in front of you, yes."

"And it's also why you—" He simulated fondling his own breast.

"Lathered up my tits with both hands like an idiot, yes. So now you know."

Joe felt enlightened. "That explains everything."

"Not everything. I have a question for you."

Joe raised an enquiring eyebrow. "Oh?"

"I want you to be honest. Why were you so repulsed by my tits?"

"Repulsed? No way. I think you've got beautiful breasts. I was just shocked, that's all. One second you were sitting quietly on the sofa, the next you were fucking thin air. I thought you'd finally lost it."

At that, they both laughed.

Joe then said, "Look, sorry, but I'm not too keen on the coming over your tits idea. So how about we stop off at a late opening chemist for some condoms?"

"Okay, Joe. You win," she said with a wicked grin. "Late opening chemist, it is."

Chapter 16

Lust and Romance

It was weird. A few hours ago, Patience Hope had given up on her quest to lose her virginity. And now, that same few hours later, she was all set to lose it to Joe, a best friend promoted to lover. Actually, lover sounded a little sordid. Lovers were usually other womens' husbands. Or other mens' wives. He was far more important to her than just a secret sexual plaything, a cheating heart, or a convenient sexual reproductive organ. No, no, no. It was official. Breaking news. Hold the front page. Joe was now her boyfriend. Her sweetheart. Her other half. Her partner. The love of her life. And her absolute soulmate.

Wow. She had a boyfriend. A real-life, bona fide, genuine boyfriend. Mmm. She liked that word. Boyfriend, boyfriend, boyfriend. Somebody to love. A good man who also loved her in return. Wow again. It had only taken twenty-five years to achieve a loving relationship with a member of the opposite sex. She longed to pinch herself to check whether or not she was dreaming. But then thought, no. She'd rather let Joe do all the groping. Insert wink here.

As a sexed-up Patience and Joe dashed hand in hand with virile haste into the flat, she thought about all the disasters she'd been involved in over the past few days. One sexual catastrophe after another. Out of the sordid frying pan and into the sleazy fire. Groan and double groan. What a complete dickhead she'd been. All that chaos could have been totally avoided if she'd simply stepped back and blessed herself with a little patience and a little hope.

Then OMG! Realisation kicked both her buttocks hard. A little patience and a little hope had been all she needed to secure Joe's heart. Patience and hope. She couldn't believe she'd been so blind. Patience

Hope was not just the name she had been given at birth. It had also helped to seal her fate. And her destiny.

So many factors could have easily scuppered their plans for horizontal gratification. Just like all the other times with Geoff, Tom, Nathan, and even Dave. But nothing tonight had got in their way. Not this time. Phew. Well, except a dodgy car battery. But that had been sorted out with Patience's patent pending thump start. And now, here they were. The two of them. Alone yet together. In Patience's bedroom.

She closed the door. Locked it. And threw the key across the room. All preventative measures to stop the Demon Of Fucked Up Sexual Opportunities from — well, you know — fucking up the ultimate sexual opportunity. That arsewipe demon was not going to get his own way tonight, period.

They both stood motionless in the centre of the room. Silent. Shy. Uncertain. Staring at each other in open-mouthed awe. Neither one quite sure where to go from here. Oh, God, Patience thought. This was definitely it. Her time, her moment, her everything. It was finally, finally, fucking finally going to happen. Sex with Joe. Two people in love. Which meant it was not just destined to be plain, common or garden sex. It was destined to be making love. Making sweet, passionate, heartfelt love. Ooooooh! She could hardly wait.

Note to self: Fuck this one up and I will never speak to you again. You got that, bitch?

It was no good. Patience needed to seize the moment. Take control. Otherwise they'd be playing bloody statues all night. She lunged forward like a mad woman and threw herself at him, wrapping her arms around his body. Joe stumbled backwards. Lost his footing. And they both landed on the bed.

Crunch!

It collapsed under their weight. They both found themselves in a graceless heap on the floored mattress, surrounded by ruffled bedding, a buckled headboard and splintered stakes of wood.

"Shit," gasped Joe, goggle-eyed. "We've just broken your bed."

Typical. Even her trusty single bed, a companion of hers since she'd staggered awkwardly into her early teens, was conspiring to prevent the taking of her virginity. Grrr. Was everybody and everything in on it? She bloody well hoped not.

"Who bloody cares?" said Patience, clambering on top of the man, determined to get her own way and succeed in her quest. "We'll do it on the floor."

They gazed into each other's eyes.

They shared an amazing moment.

"I love you, Patience."

"I love you too, Joe." Then she snapped out of it. "Let's cut the lovey-dovey slush and get down to it."

And so they did.

Hot, fervent lips pushed together in a seemingly eternal kiss as their arms wandered and writhed freely around each other's bodies like curious serpents. Oh, this felt good. Fucking good. Much better than her previous encounters with — well — mostly strangers. Sizzling electricity buzzed around her body upon every touch, every grope, every brush upon her torso with his eager fingers.

One by one, Patience began to undo the buttons of his shirt. Joe cupped her breasts, admiring their shape and form through the thin cotton prison that was her blouse. She tugged at his open shirt. He raised one arm to free it from a sleeve, then did the same with the other. The garment came away, revealing Joe's bare chest.

She kissed and licked the contours of his upper torso. He continued to fondle her tits, pushing them, squeezing them, kneading them hard. She found one of his nipples and enveloped it with her soft, warm lips. As she nuzzled, he unbuttoned her blouse and pulled it away from her smooth body, displaying bosoms cupped in black lace, with erect nipples like bullets making their mark on such flimsy semi-transparent material.

Patience worked her way down his body with a hungry tongue. Oh, how she was enjoying this. He tasted good. She wanted to eat him so badly. Upon reaching his navel, she unzipped his trousers and pulled them right down. Joe kicked them free with a few flicks of his legs. Then off came his underwear, revealing his hard cock. Oh, and what a cock it was. Patience beamed, impressed by its mass.

"Nice size."

"Thank you."

She wrapped her fingers around his rigid member and worked it with gentle strokes of her hand as she tongued all around his swollen tip.

"Ooh, you're talented for a first-timer," he remarked, thrilled by her mouthplay.

She looked up at him and smiled. "Let's just say I've picked up a few tips along the way."

A massive grin. "I bet you have."

She then opened wide. Joe cried out with delight as the majority of his cock disappeared inside her mouth, only to see the light of day again—or rather, the artificial lamp light of night—upon the upward cycle, just before surrendering to the darkness of her throat once more.

Patience fell instantly in love with Joe's spectacular cock. She loved its size, its warmth, its taste, everything. She hadn't really noticed a taste with other cocks. But it was weird. Joe's seemed to taste like chicken. Hmm. Maybe it was just her warped and barmy mind playing tricks.

"Oh, Patience, let me taste you too."

Continuing to suck his dick, she used one hand to discard her skirt and knickers. She then twisted her body in the opposite direction until her groin was mounted upon his waiting mouth. He lolled out his tongue. It made contact with her pussy lips. Patience groaned with pleasure as he lapped feverishly at her crevice like a thirsty cat with a bowl of milk. The faster he licked, the harder she sucked. It took teamwork to a whole new level.

And then his tongue found her clit. Oh, my fucking God, the electricity tore through her groin like a lightning bolt as he sucked on it, lapped at it, chewed at it. This made her suck, lick and chew his stiff weapon with wild and feverish relish.

They could have gorged on each other's delights for hours, but Patience wanted something else. Her body was yelling, shouting, screaming to be fucked hard. She needed his stiff shaft up her virgin, pure, undiscovered pussy right now.

"Fuck me, Joe," she growled, unhooking her bra and casting it aside to enjoy total nakedness. "And fuck me good."

It was one hell of an invitation. Her man complied straight away. He went about placing a condom over his dick. It took a little longer than expected. After all, it was the first time he'd ever handled a rubber. It was awkward and fiddly. Bloody thing. But at last, success. Rolled on and ready for action.

Patience lay on her back. Joe lowered himself onto her waiting form. She parted her legs and reached for his shaft, clutching it in both hands, positioning the rocket for lift off.

And then she froze. "Wait."

Joe looked alarmed. "What's the matter?"

"Shhh!" Her eyes looked left, looked right, then back at him again. "Can you hear that?"

Joe put his ears into action. Then a quizzical look. "Hear what?"

"It's the sound of nobody trying to stop me getting laid." A huge grin, almost idiot level. "One big fucking silence. Isn't that great? Now fuck me 'til I come, big boy."

He attempted to push his penis through the moist gates of heaven. It slipped out. Oops. Patience sighed as she put it back into position. Another try. Another slip-out.

Oh, please, God, she prayed inside her worried head. Don't do this to me. I've been a good girl. Well, most of the time, I have. And I've never done anything truly wrong. Nothing that could be considered bad, sinful, wicked, evil, whatever. Look, I promise I'll be a better person, okay? A model citizen. Who knows? I might even come to church. Or at least contribute some spare change to your leaky roof fund. Just let me enjoy this moment, okay? Please. Pretty please, even. Is it really too much to ask?

Joe straightened up, pushed again. And—

—ooohhhhh, it was in! OMG, fucking yes, success. Patience barked loudly with glee as his rock hard cock slid deep inside her body. He pushed it in as far as the girl could take it, then pulled back and pushed again. And again. And again. And again.

"Oohhh, yesssss!" she howled, a fusion of joy, rapture and sheer bloody relief.

Yay! At last. Finally. It was happening. She was having sex. Yes, actually having sexual intercourse. An amazing fuck-session with somebody she truly cared about. Oh, why had she waited so long for this? Why before had she turned up her nose at the act of fornication? And why the fuck had she been such a prude? Yes. That's right. A prude. Penny had indeed been correct with that particular observation of character.

She wrapped both arms tightly around his body and scratched the warm flesh of his back with eager nails as she felt her virginity being pumped away to nothing. He thrust with all his might, in and out, in and out, in and out, pummelling her willing hole with his rigid staff. She bore down with her pelvis as he thrust upwards, discovering rhythm, harmony, shared movement, everything. Oh, God, she could feel the juices down below beginning to build up, flowing downward like hot molten lava bursting free from a pressure-packed volcano. She gasped, she panted, she shrieked, she yelped. Oh, wow, fucking yes. Nothing before in her whole life had every felt this amazing. Ever.

"I fucking love you, Joe!" she squealed at the top of her voice.

He pounded harder, faster, deeper inside her, as if the yell was a cue to up his game. Her eyes slammed shut, her head rolled back, a crazed smile filled her face as she allowed him to bang her pussy, yelping loudly with delight at each smash.

Patience twisted to one side, taking Joe with her. They both rolled off the felled mattress and onto the carpet. The man landed on his back, the girl on top of him, penis still deep inside.

"My turn to be in control," she whispered suggestively.

She sat up straight and spat out shrieks of pleasure as she rode his stiff weapon for dear life. Joe clutched the girl's hips and leered with excitement, watching his throbbing cock being swallowed whole upon every downward plunge.

He reached upwards and cupped her breasts with clammy palms. She moaned with pleasure as he fondled, squeezed and pressed hard on her bosoms. This made her want to fuck him harder. She crashed down upon his willing cock, just as she had done in her sexual fantasy. He seemed to love it, sporting an idiot grin and wild, sparkling eyes as his woman continued to gyrate.

Oh, God, Patience was in sexual heaven. She'd found her nirvana for sure. Talk about tingly-wingly, oogly-woogly, fuzzy-wuzziness. Countless armies of endorphins danced all over her body, electrifying her senses, blowing her mind. If she died right now of sheer ecstasy, she wouldn't mind. It couldn't get any better than this.

All of a sudden, he pushed her away. She tumbled sideways, but managed to roll over and land on all fours like a cat after its leap of faith. Joe grinned as he knelt directly behind her, both hands placed firmly upon her buttocks.

"I want to take you like a dirty dog," he growled, headstrong, authoritive, back in charge.

His totally out of character performance surprised her. But in a good way. She'd never seen him like this before. Could she get used to it? Oh, absolutely.

Joe rediscovered her waiting hole and stabbed it once again with his sword of flesh. She was soaked down below. It slid in with ease. He pushed it right to the hilt. Then out again. And back in. And out again. She yelped with pleasure as she took the punishment for her man, plunge after plunge after plunge. They grunted, they gasped, they moaned and they rasped as he relentlessly smashed his stiff cock into her dripping wet pussy.

For Patience, the pressure inside was building up to bursting point. Tingling sensations raged all over her legs, her inner thighs, her groin, everywhere. Her body began to tremble violently. It wouldn't be long before she reached her orgasm.

Joe quickened his pace, tenfold. Upon each powerful thrust, his balls slammed hard against her clitoris, stimulating the pea to the point of ecstasy.

"Oh, God, oh, God," he shrieked. "I'm going to come!"

"No," she snarled loudly. "We come together." It was an order.

"I can't help it!"

"Joe! Hold back, for fuck's sake! I am so close!"

"I don't think I can!"

Uh oh. Emergency measures needed to be taken. Patience lifted a hand and reached for her clitoris. She rubbed her love bud as hard as she could as Joe continued to pound her pussy with his stiff meat.

"Hold back! Please! Come together! I'm almost there!"

"Oh, fuck!" he screamed. "I can't hold it much longer!"

"Nearly there, nearly there!" she squawked, buffing herself into a hectic frenzy.

"I'm going to explode any second now!"

"So am I!"

Both bodies quivered. Then tensed. Their eyes slammed shut.

Their mouths opened wide. They threw out silent screams. And then —

— Patience shouted, "Oh!"

Joe yelled, "My!"

Patience. "Fucking!"

Joe. "God!"

"I'm coming!" they both shrieked at the top of their voices in perfect unison, as if they'd rehearsed the line for weeks.

Joe pushed his cock deep inside the girl and froze on the spot, steeling himself as his seed was fired from the cannon. Patience polished herself with her fingers like a crazy woman as she rode the hectic waves of the greatest orgasm she'd ever experienced.

Ecstasy. Satisfaction. Contentment.

Love.

And then it was over.

They both collapsed into a sweaty heap on the mattress, gazing up at the ceiling, gasping, puffing, eager for cool air to fill their lungs. Joe laughed. And so did Patience. Minor chuckles at first, soon building up into unbridled, fanatical hysterics. No real reason. They just fancied laughing, that's all. And loudly.

Sod the neighbours.

And so they continued. Giggling like children for as long as they could manage. Until such time they both fell asleep. On a collapsed bed. In each other's arms. Very much in love.

Patience Hope was no longer a virgin.

Her quest was complete.

If you enjoyed this story, you can sign up for a free membership at ForbiddenFiction.com and discuss it with other readers and the author at the *Patience is a Virgin* story page at http://forbiddenfiction.com/library/story/MJ1-1.000039.

We do our best to proof all our work, but if you spot a text error we missed, please let us know via our website Contact Form at http://forbiddenfiction.com/contact.

About the Author

Mikey Jackson is a novelist, scriptwriter and coffee addict from the seaside town of Worthing, near Brighton, on the south coast of England where the sun sometimes shines, but it mostly rains. Aside from novels, he writes both comedy and drama material for TV, radio, film, theatre, print and web. He has also had short stories published in print, ebooks and on phone apps.

About the Publisher

ForbiddenFiction.com is a publisher devoted to writing that breaks the boundaries of original erotic fiction. Our stories combine intense sexuality with quality writing. Stories at ForbiddenFiction.com not only arouse readers through sensations, but also engage them emotionally and mentally through storytelling as well-crafted as the sex is hot.

ForbiddenFiction.com is also designed to be a social reading environment. You'll have fun even if just reading the latest post each day, yet you will have the chance for so much more. Readers and authors can be part of ongoing discussions of specific works and individual authors as well as more general topics.

Sign up for a FREE Membership today at ForbiddenFiction.com.